ALSO BY STEPH NELSON

The Final Scene

Last One Out

Make No Mistake

DON'T ASK WHY

STEPH NELSON

Published 2026 by Ticking Clock Press

ISBN: 979-8-9896154-3-8

For Heidi Hildebrand

May your Leo fire always burn bright

Content advisory: This novel contains depictions of depression, anxiety and panic attacks, suicidal ideation, violence, kidnapping, terminal illness, drug use, and coarse language. Please read with care.

Swim faster, I think. *Just a little farther and you can hide in the mangroves.*

My lungs burn. I gasp for hot and sticky breaths, my heart-beat a steady count as I swim parallel to the beach.

Stroke-stroke-breath.

Stroke-stroke-breath.

Thirty yards or so and I'm there.

Thank god for the blanket of darkness the new moon provides. I can't see him, and I pray that means he can't see me.

I thought I'd be safe on this island. That he couldn't find me.

"He won't stop until he's behind bars."

My sister's words float into my mind like an accusation. She said this only yesterday while we were tanning on the beach, but I didn't believe her. I couldn't help but feel a sense of safety here on the island.

Which is why I walked the beach solo with a margarita in hand late tonight, like countless nights prior. Why didn't I pay attention to how far from the house I'd strayed?

I'd wandered almost to the mangroves when I heard move-ment coming from the stand of palmettos behind me.

He was fast, on me instantly.

I scrabbled in my shorts pockets for the pepper spray I've started carrying all the time, and when I sprayed it into his eyes, he released his crushing grip on my arm.

I had a single moment to decide: sprint back along the beach toward the house, or swim the Gulf of Mexico. It's two miles to the nearest shore.

If I stayed on the beach, he'd catch me, but a two-mile swim was out of the question at night.

A third option emerged: that secret spot in the mangroves.

I glance back. Did he follow me into the water? I don't see him, but it's dark, so I'm not sure.

Don't slow down. Don't think about that. Just swim.

I'll hide, and in the morning, go to the police. Yes, that's a good plan. They'll have to help me now that I have "concrete evidence" that he's stalking me.

After a few moments, I still don't hear anything coming from behind. Why isn't he following me?

Relief is a temptation I can't give in to, and so I let my thrumming pulse propel me forward.

I surface once more for breath, and my eyes land on the black spot among the shadowed mess of branches—the opening of the mangrove tunnel.

My heart leaps, and adrenaline drives me harder.

I turn into the mangroves, swimming the length of the tunnel, passing spindly trees half-submerged in water, and once again push away thoughts that I might finally be safe.

I learned my lesson. Safety is an illusion unless he's in jail.

When the tunnel splits off, I take a narrower one, and the water grows shallow until I can no longer swim.

When I kayaked through here earlier, the tide was in, but now I have to crouch low, walking as fast as I can through the shin-deep water without splashing too loudly. This tunnel dead-ends in a little clearing where I can hide.

I step into the small circle of mangroves surrounding a patch of silty sand—it's as if someone simply plucked a few trees to create this protected spot. I pull my knees to my chin, tucking myself into a ball, and pray he's gone. My ribcage expands with every gasping breath. Tree crabs scuttle up branches. Mosquitos buzz. Water slaps against the prop roots that anchor the mangroves to the sand.

My breathing slows. Maybe I've done it. Maybe I've lost him. If he didn't see me turn into the tunnel, he won't know where to find me.

Then I hear a paddle strike water and almost gag. He's in a kayak.

That's what he was doing. Retreating down the beach to get a kayak so he could come after me.

"You picked the perfect spot for our first date—so romantic!" he yells.

I feel bile rise in my throat as his words come from all around and nowhere at the same time. He must have seen me turn in. He's already in the mangrove tunnel; the swamp is distorting the sound. I whimper and cover my mouth.

"I've been looking forward to this since we met."

I squeeze my eyes shut and clench my teeth.

Please god, please don't let him find me.

I can't stay here. This nest of safety becomes a prison if he finds me. I glance around furiously, but it's no use. There's nowhere to go except the direction I came from. The channel of water he's now in.

I have to do something. Maybe I can squeeze through the tangle of branches that stretches inland.

I stand and try to step between the branches but plant my bare foot on a spiky root hidden in the shallow water. *Shit.* I wince but manage to keep my mouth shut. Stumbling, I grab a branch for support.

Then the realization hits: It doesn't matter where I go. I'm his little mouse, stuck in a cage as long as I'm on this island.

His paddle sounds get sloppier, louder.

"We have all the time in the world now."

I can tell he's in the second tunnel. I hear him getting out of the kayak and sloshing forward. Fresh tears warm my cheeks.

Since mangrove branches have some give, I desperately try to pry them apart to create space for my body, but they're too densely woven and my arms won't stop shaking from the intense swim.

Push. This is it. Your last chance.

His laughter assaults me from right behind.

Still, I shove my body forward, bare arms scraping the ridged bark as I try to pull my hips through the narrow opening.

His huge hand wraps around my hair. It tears at the scalp as he yanks me backward. A bolt of pain hits my neck as he wrenches my body, twisting my face around to meet his.

His breath is hot even against the warm night air.

"Hi there, beautiful. Don't worry, I'm not going anywhere. And neither are you."

I scream, but the sound is swallowed up by miles of sea.

ONE YEAR LATER

1

COURTNEY

Girls' trips conjure images of carefree moments spread across days of cleared schedules. They're day drinking and laughing until stomachs hurt. They're late nights and late mornings and deep secrets told. But mostly, they're an opportunity to claw our way back to the glory days—the days before the monotony of life steamrolled in. They're a chance to rediscover ourselves.

But this isn't that kind of girls' trip.

My friends and I all live in Boise, Idaho. I see them almost daily. Only one of us—my sister-in-law, Paige—has a kid, and she's a young adult now. We aren't getting away for the hell of it, or for self-discovery. We're on this oversized fishing boat cruising through the Gulf of Mexico to fulfill my husband's dying request.

Bryce confided in Paige, his older sister, that he wanted her to take me away immediately after the funeral. He found a small private island in the Florida Keys and made the arrangements. The only thing she had to do was to book it when the time finally came, and I had no clue any of this was in the works until Paige approached me about it a month ago.

The day after his funeral.

It was so like my husband to organize a trip to a tropical paradise for me even when he was facing the end of his life. Even when he knew he wouldn't be with me to enjoy it. He planned a lot of trips for us over the fifteen years we were married—Mexico for our honeymoon, Paris to celebrate the pinnacle of my journalism career: an article I wrote about the Salmon Falls school shooting in 2019.

I close my eyes and try to feel something. Anything. But all I get is the vibration of the boat as it cuts through the Gulf. The sound of its motor roaring, the breeze warm and wild as we move toward our destination. Otherwise, it's a vast, flat canvas of nothing.

Except tears. So many goddamn tears. Before Bryce died, I didn't know how involuntary crying could be.

My eyes sting, already so tender from the past month. From the slow death march with Bryce prior to that. I've known for four years it would end this way for him. But hope, like love, is delusional, and so it still landed like a bombshell.

The wind wags my chin-length hair so it brushes my damp cheeks. I think the last time I actually felt anything was after Bryce's funeral. I spent those days curled up on our couch, wearing his vintage Marlboro tee shirt, getting shitfaced on whipped cream vodka while listening to "These Arms of Mine" by Otis Redding on repeat.

Now I'm supposed to be on vacation. In a warm, happy place, when all I want to do is disappear.

But I'm here for Bryce.

I'm sure when the idea came to him, he thought it might be a relief to get away soon after his passing and the many years I'd spent taking care of him.

Bryce always overestimated me. He saw me as strong and capable. I could never convince him that any grit I had was because of him.

But it's only four days. And it's on a private island. I can stay holed up in a bedroom the whole time if I want to.

Plus, what's the alternative? Stay home?

What's home without Bryce?

I clench my teeth and a new torrent of warm tears wets my eyes.

"Perfect day to spot a sea turtle, or maybe even a manatee," the boat captain says into his handheld mic. He's probably in his early sixties, with his leathery tan skin and deep crow's feet. He wears flip-flops, board shorts, and a sandy brown tee shirt that says "Huk" in large letters across the front. "Just a couple more minutes and we'll be there."

I scan the water but don't see anything except the piece of land ahead. Certainly no manatees.

When I glance back, Paige is staring at her phone, wearing huge black sunglasses. She holds her long, dark hair in a ponytail with the other hand. It takes her a moment to notice me and then she quickly hides her phone in her purse and lifts her hand to wave. Her hair swirls in the wind the moment it's released.

Paige is supposed to be taking some time off work this week. She owns a wildly successful astrology-based dating app called SoulMatch, and she struggles to delegate. I've been telling her for months she's going to burn out if she doesn't make some changes. But if I'm honest, I expect work will find her here, too. Our other friend, Tori, works for Paige at SoulMatch, and the two of them constantly bicker about the company. She's coming to the island later.

Normally this pending dynamic would be stressing me out, but right now it just bounces off my brain as a fact I can't do anything about.

Reese sits next to Paige, her blonde hair gathered on top of her head in a pile, blunt bangs swishing in the wind. She's looking back in the direction we came from. Maybe she's searching for sea life.

Reese and I have become friends over the past year while she took care of Bryce as a full-time live-in nurse. Paige hired her and didn't totally understand why I wanted Reese to come on this trip with us. I can't tell her the truth, but it's because Reese is comfortable with emotion. She never makes me feel like I'm a burden and lets me be what I am right now: a lump on a log. A very teary lump on a log. Maybe there's a part of me that isn't ready to let Reese go, too. It feels like another layer of letting Bryce go, and I'm not there yet, even though his illness offered a long runway to grieve him.

Paige is taking an almost opposite approach to her brother's death than I am: acting like nothing happened. She was able to organize this trip while helping me with Bryce's funeral. I don't judge her—we all manage grief differently—but something deep inside me does wonder how she can be so strong.

On the boat, Reese shoves her hands between her clenched knees, and I notice she's not looking around as if for manatees, only backward toward Marathon, where we came from. Is she okay?

The island comes into clearer view, and it's unbelievably beautiful. A tropical paradise with sugar sands bordering out to gemstone water. The lengthy expanse of sand is punctuated with palm trees bursting upward as if in praise to the sun on one side, while lush vegetation covers the other.

Reese lifts her cat-eye sunglasses to scan the shoreline too. Her eyebrows shoot up and I feel like I can read her mind—*morning walks*. They're practically her religion.

The boat aims for a long dock where an American flag hangs from a pole at the end.

"Perfect, right?" Paige calls out from the stern, pointing to the island.

I nod, mirroring her big smile, and my face stretches tight at the foreign sensation. The skin hasn't been called upon to do this in forever.

Fake it 'til you make it, Bryce would say, brown eyes dancing. I picture him buttoning up his uniform. The burly federal agent who spoke in silly idioms and cliches. Who loved herbal tea and candy bars and listened to 1960s soul music.

We're close enough that I can read a key-shaped sign perched in the sand:

Welcome to Lost Key

Est. 1956

The dock morphs into a boardwalk running perpendicular to the shore, then disappears into the palm trees. It probably leads to the house, but I can't see anything except beach and lush vegetation.

The captain cuts the engine about a hundred feet from the dock, and Jimmy Buffett's "Margaritaville" blares over the speakers. The boat lurches to a stop. Paige stands, bracing herself with a hand on the back of a seat as the boat bobs and drifts. "Why are we stopping way out here?"

"It's two miles from the island back to Marathon," the captain announces, turning down the music. "That's your closest access to the mainland."

"Okay … ?" Paige says, drawing the word out like a question. Of course Marathon is closest. We know that. We just came from there.

The smell of engine exhaust swells, and the captain turns toward Paige while keeping one hand on the steering wheel. He adjusts his faded NASCAR ballcap.

"What I'm about to say—well, don't mention where you heard it."

I stand and slowly make my way toward the stern of the boat so I can hear better, using the seatbacks for stability as the boat rocks in the water. Reese scoots over on her mini bench and I plant myself next to her.

Paige removes her sunglasses. "I'm not following."

He says, "If I were you, I wouldn't be staying here after what happened. But hey, it's your funeral."

2

COURTNEY

I stare at Paige, thinking, *What the fuck?* and she shrugs, like *No idea.*

"Well, what happened?" Paige asks. She sounds calm, but I sense her unease.

"Family stayed here recently. Rich like … " He trails off, looking Paige over, as if insinuating *like you.* He doesn't acknowledge Reese or me, and if Paige notices, she doesn't let on. "Anyways, island's small, but that doesn't mean bad things can't happen here."

Paige's gaze goes hard. She's doing her CEO thing. Or at least, that's what I call it, because she never did that before she became the owner of a multimillion-dollar corporation. She used to be timid and unsure. Now it's second nature to ice people with awkward silence until they overshare.

"Like I said, I'm not supposed to talk about it, but you girls seem nice, and I think you deserve a heads-up."

Another pause grows long as we wait for him to tell us more, but instead, he turns away like he's going to start the boat up and take us to the dock.

"So, what happened to the family?" Reese asks.

He doesn't answer, and instead the ignition comes on, ruining the chance for any conversation. He trolls slowly to the dock, then moves to the side and drops the buoys.

"You're really not going to tell us after all that?" Paige asks.

He works fast to catch the dock and tie the boat up and then he faces us. The water moves gently, rocking the boat, and the captain offers a hand to help Paige out.

"No thanks." Paige grabs her black suitcase and takes a huge step, her wide-leg pink linen capris straining with the reach.

"Tell us what happened," Reese demands from her seat.

"A girl died here," the captain blurts.

"Whoa. How?" Paige fires back. "Did she drown?"

"Worse."

My heart climbs into my throat. This is the first time I've felt something intense in a long while. What if someone was murdered? Why else would the captain feel like he needed to warn us? In my periphery, I catch Paige looking at me with a *What the hell?* expression. But I don't make eye contact. I can't stop staring at the captain as his words reverberate in my mind.

Reese reaches for her bulky army-green duffle bag as if she's satisfied with this answer. It's not really her style to freak out or get emotional. At least not that I've seen, and she's had a lot of chances to do so, especially during Bryce's last days.

Paige stands on the dock, her arms limp at her sides, and glares at the captain. As he turns away from her, I swear there's a smirk on his face.

"Okay, yeah, you're just fucking with us," Paige says. She must have seen it too. "Leslie would have told me about something like that."

Leslie is the house manager who'll be staying with us and cooking our meals. I don't know her, but Paige has been emailing with her for weeks to coordinate, and they've discussed everything from transportation to menu plans. I raise my eyebrows at her comment, though. She of all people should realize that "a girl died here" isn't exactly a selling point from a business perspective. Of course Leslie wouldn't have told her. What's she supposed to say? *"Come stay at our expensive-ass secluded property where you too could get murdered!"*

The captain scrunches his face like he doesn't know who Leslie is, or maybe he doesn't care. He turns to help Reese lift her bag onto the dock, but she ignores his outstretched arms as well. She tosses her bag with strength and style that announces *I was in the Army!* and steps out of the boat.

Not only was Reese in the Army, but she never misses a day of CrossFit, either. It always amazed me how she could handle Bryce when she needed to bathe him, even though his frame did diminish and become very slight toward the end.

I'm the last to get off the boat. He doesn't try to assist me when I lift my lemon-yellow hardshell onto the dock, but Reese stretches her hand out to help me step over the gap between the boat and the dock, and I take it. When our eyes meet, I don't see her usual kindness. I see something else. A bright spark of fear.

"Thanks," I say, forcing a smile. "You okay?"

"Yeah. I just want to know more about that girl."

The boat motor starts up, and Reese shouts at the captain over the noise. "How long ago did it happen?"

But he's already unhooked the boat and is shoving off.

"Hey, wait! You can't just say that and leave us here!" Reese yells as the three of us stand there, watching him go.

Normally I would latch on to this mystery of a murdered girl, craving more information. But I can't bring myself to that level of curiosity right now, even though it's got reporter-bait stamped all over it.

I sigh and stretch my neck, then straighten out my yellow-and-white floral sundress. Together, the dress and luggage scream *happiest person on the planet*—totally the opposite of my current vibe. But Bryce always loved yellow, so this is my way of telling him I'm thinking about him. That he completed me and I'm really nothing without him. That I'm only moving forward because he made me promise I would.

By the end, he could only communicate with an eye-gaze device because the disease had progressed so far that it'd removed his ability to speak or use his hands to type.

Guilt and regret crash against me like a deadly tidal wave. *Whatever you do, don't think about that.*

I cram the memories back into the box of things I'm not ready to unpack yet.

3

COURTNEY

WE STAND THERE, DUMBSTRUCK ON THE DOCK, WATCHING THE captain fly across the water much faster than when we were with him.

"I've never heard such bullshit." Paige is the first to speak.

I remember something she mentioned before we left Boise. "Didn't Leslie say we're the first ones to stay here in a long time? That the place was closed for renovations?"

"Yeah, see? It was being remodeled," Paige says.

I wasn't trying to strengthen her argument, but that's how she takes it.

"Why did he wait until we got to the dock to tell us someone died here?" Reese adds, still looking out at the Gulf of Mexico.

"Exactly. That's why I think he's fucking with us," Paige says. "He clearly has a thing against tourists."

"*Rich* tourists." I nudge her ribs and notice that even when I'm trying hard to be playful—to be normal—my words sound hollow.

"Whatever." Paige's slight smile is hard to miss. "I'll ask Leslie about it when we get up to the house. For now, let's just relax and take in all the sunshine we can. Bryce would want that." She smiles right at me this time.

She's right. We don't know for sure that it was a murder, and I don't want it to put a damper on the whole trip. Hopefully Leslie can shed more light on what happened.

Paige marches ahead of us, her pace faster than I feel like keeping.

I follow, and my suitcase *clunk clunk clunks* as the wheels hit the dock's wooden slats.

When we get to the shore, it seems the boardwalk leads up through the palm trees and to the house. If we peel off to the right, we'd be on the beach. Paige pushes on toward the house, so we follow.

The palm trees are picturesque, and there's a hammock stretched between two trunks that lean outward at the base, but curve back toward each other at the top like lovers. Old buoys hang from thick ropes—yellow, red, blue, and white circles along with bullet shapes strung like beads—dangling from branches. The muggy air feels nice, like a steam room, even though I'm sweating.

Reese and I walk together in silence, Paige keeping her pace up ahead.

"You okay?" I ask Reese again.

"Of course. I'm grateful to be here." Her response is tight, but she quickly adds, "The more important question is: How are you?"

"Oh, you know."

Just then, Paige takes off her black wide-brimmed hat, throws her arms out, and shouts, "This is fucking paradise!" She spins. "Four days without a company to run. Four days in the sunshine. I'm not letting anything ruin this trip." She turns again to recover her fast pace.

Her sudden self-focus feels like whiplash, and a distant part of me notes that she's acting like her beloved brother didn't just die.

I wait for irritation to bloom, but nothing happens. I'm a robot, going through the motions of life.

"That was a one-eighty," Reese says. Paige is too far ahead of us to hear.

I don't want to talk bad about Paige or, worse, explain why I'm not upset by what she said. "I'm sure she's stressed about being in charge of the vacation."

"Paige? Stressed about being in charge?" Reese smirks. "Sometimes I felt like it took everything in her to not take over Bryce's care. Like she would have hip checked me to change out his IV herself if she'd known how to do it."

I smile, and it's genuine. I love that she isn't afraid to bring up Bryce. Reese has never tiptoed around him, his diagnosis, or his death. "True," I say. "But I'm glad she's excited. I want everyone to have fun."

And fun might be in short supply once Tori gets here.

Tori was supposed to meet us in Marathon. She's been staying in Key West for the past two weeks, using up her PTO, but she sent me a text this morning saying she wasn't going to make the boat and will charter a later one, and that she's bringing some guy she met. I told her it was fine even though she didn't exactly ask permission. I don't love the idea, but I didn't have the energy to argue about it. I'll probably be in my room or on the beach the whole time anyway. When I told Paige, she said, "Nope. No fucking way Tori's dude is crashing our trip."

So I have that conflict to look forward to. Plus, Reese doesn't really know Tori, and they've only met in passing a few times, so I have no clue how they'll get along.

"Weird that Leslie wasn't on the dock with margaritas like she said she would be." Paige tosses the words over her shoulder. "I bet she'll have them at the house."

There's a slight hesitancy in her tone. When it comes to organizing events, people, or projects, Paige gets nervous if she doesn't know what to expect.

We follow the slightly elevated boardwalk as it meanders through thick tropical vegetation. Path lights dot its sides, tiny three-tier pagoda-style lanterns, their metal corroded by the salt air. We're surrounded by all sorts of palm trees, some tall and some squat, and other trees with red bark peeling off. Their huge branches are crooked and low like benches. We pass a stand of trees with round leaves and what look like clusters of green grapes hanging from them.

Soon, the foliage gets thicker and branches stretch out overhead like an archway, the Spanish moss hanging low enough you almost have to duck. It reminds me of a bayou. Does Florida have those?

We've only been walking a couple minutes, but these days, it's like my body is moving through wet concrete everywhere I go. After the long flight yesterday, an early morning, finding out there was possibly a murder here, and news that Tori's bringing an unexpected guest, I just want to find my room and melt into bed. A headache is starting to come on, and I'm not sure if it's from the heat or all the crying I've done today. Probably both.

The house comes into full view, and gorgeous doesn't begin to describe it. It isn't as big as I imagined, but it's beautiful. It's posh for a beach house. The whole thing is painted white and set on stilts with wide stairs leading up to a wraparound porch. The roof is plastered with solar panels, and the place looks like the result of a love affair between a southern plantation and a treehouse. Birds of Paradise and orange flowers with clustered tubes surround it. I even see short plants with little yellow flowers that remind me of the buttercups I know from my childhood on the West Coast.

"Holy cow," Reese says, echoing my thoughts.

We're at the bottom of stairs leading to a front door painted robin's-egg blue. It stands out against the clean white of the house. The windows on the second level have wide slat shutters —blue, to match the door. The stairs and the porch itself are painted a light concrete gray.

To the right of the house, there's a stretch of dirt making a narrow road, leading away. It seems like it might access the rest of the island.

Reese is peering down the dirt road in search of something. When she sees me notice, she quickly returns her gaze to the house.

"What is it?" I ask.

"Oh, nothing." She flashes a smile, but it's forced. Lately I've become an expert on forced smiling, but it doesn't feel like the time to press her.

Paige props the screen door open while she enters the house code, then pushes herself inside. She moves fast down the hall, abandoning us in the entryway without a word, as if we aren't even here. Reese catches my eye as if to ask, *What's she doing?*

"She has to check everything out and make sure the place is in order before she can relax," I say, collapsing the telescopic handle on my suitcase. This is Paige's way. I don't mind. Whatever she needs to do to feel good about things.

"Leslie?" Paige calls out, climbing the stairs.

We follow, and I think again about a nap. Almost there.

Reese and I are in the entryway, and I'm pulling the door closed behind us when Paige appears at the top of the wood-banister staircase, tossing her hands in the air. "She's not here."

4

COURTNEY

"I'm sure she's somewhere close," I say, resisting the urge to massage my temples. I don't want to seem annoyed. I doubt I could even *feel* annoyance these days.

"Where else would she be?" Paige speaks fast, clearly concerned. "Leslie swore she'd greet us at the dock, and she wasn't there, either."

"There's a garage," Reese says. "Maybe there's also a vehicle and she's somewhere else on the island."

Paige comes down the stairs to stand with us. "What do you mean?"

"I saw tire tracks near that little building next door, which looks like a garage, but it's not big enough for a car. That and the fact that there's a dirt road makes me think Leslie has an ATV or something that she uses to get around," Reese says.

That must have been what Reese was looking for when I caught her staring down the dirt road. So what was with the fake smile and brush-off?

"Why would she be running around right now? She knows

our arrival time." Paige says it as if Leslie's absence is Reese's fault.

"Maybe she had something to take care of real quick. There could be a lot of reasons why she's not here, Paige." I can't think of any, but I need to take the tension down a notch. We've only been here for like three seconds.

She groans in irritation then turns into the kitchen.

Looking around, I only see the large living room to the left, the doorway to the kitchen on the right, and the staircase ahead. The bedrooms must be upstairs.

The style of the house isn't breezy and light like you'd expect from a tropical vacation rental. There are no "Life's a Beach" signs. No onslaught of decorative anchors and seashells. The horizontal wood slats are dark honey-colored, not the typical bright, whitewashed wood. It feels more like an Idaho cabin.

Then my eyes catch a picture hanging on the wall. It's a young family. A mom, dad, and two small girls caught mid-laugh while building a sand castle against the backdrop of a cerulean ocean.

Reese seems to notice it at the same time because she steps over to inspect it.

"Kind of weird when vacation rentals do that," I say, moving closer. "Decorate with pictures of real people."

"It's probably the owners." Reese points to the far corner of the image, where there's a bit of dock, and then the backside of a sign. The shape and size is unmistakable. A key lying on its side —the same sign that greeted us at the dock today.

The girls have pointy chins, sunburned noses, and summer-bleached hair. They're happy. I can see it in their eyes, and I recognize it from once upon a time in my own life, too. Sheer joy with not a care in the world.

"You will find happiness again."

The words Bryce spoke during our last conversation ambush me, and I feel the pinch of tears.

"I found a note!" Paige's voice sails through the house.

I wipe my cheeks, grateful for the interruption.

In seconds she's next to us, holding a piece of paper. She clears her throat and reads. "Sorry I wasn't here to greet you. I'll be back later tonight. —Leslie."

Paige shakes her head and sighs loudly, giving a carnival of an eyeroll. "What the hell? She swore up and down she'd be here to greet us. On the dock. With welcome margaritas. She made a big deal out of it. Where's my purse? I'll email her."

I'll admit it's not ideal that we haven't even unpacked and we're already fielding a curve ball. But I'm also fine skipping the welcome margaritas in favor of crashing out for an hour or two.

When Paige walks out of earshot again, Reese says, "This feels like a lot of red flags."

"You think?" Normally, I'd be trying to manage everyone's worries. I'd be trying to smooth things over and create peace and calm. But I don't have the bandwidth for it right now, so I just let her talk.

"What the captain said, combined with the Leslie thing. We haven't even been here an hour and—"

Reese stops talking as Paige returns with her phone and holds it up.

"So, the Wi-Fi password doesn't work," she says. "I saw the router in the kitchen. I'm going to try and restart it."

I don't like how her tone has shifted from annoyed to worried, and unease roils in my stomach.

"Leslie must have all of our supplies—food, drinks, everything," Paige says. "She was supposed to stock the fridge for us, but it's empty."

"Wait, there's no food?" Reese's voice rises in pitch.

"I mean, there might be stuff in the pantry. The odds and ends every vacation rental has. I don't know. But Leslie was planning to bring all the food in from Marathon before we arrived. We worked together on a menu."

"It'll be fine," I say, even though this is admittedly unnerving. I feel my old urge to de-escalate kicking in. "We had a big breakfast, and I'm still stuffed. I'm sure we can wait until tonight for food." My stomach chooses that exact moment to growl, reminding me that I picked at my omelet instead of eating it.

Reese turns toward the photo again, and my eyes gravitate there as well.

"What are you guys looking at?" Paige asks.

"Nothing. We were talking about what the captain said," Reese says.

"Leslie can clear that up, too. We don't even know if it's true," Paige says quickly, like she's hoping we'll forget about the whole thing.

"Maybe you're putting too much trust in Leslie." Reese's tone is tight. I've never heard her talk like that before, especially not to Paige.

"What does that mean?" Paige turns to face her.

The rising tension squeezes at my nerves. Maybe they just need to argue it out, but I don't want to be here for it.

"I'm going to rest for a bit and then hit the beach if anyone wants to join."

I don't wait for them to reply before starting up the steps with my suitcase. When I turn the corner at the top, the hallway opens up to four doors. My body softens at the prospect of a nap. But then I hear my name coming from downstairs.

"Look, we don't know each other well, but I know Courtney *very* well," Paige says. "I'm super grateful for the care you gave my brother. But Court needs us to be supportive and fun right now. She doesn't need you dredging up all this worry about an imaginary problem. Especially when there are *real* problems to solve."

I shouldn't listen, but I can't help it. I stop, and my eyes fixate on the wooden canoe paddle hanging on the wall next to me.

"Imaginary problem?" Reese asks.

"Yeah, all this murdered-girl shit. Court hasn't been herself lately. She's always been sensitive, but since Bryce died … I don't know. She's not handling things very well."

Not handling things very well?

What the hell? My husband just died. Of course I want to curl up and die, too. And considering he was her brother, I'd expect more devastation from her as well.

"She's stronger than you give her credit for," Reese says, her tone softening.

Paige scoffs. "Okay, well, get back to me in fifteen years when you've known her as long as I have."

I roll my eyes. It's a shitty comeback. In fifteen years, Paige will still have known me longer. She's reaching.

"I'm sorry," Reese practically whispers.

Silence grows, and I can practically feel Paige trying to decide whether to pull back.

"God, no, I'm sorry," Paige says. "I'm just so on edge because of this Leslie thing. And as soon as that's resolved, we'll be dealing with Hurricane Tori's arrival."

Hurricane Tori.

I squeeze my eyes shut, so glad to not be down there.

"I just want this week to be perfect for our Court," Paige adds.

"Same."

I lean my shoulder against the wall and pinch the bridge of my nose. I'm way too spent for this.

5
____

COURTNEY

After lying there for a while, staring at the ceiling fan, it becomes clear that I'm not pulling off a nap, so I get up and put on my bikini, then the kaftan from Paige. She bought one for each of us—a flowing frock that acts as both a swimsuit cover and a dress. Mine is solid yellow with a deep V-neck and short, batwing sleeves. Whenever we travel together, Paige buys everyone some piece of clothing that matches. Granted, it's been a few years since we've traveled.

Downstairs, I find Reese in the kitchen, facing the open pantry with her back to me. She's in her kaftan too—an indigo one with huge gold lamé paisleys. Not really her style, but Paige doesn't know her well enough to know that. Reese has one hand on the doorframe and a full bottle of el Jimador in the other.

"Whatcha doin'?" I ask.

She startles and spins all in one motion, placing her free hand on her chest. "Jesus, you scared me."

I smile, and it makes breathing feel easier for a moment.

"Just checking to see what food we have. Looks like pretty

much only pantry basics—flour, sugar, salt, some canned items, and random sauces and spices," she says.

"So, basically like every vacation rental ever?"

She chuckles, and Paige walks into the kitchen. "I don't know what to do with myself. I can't sit still until Leslie gets here with the food."

She's in her kaftan too—red with turquoise, orange, and blue patterns that look like huge butterfly wings.

"I can probably whip something up with what's here if we get desperate," Reese says with a head tilt and a shrug.

"You can whip something up from a can of chicken and Worcestershire sauce?" It's a question, but comes out of Paige's mouth like a statement.

"I have my ways." Reese wiggles her eyebrows mischievously.

"We'll be fine. I'm sure Leslie will be here soon. Let's go to the beach and wait for Tori," I say.

"At least I packed some booze." Reese lifts the tequila like a trophy. "We need tumblers."

"On it," Paige says, opening cupboards.

As they move around the kitchen, I notice both of their kaftans hang elegantly low—Paige's almost grazes the floor—while mine hits mid-calf. The curse of being a six-foot tall beanpole.

Paige holds up three lowball glasses—two in one hand and one in the other. "Let's get started. We deserve it after our shit-show of a morning."

Reese pours a generous amount into each glass.

Getting wasted doesn't seem like that bad of an idea, but when I think of Tori, I change my mind. I should be sober enough to run interference when she gets here. That's my role when she and Paige are together, grieving widow or not. Today it will be more like damage control because Paige is planning to make whatever guy Tori is bringing get back on the boat. I'm on Team Paige for sending the stranger back, but I'll be on Team Tori for the emotional fallout.

Such is the tightrope I walk.

Paige charges out the door, with Reese close on her heels.

I jog to catch up, my drink sloshing over the rim. Sweat runs down my spine almost immediately—Boise is hot, but this humidity is something else.

On the walk down to the beach, I notice again how wild the vegetation is. It's overgrown, but something about it being tropical makes it beautiful, even if it's chest-high at parts and you'd need a machete to hack your way through it. I'd hate to get lost.

Once my Chacos hit hot sand, I notice a few things I didn't when we first arrived. A shed that looks like a tiki hut—thatched roof and all—down the beach in the opposite direction of the loungers. It sits high on posts with a ladder to get up to the door. In front of it are two kayaks. Red and blue.

The three of us claim lounge chairs and lie in silence, sunglasses on, soaking up the rays. I must have dozed off, because the next thing I know, Paige calls out, "Look, a boat! It better be Leslie with our food."

"It could be Tori," I say, yawning and stretching to shake off the fuzz of sleep.

Paige groans, then stands and takes off toward the dock. The sand is too hot to go barefoot, so I slide my sandals on to follow.

Reese and I walk along the waterline to join Paige at her spot right where the dock begins. We stand side by side on the beach like some welcoming committee, though we have no idea who we're welcoming.

The boat docks, and I see Tori's red hair hanging in two long braids. She stretches her arm overhead in an exaggerated wave.

I wave back, but I'm the only one who does.

"Who is that with her?" Reese asks, and I realize I didn't fill her in on the mystery man, so I do.

Someone stands at the boat's helm—he seems like the captain, although it's a different one than ours was. There's another person with Tori, but they're blocked from view by the oversized American flag.

"I only count three," Paige says. "Maybe it's Leslie and Tori left her boy toy behind."

That's wishful thinking.

Tori climbs out of the boat and a man follows, holding her hand.

Still no sign of Leslie. Or our food.

6

____

TORI

They're all standing there, hands tented over their eyes, wearing *kaftans*, as Paige called them in the group chat. I give them a big wave, but of course only Courtney waves back.

"That's them?" Rawson asks, squeezing my hand affectionately.

"Yep. That's them."

"Why are they wearing kimonos?"

I snort a laugh. "They're not kimonos. They're kaftans. Paige bought them for us, but I left mine in Boise."

I'm so tired of dancing to the rhythm of Paige's demands that I just couldn't stomach going along with the kaftan thing.

"Paige is the rich one, right? How did she get her money, again?"

I turn to face him, trying not to show my irritation. He already knows this. I've gone on and on about Paige's app. I work there; I'm the in-house astrologer and audio talent for SoulMatch.

I'm used to people not taking the app seriously. A dating app based on astrology sounds hokey. But subscribers love it. Instead of the sky-high mounds of undatable trash to sort through on most apps, SoulMatch suggests people based on how users' astrological charts align. You can also manually input anyone's birth date and time to run their chart against yours to see if there's a match. So if you meet a cute guy in a bar, you can check compatibility on the spot.

Which is exactly what I did with Rawson. We met in Key West a couple weeks ago, and I was elated to see that we matched at the highest level possible: "Twin Stars." We laughed about it, but I was seriously cheering inside because this level of connection is rare for me. It's a soulmate match, and I never get those. Sometimes I get "Soft Glow," which means a so-so match, doable with a lot of work. But I usually get "Star-Crossed" or "Cataclysmic." I get those more often than I feel like other people do.

In fact, I've only ever matched as Twin Stars with one other person: my husband Tucker, who passed away years ago. And he really was my soulmate, so this connection with Rawson feels like validation from the universe.

As for the app, it was my idea in the first place. Paige has never really been into astrology. But she's into making money off of stolen ideas and ruling her company with an iron fist. And telling me I take astrology too seriously, which maybe I do, but I can't help it. I see its truth everywhere I go.

Paige is a Virgo sun, and she has plenty of other earth signs in her chart. The best version of a Virgo is a grounded, organized person. Someone who truly wants to help people. But Paige operates more on the shadow side of Virgo—a hypercritical and perfectionistic workaholic. SoulMatch offers content for anyone, not only singles looking for a partner. We teach users how to express their own unique selves in the healthiest way, with audio clips narrated by yours truly. So you'd think she'd pay more attention to learning how to be her highest self since her own damn app could teach her how to.

Whenever I hint at new content I've created for the self-development side, Paige always says, "I don't need a dating app," ignoring that the information would totally support her growth if she gave herself to it.

"How to Flourish as a Capricorn Moon"—which she is.

"How to Tap into Your Power as a Scorpio Ascendent." Also her.

"How to Banish the Shadow Side of Your Signs Forever." A series I developed with her in mind.

And sure, she doesn't need a dating app. I've known Paige longer than I've known Court or anyone else in my life, and she's always had a partner. Her current husband is somewhere in the Idaho wilderness for the summer, probably to get away from her. Her only daughter is far away at college and wants little to do with her because of a lifetime of overparenting. But Paige desperately needs to learn how to manage her energy or she stands to lose every close relationship.

Me, on the other hand? Astrologically, I'm designed to be a free spirit, and relationships—especially romantic ones—have always been a challenge. My Sagittarius sun sign is one of the most freedom-loving, and when coupled with the fact that my whole chart is full of fire and air signs that crave freedom—Leo, Aquarius, Gemini —I'm kind of screwed. This makes the universe pickier about who I match with. It's possible I'm not designed for monogamy at all, but if I'm not designed for it, why do I want it so badly?

Courtney would say what I'm really looking for is not a soulmate, but closure from losing Tucker so traumatically. But that was a million years ago and not the reason I'm in the market for a life partner. Never mind that she's clearly projecting her own grief onto me.

I met Tucker in college, and he was a beautiful Pisces—compassionate, intuitive, with a dreamy artistic soul that allowed him to always sense what I needed. Just looking at sun signs, a Sagitarrius and a Pisces aren't a natural match, but that's why you have to look at the whole natal chart. He had all kinds of other placements that were more compatible with mine. Tucker just *got* me. So, yeah, Court is partially right. When he died, something in me died too.

Which is why as far as Twin Stars are concerned, Tucker and Rawson are it for me, so Rawson will have to use the Jaws of Life to pull me away. I want so badly to grow old with someone. I've been alone for too long, and this is my big chance at love. Any sticking points between us can be smoothed out. I'm determined.

"Oh, she got rich off the tarot app. I remember now," Rawson answers his own question.

"Astrology," I correct him.

"Right, yeah, the other voodoo thing." His tone is dismissive as he reaches for my suitcase, offering to carry it for me. "Must be nice not to be a slave to student loans for an art degree from a private school. To be able to do what you want with your life."

I watch his face, trying to think of a reply. It sounds a little bitter, which isn't really like him.

"You're sure they'll be cool with me crashing their party?" he asks as if to change the subject.

No, I'm not sure. I know this trip is for Courtney. I know it's because of Bryce's death. But I also know that I need more time with Rawson to cement our connection. He's into me, I'm absolutely sure of that, but even though we're meant to be together, I worry that if I go back to Boise right now, he might forget about me. When it was time to leave him in Key West, I just couldn't do it. I was so glad Courtney said it was fine if he came along, because I don't know what I would have done if she'd said no.

"Course," I say as we start walking down the super long dock.

"Did you consult the stars about it?" he teases.

I just laugh.

Rawson doesn't totally believe in astrology, but it's fine. He'll get there.

7

TORI

I met Rawson at Sloppy Joe's on Duval Street in Key West. I was having a drink at the bar and reading a book. Or trying to. Turns out it's more of a live music scene. Pictures of Hemingway lined the walls, and I knew it was Hemingway's old hangout, so I assumed I'd be able to read there. But Sloppy Joe's is more focused on Hemingway's other activity: binge drinking.

It was larger inside than it seemed from the street, with a sea of tables set up in front of a stage and a bar near the entrance.

"Hey, whatcha reading?" this guy asked. He was wearing a tropical shirt, unbuttoned to show off his sun-kissed and not-too-hairy chest, and a gold chain around his neck. The look itself screamed *sleazy*, but it worked on him. His hair was effortlessly tousled.

I flipped my paperback over so he could see the cover.

"*Gray After Dark*," he said, reading the title. "Never heard of it."

"It's by the author who wrote *Ask for Andrea*. The one about the ghosts hunting down the man who killed them?"

"Hm, can't say I've heard of that one either."

"She writes amazing thrillers. They're constantly going viral on BookTok."

"Oh, well, that explains it. I don't really read *viral* books."

I set my book down and turned toward him. God, he was cute, but he didn't look like the sort to turn his nose up at genre fiction. He didn't look bookish at all, if we're operating in stereotypes. Of course, me being the Sagittarius I am, I found that unexpected, therefore intriguing and irresistible.

"Oh, really? What do you read?" I asked.

He leaned on his elbow on the bar. "I like books that have substance. You know, actual art."

I wanted to roll my eyes, but instead, I said, "Okay, give me your top three authors."

He smiled, and the way his dimples deepened confirmed it for me. Scratch cute, he was hot as fuck. My body lit up while I waited for his answer.

"What was that look for?" he asked.

My cheeks burned. "Just dying to hear your answer."

"I mostly read the classics. You know, Hemingway, Thompson, Kerouac. That, and poetry. Poetry is my church."

"So, basically dead white men."

"What? No! I love women. My favorite poet is Mary Oliver."

"Well, I happen to love her too, so I'll give you a pass."

He bowed in a sort of playful way. "I appreciate that. Truth is I'm a shameless Hemingway fan. Dead white guy or not. I even have a polydactyl cat I named Snowball." His brown eyes glimmered.

"Which explains why you're here, I suppose." I didn't know much about Hemingway beyond what I learned in high school English. I remembered liking *The Old Man and the Sea*, but that was about it.

"Yeah, can't you just feel his presence?" he said, leaning closer. "Hem lived all the way on the other side of Key West.

Legend has it that he used to walk home drunk with only the lighthouse next door to his place to guide him. Man, those were the days. You could simply live your life and practice your art. Total freedom."

Yeah, if you were a man, I thought, but I asked, "Are you a writer?"

"No, an artist. Well, really I'm a slave to a paycheck so I can pay my student loans, and sometimes I draw."

I felt a gravity between us, like no matter what I said or didn't say, we'd found each other, and this was only the start.

"So, what do you do?"

"A bunch of stuff. DoorDash, Uber, bartending. Name's Rawson," he said, extending his wide palm.

I took it and said, "Tori."

And that's how Rawson ended up in my bed on my very first night in Key West.

8

——————

TORI

As we walk the dock and get closer to the sand, I can feel my friends' disapproval radiating like heat. Especially Paige's. It's a solar flare. Her arms are crossed and her face is blank—her usual look when I walk into a room. It hasn't always been this way. When we were kids, she used to be mesmerized by me. Eyes wide with wonder as if everything I did was magical and she could only hope to one day be as adventurous and wild as me.

"Wow. They look fun," Rawson says in monotone. "Which one is Paige?"

"Long, dark hair. Carries herself like she's the CEO of the world."

Right then, Paige starts walking along the beach toward the dock.

"Speak of the devil, here she comes," I say. She can't even wait until we're on land to lash out at me.

"And why are you friends with them, again?" Rawson asks.

"Well, I've known Paige forever. She's like a sister I'm stuck with. We do have good moments, but lately they're few and far between. I'm here for Court. She gets me. I don't really know the other one."

I know her name is Reese and that she was Bryce's nurse during his last year. But I avoided anything having to do with Bryce if I could. He was a Leo, a classic larger-than-life personality who lit up any room he walked into, and he was Tucker's best friend. They met at John Jay College and discovered they both grew up in Idaho. Life brought them back together when they were both assigned as U.S. Marshals to the Boise office.

After Tucker died, it was too hard to be around Bryce, and the few times I was, I could feel that he wanted to connect over losing Tucker. To talk at length about stuff I buried to keep living.

When Bryce married Courtney, she and Paige hit it off instantly, and I was drawn into their orbit. I thought Bryce would stop trying to talk with me about Tucker eventually, but he never did. At first it was questions about how I was doing living without him. Years later, it morphed into wanting to share memories of Tucker. I still couldn't do it. The only way I've handled Tucker's death was to move forward.

Paige barely gets a foot on the dock when a loud motor roars behind me and the boat takes off for the mainland. She throws her hands in the air and spins in retreat, making her way back to the others like she was coming to talk to the boat captain, not me. I dodged whatever that bullet was.

"Heyyy!" Courtney calls out.

I wave again and get a little flutter of excitement. When we get to where they're standing, I say, "Everyone, this is Rawson." I squeeze his hand.

He extends the other one. "Friends call me Raw Dog."

I whip to face him. Where did that come from? I haven't heard him use that nickname even once. Also, for the first time I notice a little accent in the way he extends the O in "dog."

His smile twitches.

"Hi … " Courtney stumbles awkwardly after the greeting like she's trying to decide whether to call him by the nickname or not. She smiles, but it's tight and disappears quickly. Then she says, "Tori, you remember Reese."

I nod and we shake hands even though I've met her before. "I'm excited to get to know you better this week," she says. Something about it is childlike and innocent. I wonder if she has a Gemini placement in her chart.

I don't get a chance to reply before Paige butts in. "So, Rawson, why are you here?"

"Court didn't tell you he was coming?"

She glares at me and then just watches Rawson.

His eyes shift toward me subtly, and I can feel what that look is saying: *You promised they'd be fine with me coming.*

I told him there might be a small speedbump at the start while they adjust to the idea of him being here, but then it'll be fine. I give him a bright, reassuring smile and answer Paige. "Since you said we have the whole island to ourselves, I thought it wouldn't be a problem to bring him along. He won't be any trouble."

I shove Rawson playfully, but he doesn't budge.

"Right. Why not invite a stranger to the vacation rental your friend paid for on a trip you're only taking because your other friend's husband died? It makes total sense," Paige says.

My cheeks flush, and frustration turns to anger. I didn't expect her to be like this right out of the gate.

Courtney's hand snakes out and gently grabs Paige's elbow. Good old Court. Her natal chart screams peacemaker extraordinaire, but with a shadow side of people-pleasing. She's a Libra sun, Pisces moon, and Libra rising, which means she'll always steer things away from conflict.

"Good to see you, Tor," she says, hugging me.

"How are you doing?" I whisper, holding her for a beat longer.

"I'm making it." She pulls away, forcing another smile. There's an awkward pause. I see Paige's jaw ripple, and then I notice Reese tilting her head to the side. She's been staring at Rawson this whole time. Is she checking him out or sizing him up? She's definitely not his type, so no threat there. Too athletic. With those biceps, she could probably take him in an arm-wrestling match. She looks amazing, but Rawson has made such a big deal about how much he likes the soft parts of my body that I know she won't tempt him.

Courtney surveys the little circle we're standing in for a moment, then says, "Let's get you guys settled in."

"You should know, there's nothing to eat or drink," Paige says matter-of-factly. "That boat captain took off before I could ask him about Leslie." Then she quietly adds, "Or send this guy back."

"Who's Leslie?" I ask. Paige does that a lot—talks about people you don't know as if you do.

"The house manager. She was supposed to show earlier with our supplies. I hope you're not too hungry," Courtney says.

I look at Rawson and try to hold back a wince. I promised him we'd eat first thing when we got here because we were running so late we had to skip lunch.

"Nah, we're good," he says with a smile.

My body relaxes. This'll be fine. Rawson is great with people, and he's going to win my friends over, no problem. Paige doesn't count.

9

———

TORI

AFTER HIKING THE NEVER-ENDING BOARDWALK THAT LEADS TO an adorable house, Rawson and I follow the others up the porch stairs where Paige stands, having far outpaced us with her classic power walk, holding the front door open.

Reese and Courtney go inside, and when it's our turn to follow, Paige steps in front of me and puts a hand out. "Tori, can I talk to you real quick?"

Whenever people say this, especially if they use my name, I feel like a kid in trouble. Then I get mad, because fuck them. Who are they to make me feel so powerless? Doesn't help that Paige is my boss.

Rawson hesitates just outside the door.

"Can you excuse us, please? I need to speak with her alone," Paige says to him.

I smile to say it's okay, even though it isn't, and he goes inside.

"What the fuck are you doing?" Paige spits out. "Bringing a man on our girls' trip? How does that make any sense, even for you?"

"We got Twin Stars on the app." I feel like she might understand this, or at least get what it means to me.

"You're so immature." At least she's skipping to the end of the argument. The part where she flat-out insults me. "You're so selfish. You wouldn't know a boundary if it clotheslined you."

Selfish? Like she's one to talk. I scoff a laugh. Why did I think she'd understand? Paige doesn't value relationships anyway. "It's not a big deal. You'll love him once you get to know him."

"I don't want to *get to know him*. I want to focus on our friend who just lost her husband, my brother. You know—the whole reason we're here."

"Why *are* we here, Paige?" I ask, lifting my eyes to meet hers.

"What?"

"Why are we *here*?" I wave an arm. "In Florida, of all places?"

"I don't know what you mean." Paige crosses her arms. "The trip was Bryce's idea—he chose it."

"Sure. Okay, well, how about you go manage someone else. You're not my boss right now. I'm on vacation."

"Is that why you brought him? To get back at me for something about work?"

Seriously? I accuse her of making the trip about herself, and she denies it by making it about herself.

"Yeah," I say in a mocking tone. "I went out and found the love of my life so that I could crash the party you claim you're throwing for Courtney all because I'm mad about work. Come on, Paige."

"You're one to talk!" Paige is close to yelling, but there's restraint in her tone. "You never think about anyone else's feelings."

I shake my head and step toward the door. "I'm done here."

"He needs to leave," Paige says. "When Leslie gets here, he's on the boat back to Marathon."

I force my face to stay neutral. Rawson isn't going back. I don't care how mad Paige gets, so maybe it's time to play the one card I have. I've been holding it for months, waiting for the right time. I straighten my back and say, "Rawson stays or I'm done keeping your secrets. You know what I'm capable of."

10

COURTNEY

Once we get inside the house, I realize how famished I actually am. I don't want to worry about the food situation, but I am worried. Where could Leslie be? Is she in trouble?

I watch that guy—*Raw Dog*—get himself a glass of water while he waits for Tori. He's cute, I'll give him that, even though I can't see his eyes since he still hasn't taken off those dark aviators. He's definitely Tori's type. Good-looking, a little aloof, and slightly goofy. I'm happy for her, but that doesn't mean I want to be around him. I'm already so exposed emotionally that this is an extra mile I just can't go, even for Tori. I'm glad Paige is sending him back.

I relax at this thought, and a rush of appreciation for Paige floods me. Most people only see her as bossy, but she's also loyal and generous. She was my backbone through Bryce's illness, covering all our expenses for four years so I could be home with him. I owe her everything.

I head up to my room to get my phone—I need to know what time it is, because the Leslie thing is really nagging at me.

My room is the last one on the left, and when I walk in, all I see is a mess. The bedding is crumpled and my bag already looks like it's been pawed through for days. I grab my phone from the nightstand and tap the screen to wake it up.

Seven forty-five. I groan. Is it that late? What could possibly be taking her so long?

Then I smell something cooking. It's like fried bread, but not quite pancakes. I go downstairs and into the kitchen to find Reese at the stove with her back to me. I can't tell what she's making, but it smells so good.

"Any word about Leslie?" I ask even though I think I know the answer.

"Nope. I thought I'd whip something up real quick before my stomach decides to eat itself," Reese says, not looking away from whatever she has in a frying pan.

"With what? There's no food."

"Oh, I found a couple things in the pantry. It'll be strange"— she lets out a small laugh— "but at least we won't be hungry while we wait for real food."

I step over to peer into the pan, and she flips what definitely looks like a thick pancake. On the other burner, a pot of water is boiling next to three packages of ramen noodles stacked on the counter.

"All that came from the pantry?" I ask.

"Yep."

"I don't remember seeing pancake mix. Or ramen."

"These aren't pancakes. It's just flour, oil, water, and salt. Super bland, but filling."

Past the noodles, I see more ingredients she's pulled: a jar of alfredo sauce, a can of chicken, a half cube of butter with its waxed wrap folded up against where someone previously cut it.

"Are you making chicken alfredo?"

She laughs again. "More like chicken alfredo's weird cousin."

"How did you come up with this?"

"I mean, it's not that hard to figure out. I saw the sauce and went from there."

I swear there were no ramen noodles when I looked earlier. And I don't remember her ever cooking during the year we lived together. She was only responsible for Bryce's care while I managed the house and made our meals.

"That smells good," Paige says, walking into the kitchen. "I'm starving."

"Just doing my part." Reese salutes, then looks around and whispers to her. "You get *Raw Dog* squared away with his trip back to the mainland?"

Paige bites the inside of her cheek. "He's staying."

"What?" I blurt.

"I don't want to talk about it. Tori promised to keep him out of our hair." Then she leaves the kitchen before we can say anything else.

The numbness that's become my default had just started to leave, but now it's returned, and I stand there with my arms limp at my sides. Tears well up.

"What happened? Why did she change her mind?" Reese asks, but I just shrug and turn to try to hide that I'm crying again. The whole way up to the house, Paige talked about sending Rawson back on whatever boat brings Leslie in. It didn't seem negotiable.

It *shouldn't be* negotiable.

Heat surges through me, and I swallow hard to try to stop the tears. Paige's about-face makes me feel like she doesn't have my back. But then I get annoyed with myself. I'm sure Paige knows what she's doing. This trip can't be all about me.

I clear my throat and wash my hands. I'll focus on helping Reese get the food ready. Really, I'd rather go lock myself away in my bedroom, but that feels selfish.

We eat our makeshift meal on the second-floor porch—the one off Paige's room—because it's west-facing and we can watch the sunset. This is a cozy setup with patio couches, chairs, and even a rocker. Hazy pewter clouds expand over the horizon. Probably a quick tropical rainstorm coming.

Rawson hasn't said much but helps himself to seconds.

Paige and Tori are nearly silent. They haven't spoken since their talk on the porch, which we still have no details about.

Now that I've eaten something, I feel like I've adjusted to the idea of having Rawson here. It's not ideal, but I'm not going to fall apart over it. Still, how in the world did Tori change Paige's mind about sending him back?

A knock comes from downstairs, and Paige jumps up. "Leslie! Finally."

The three of us leave Tori with Rawson, who is still stuffing his face.

Paige opens the door but says nothing. She blocks my view, so I crane my neck to see, expecting Leslie, but, no—

It's a man.

"Hi, I'm looking for Paige," the man says.

"That's me."

"Oh, hey, I'm Leslie."

11

COURTNEY

Did he really just say he's Leslie? He stands there in cargo pants and a faded blue tee shirt with a shark graphic on the breast pocket. His shaggy salt-and-pepper hair tufts out from underneath a backwards ball cap. Dark sunglasses hang from a neon green strap around his neck. He's probably in his mid-fifties.

"I'm sorry, what?" Paige asks.

"I'm Leslie. The house manager." He looks down and grabs the screen-door handle, as if he's just going to walk in.

"Wait," Paige says, grabbing the door from the other side to stop him. "Just … I'm sorry," she repeats, and puts on a fake smile. "I was expecting someone else. You're Leslie Seaver?"

"In the flesh." The man spreads out his arms, and I half expect him to spin like a model, but instead he smiles big, showcasing crooked, nicotine-stained teeth. "And I've got your groceries on the four-wheeler."

I feel a wave of relief coursing through not only me, but Reese and Paige too.

"Okay, but Leslie is a woman," Paige blurts.

I can practically see her scrambling to make sense of this. As if she's mentally scrolling email threads, trying to pinpoint where she went wrong.

The man laughs, and it booms in echoes on the covered patio. "Not sure what gave you that idea, but I promise I'm not a woman."

"The person I emailed with was female. Named Leslie."

My stomach dips. She sounds angry. Borderline bitchy.

He shrugs. "It's a male name too, so I'm not sure what to tell you, lady."

Paige and Reese look at each other, and something passes between them. An understanding of sorts.

Fat raindrops plink on the stairs behind Leslie, and he turns to look at the sky. That's when I notice the ATV parked off to the right of the house, on the tiny dirt road.

"We need the food," I say to Paige.

"Yeah, and it's about to get drenched," Leslie adds.

"You can set everything right outside the door, there on the porch." Paige tilts her head to indicate the spot, as if letting him bring anything inside is somehow an admission that she's wrong.

He nods, and once he's down the steps and out of earshot, Paige turns to us. "That's not Leslie."

"What?" I say. Is she serious? I look at Reese, but her face is set, no expression.

"That"—Paige throws a finger in the man's direction—"is not the same person I've been emailing with. My Leslie is a woman. We talked about our husbands, kids, recipes. I'm telling you, that's not her."

"Why does it matter if Leslie is a man or a woman?" I ask. So, she got the gender wrong, big deal.

"It matters because I feel like this is a totally different person than the one I've been in contact with. Don't you think that's a little creepy?"

"Paige … " I whisper, speaking very carefully, because she's starting to sound a little homophobic, which I know she isn't. "Are you sure you didn't just make an assumption based on the name 'Leslie' being more common for women? He could still have a husband. And kids. And plenty of men love to cook."

This possibility seems to take the wind out of her. She steps back and chews on a thumbnail.

I lean to look out the open door. Leslie is removing crates from the ATV, his blue tee shirt already rain-plastered to his body.

"We should help. It's our food, and this rain is intense," I say.

"Who is it?" Tori asks, coming down the stairs with Rawson following.

"Leslie, the house manager," I say.

"That's not Leslie," Paige hisses at me.

"I'm right here, you know," Leslie says with a laugh, and yeah, he's suddenly standing there on the porch. He sets down a black crate holding cartons of chicken broth, cans of black beans and corn, and two loaves of bread in rain-streaked plastic wrap.

"Hey, man, you need a hand?" Rawson asks, approaching the door.

"That'd be great."

Rawson is shirtless, but he's finally taken off those aviators. He slides his flip-flops on and goes out into the rain, following the man down to the ATV.

Paige turns to grab her phone from the entryway table.

"No Wi-Fi," Reese reminds her.

"I know. But I should still be able to see my read emails. How did I miss this?"

"What's going on?" Tori asks, looking at each of us for an answer.

Reese fills her in, then says, "Forget the gender thing. It's his vibe. The way he called Paige *lady*. I don't have to run a business to know you don't address a customer like that. And the way he tried to barge into the house without asking. What the hell?"

Paige looks up. "Right? That was so aggressive."

I agree that *lady*—with the tone he used—is a weird way to talk to someone paying you for a service. But they're panicking. I have to de-escalate.

"It's raining out. Of course he wanted to come inside," I say.

"He was under the porch cover," Reese corrects. "And it wasn't raining yet."

"Okay, but he's the house manager. Why would it be weird for him to come inside?" I ask. "He's going to be cooking our meals and staying with us." This whole thing is spiraling out of control.

"I don't know, something feels off," Reese says, shoving her hands into the pockets of her jean shorts.

"But does it? Or are we being paranoid?" I ask, trying not to make it sound like an accusation.

"Look at all these emojis and exclamation points." Paige turns the phone to us.

"You assumed he was a woman because he used emojis and exclamation points?" Tori says. "What real proof do you have? Did you discuss perimenopause and mammograms?"

Paige glares at her.

"This isn't a big deal. Let's get the food inside and see what kind of alcohol we get to add to our stash," Tori says.

While we're unloading groceries in the kitchen, the men leave more crates on the porch, along with a massive red cooler. When I open it, the ice is practically melted. I touch one of the bags of sliced turkey, and luckily, it's still cold.

Minutes later, Leslie knocks on the doorframe and says, "Okay, see you guys tomorrow."

"Wait," Paige calls out before rushing over to talk to him, and I follow. "You're not staying here?"

"Nah. Change of plans."

There's a beat of awkwardness, and I can feel all of us reeling with this new change in plans. Paige could have gotten his gender wrong, but this strikes me as weird.

"Okay … How do we get a hold of you?" Paige asks.

He says, "Be right back."

Seconds later, he returns with a walkie talkie. "Use this if you need to, but I'll be here first thing to check in, too."

"Where are you staying?" Paige asks. "I thought this was the only house on the island."

"Don't worry about me. Just call if you need anything." He points to the walkie in Paige's hand and again turns to leave.

"Hold on!" Reese says this time.

He spins slowly, his face broadcasting annoyance.

"Do you know anything about a girl who died here recently?"

He scoffs and shakes his head. "That's just a nasty rumor going around since the place was closed for repairs for a year."

"That's what I suspected," Paige says.

When Leslie is out of sight, she turns to us, and says, "There. Mystery solved. It's weird the plan changed, but I'm fine not having that guy stay here. We have food." She lets out a breath. "Now we can relax."

DAY 2

12

COURTNEY

The morning sun shakes me awake. Beams of light stream in even through closed horizontal blinds.

I feel the empty space beside me and think of Bryce. Tears are already coming by the time I turn my face into the pillow.

It's been forever since I shared a bed with him, because toward the end, he slept in a hospital bed in the spare room. I spent late nights and early mornings beside him in a recliner. Ten months since Bryce and I slept in the same bed, and still, every time I wake up, I expect to feel him next to me.

I cry harder. Every day holds some memory or realization that reopens the wound. Nothing but the passage of time can ease my pain, and even that, I question. I feel like I'm half a person, empty and aimless without him.

Birds sing outside. The delicate chirping is layered with what sounds like the cooing of doves. It's a reminder that I'm in paradise, yet I don't feel anything. At least I can admit it's beautiful.

I move out of bed and decide my cropped yoga tank is

modest enough for mixed company, so I pull on some running shorts and make my way downstairs for coffee.

I get to the bottom of the stairs and startle when I see movement through the privacy glass. Two people-shaped shadows. Then a knock.

I tuck my hair behind my ears as I walk toward the door.

I open it to find more men.

They're wearing dark-green khaki polos tucked into matching cargo pants; the shirts have gold badges on the left breast—or rather patches that say "U.S. Border Patrol." One of them wears a khaki ball cap and the other has sunglasses perched in a nest of short, dark hair.

He speaks first. "Hi, I'm Agent Delgado, and this is Agent Pierce. We're looking for Leslie Seaver. Is that you?"

"I'm sorry, what's this about?"

"We're with the U.S. Border Patrol. We got a call about suspicious packages found on your beach. We're here to pick them up."

"Okay. Leslie is the house manager; we're renting this place for a few days. What do you mean, *suspicious packages*?"

"Who is it?" Paige's voice comes from inside the house.

I turn sideways so she can see. "Border Patrol. They're looking for Leslie. Something about suspicious packages?"

"What?" Paige asks, smoothing back her wild sleep hair. She's in a pair of pink sleep shorts and a black tee. "What kind of packages?"

I turn to the men, waiting for them to answer.

"Probably drug wash-ups, based on the description we have. Been getting lots of calls like this thanks to Denny," Agent Delgado says.

"Who's Denny?" Paige asks, crossing her arms in a classic *I forgot a bra* move.

"Hurricane Denny," Agent Pierce says.

Right. The category four that touched down in Miami right around the time Bryce passed away. When Paige first told me that he had asked her to take me on this trip, she was worried we'd have to put it off because of hurricane damage. Except it turned out the Keys—especially on the Gulf side—were only lightly affected. Some high winds, rain, and minor storm surges.

"Oh." Paige squints, and I can't tell if it's the sun in her eyes or if she's as confused as I am. "So when you say drug wash-ups, you mean … "

"Exactly what it sounds like. Smugglers sometimes offload the bricks when they see the Coast Guard. But it's more likely this is because of Denny. Boats caught in the storm, and the like. Can we talk to Leslie?" Delgado says.

"I don't know where he is, but you're free to look around."

The men glance at each other, and I read something along the lines of: *Oh yeah, we'll just walk three square miles real quick.* "We were hoping Leslie would take us directly to the wash-ups so we could get on with our day." Delgado again.

"Right, but I don't know where to *find* Leslie," Paige says slowly.

"We could call him on the walkie-talkie," I suggest.

She nods and turns to go get it, but I say, "Paige, wait." I hear what sounds like an ATV motor.

"Excuse me," Paige says, and steps between the men out onto the porch at the edge of the stairs, leaning to see.

The ATV comes into distant view down the road.

"That's him," she says, and Leslie pulls down his tethered sunglasses, allowing them to drop against his collarbone.

Agent Pierce signals Leslie with a hand in the air, and both officers take the stairs down to meet him, but Paige and I stay standing side-by-side, watching.

"Have you ever heard of a drug wash-up?" I ask her, not removing my gaze from the men.

She turns to find my eyes. "Of course. Do you remember who my mom and brother were?"

Shit, I walked into that. I look down and nod. Both her mom and Bryce were addicted to meth. Bryce had a quick run with it when he was still in high school, way before the time I met him. He always stayed involved with AA though, sponsoring upwards of fifty men. Their mom died of a drug overdose.

We can't hear what the men are saying, but it isn't long before Leslie parks and waves them into the garage.

"God, this has been a weird vacation," Paige says, eyes fixed on them.

"Seriously. Why did you pick this place?"

"I didn't, remember? Bryce did."

Right. Wow. Grief brain for the win.

"Do you know how he found it?"

"No clue. He wouldn't give me any explanation, just said it had to be this place. I guess he thought you'd like it."

I keep mentally bobbing in and out of the fact that we're here because of Bryce's death. I'll completely forget, like last night during the whole Leslie-isn't-a-woman scene, but then it'll get quiet, and my mind goes right back to him, and it feels like being swallowed up by quicksand.

"What's going on?" Reese asks, appearing behind the screen door in shorts and a tee shirt, her blonde hair in a high ponytail. She pushes the door open and joins us on the porch. "And why hasn't anyone made coffee?"

"Cops are here. Something about a report of drugs washing up on the shore," Paige says.

Before Reese can comment, Leslie and Agent Pierce come out of the garage. Agent Delgado follows, holding a brown rectangular package in his gloved hand.

13

TORI

I CAN VAGUELY HEAR PEOPLE TALKING DOWNSTAIRS, BUT NOT what they're saying. I think it's Court and Paige. Rawson rolls off me as soon as he finishes and reaches over to the nightstand on his side of the bed for a cigarette, showcasing a full view of his naked back and ass. There's a sheen of sweat on his skin. I usually love morning sex, but today all I feel is irritation.

"Please don't smoke in here. Paige will smell it and I'll be in even deeper shit," I say.

It isn't really about him smoking in the vacation rental—I can handle Paige's anger. It's that I'm so frustrated that the last couple times we've had sex, he just collapses when he's done and doesn't even try to get me off.

Rawson is an Aries sun, and I adore that energy. It's all passion and courage. But *his* Aries sun is conjunct Pluto, so that Aries drive to assert itself, amplified by Pluto—the planet of power and control—is a recipe for *me first* energy. His Libra moon hides this selfish streak pretty well, but when it shows up, it's annoying as fuck.

Rawson takes a pull from his cigarette and saunters over to

the window, stark naked, and opens it. He blows the smoke outside. He's lean to the point of being skinny, but he's strong so it doesn't matter. As I watch him, my body is still dealing with having gotten turned on and then dropped off, unsatisfied.

With the window open, I hear waves lap the shore like they would at a lake, not how I imagined a Florida beach. But my weeks in Key West taught me that it can be like that on the Gulf side.

The morning sun isn't fully hot yet, but it's bright with promise that it'll get there. I close my eyes and take a deep breath to connect with myself and let go of my irritation with Rawson. I reach for my tarot deck on the nightstand to get a little encouragement from the universe.

I flip over a card and stare at it. Temperance. The winged angel is reminding me to be patient, and keep the long game in mind.

Right. Let this go. Focus on our overall compatibility. Twin Stars.

"Since when do you care what Paige thinks?" Rawson asks. His cheeks hollow as he takes another pull from the cigarette.

I sit up and hold the milk-white sheets against my bare chest. "I don't *care*. It's more like … I already annoy her naturally, so I don't need your help in the effort."

"Well, you sorta enlisted me to help you *in the effort* when you brought me here even though you knew they'd be mad about it." Then he holds the cigarette between his lips and braces his hands against the white-trimmed windowsill to lean out into the open air.

"Do you hear that?" he asks.

"Hear what?"

"People talking. Sounds like men. I can't make out what they're saying. I thought Leslie and I were the only men on the island." His tone is borderline possessive.

"Can you see anything?" I ask. He shakes his head and walks over to my nightstand to drop his cigarette into the glass of melted tequila ice from last night. It sizzles.

"The porch overhang is in the way."

"I'll go see." I move out of bed and pull on the white terry robe I found hanging in our closet last night.

Rawson rummages through his pile of discarded clothes on the floor and picks out a pair of palm-frond boardshorts. "Hang tight, I'm coming with."

At the bottom of the stairs, I can see my friends huddled on the porch, all of them with their arms crossed, staring off to the right of the house.

"What's going on?" I ask, opening the screen door to join them.

"Leslie called Border Patrol because he found drugs on the beach," Courtney says. "They're here to pick them up."

Paige seems to be entranced with the men, like she's straining to read their lips or something.

"Oh yeah, probably a wash-up. What kind of drugs?" Rawson asks. I cringe inwardly at the excitement in his tone.

"Shh!" Paige hisses.

I roll my eyes. How the hell am I supposed to deal with her for the next three days?

"I'm trying to listen," she explains.

I move to cross my arms, but remember everyone else is doing that, so instead I stuff my hands into my robe pockets.

"They don't know what kind," Courtney whispers to answer Rawson's question. "You're right though. They called it a wash-up and said it's likely coke or marijuana, but it could be fentanyl."

"It's not fentanyl," Rawson announces. "They don't usually move fentanyl across large bodies of water. It's too fragile. Just a little moisture would degrade it. I'd put my money on it being coke."

I turn to face him. "Whoa, illegal drug expert."

He shrugs. "I wouldn't say *expert*. But it comes with the Florida Man territory. You know, gator wrestling, kayaking through a flooded golf course, getting in fights outside of Waffle House—not my finest moment, by the way. Don't y'all worry though, I left my *Swamp Rat* hat at home."

His Florida accent is in full effect, and this image doesn't match the one he projected at Sloppy Joe's—his opinions on literature or his obsession with Hemingway. Am I dating a secret redneck? I know Florida has a reputation, but I guess I didn't see it in him before.

This little voice in my mind reminds me that I don't really know him, and I can acknowledge that there's some truth to it. Most people can't fully know someone in such a short time, but our connection is different. We're Twin Stars.

I mentally scan his chart and remember that he's a Gemini rising. I relax. Geminis are adaptable and quick-witted, able to talk to anyone about anything and make you feel like the most interesting person in the room. Since it's his rising sign, that's how he presents himself to the world. And yet, every Gemini has a couple sides to them. So what if Rawson's are "artist" and "Swamp Rat?" I look over at him and smile. It'd be kind of cute, actually.

At this point, the matchy-matchy—and supremely hot, I might add—Border Patrol guys walk back toward us. For a minute I imagine this is a bachelorette party and they're actually here to give us a surprise strip show. I chuckle to myself.

"What?" Paige barks at me.

"Nothing."

She hates it when I laugh during serious moments. The problem is, literally everything is serious to her.

"Sorry to bother you all," the one in a ballcap says. "It looks like we got what we came for."

The other agent holds up the brown brick, and there's a huge picture of SpongeBob on it. *What?* The cartoon's gaping face takes up almost the entire surface area. "If you find any more of these, just call us."

"We don't have phone service," Paige says.

"That's true. How did you call them?" Reese asks Leslie.

"Did it from Marathon."

"Well if you find more, leave them on the beach exactly where they're at," the one holding the brick says. "Don't even touch them."

"We don't have a boat, either," Paige says flatly. "So how would we get to Marathon to call you?"

"I have a boat on the other side of the island," Leslie says.

"You do?" Paige asks.

"Well, yeah, how else do you think I got here?"

Right. Of course he has a boat. The Border Patrol men offer a wave and head down to the dock. They speed off in their boat.

Leslie gets back on the ATV and disappears down the road. Is he not making us breakfast?

Reese turns to Paige. "Did you know anything about a second dock?"

"No. It turns out there's a hell of a lot I don't know about this place."

14

REESE

A SECOND DOCK.

Another boat.

I know what I have to do. I turn to the girls and that bozo, Rawson. "I'm going on a walk before it gets too hot. Anyone want to join?"

It's pushing 1000 hours and I want to find the other boat, just to know what we're dealing with and whether there's a way to leave the island if there's an emergency.

There won't be an emergency, says Rational Reese. This is the Reese who was stationed in Afghanistan and could help a team launch out seven minutes from the first crackle of the radio alerting, "Medevac, medevac, medevac."

I know how to stay calm. How to operate under extreme stress. The problem is I'm only like that in *those* situations. Otherwise, I'm hypervigilant. Constantly scanning for threats, trying to gain intel. I'm always overprepared, and when traveling, that translates into packing stuff normal people would never bring, and always having an exit strategy. It's what I have to do to calm my nervous system because of my past. And it's not just from my time in the military, either.

But this is a vacation. It's supposed to be fun, Rational Reese says.

Fun. Yes, I should focus on that. And I will, as soon as I get the lay of the land.

Paige made such a big deal about how there would be no boats in or out until the end of our stay that I assumed the one dock was the only access point. And I assumed that anyone else on the island—employees, etc.—would be dropped off like us. But Leslie's boat and the second dock mean we aren't totally stuck on this island with no way off for days. Thank god.

Then my stomach drops because another access point doesn't only mean we can use it to leave. It means people can get to the island without us knowing. We're more exposed here than I'd like.

"I'm in," Court says about the walk. "But I need coffee."

"Same," I say with a smile.

I follow her into the kitchen. She goes right for the machine, then looks around, presumably for coffee pods. I open a cabinet and reach for an oversized burgundy mug, then hand it to her.

My mind keeps pinging, running my anxiety up. Like the whole Leslie thing. I can entertain the idea that Paige got confused because the man's name sounds female. But she was *so* certain, and I know how important it is to trust my own gut, so I've learned to recognize when others are leaning into theirs.

For me, it's the way Leslie interacts with us, as if we're a nuisance. How he's not staying in the house. How he took off before offering to make us breakfast even though that's supposedly why he's here. I know these things aren't concrete proof that he's dangerous or anything, but they do make me distrust him.

Courtney is opening cabinets, still looking for coffee, and I remember I saw coffee pods in the pantry yesterday, so I walk over there and pull out a clear bin full of them.

"Your favorite—instant coffee," I say with a smirk. Courtney is a coffee snob.

She hangs her head and then nods, but doesn't look at me. It isn't until she swipes at her face that I realize she's crying.

"Oh, are you okay?" I ask, setting the small bin down next to the coffee machine.

Between the food scare, Rawson appearing uninvited, the Leslie mix-up, and now the drug bust, it's been a busy twenty-four hours. Bryce slipped my mind.

"Yeah," she says, lifting the lid and getting a coffee pod. She sets her mug on its perch. "Bryce made the best coffee. He always got the proportions perfectly right."

I wrap my arms around her shoulders in a hug.

Courtney is one of the most loving people I've ever met, and outside of my crewmates from my 2011 deployment, who I only keep in loose contact with, she's the closest thing I have to a friend.

"I know you miss him. I do too," I say.

The sound of Tori and Paige bickering on the porch filters into the kitchen, but I can't hear what they're saying.

"I hope they aren't like this the whole trip," Courtney says, turning to watch the machine groan out her coffee in drips and spurts.

"They won't be," I say. "I'm sure they'll work it out and find some kind of truce." But I'm not sure. Not at all.

"I don't want him here."

Him. Rawson.

I nod while reaching for a hunter green mug. It's rare for Courtney to have an opinion that might upset anyone.

"I suppose it's my fault for saying she could bring him. But she means a lot to me, and I didn't want to upset her."

"What's your fault?" Tori asks, standing at the entrance to the kitchen.

I catch a gasp before it's audible. How did we not hear her come in?

Courtney stands at attention. "Oh nothing, I … " Her eyes fill with tears. She doesn't make a move. She's been caught.

I have no idea how to make this better. Tori is watching Courtney with eyes wide, chewing on her bottom lip, as if waiting for Courtney to say something.

"Are you mad at me about bringing Rawson?" Tori asks, stepping closer. Before Courtney can answer, Tori adds, "I know this is your trip. And I know you just lost Bryce, but I guess I thought that's why—I mean, because of your connection with Bryce—you'd understand. Have I overstepped? I can send him back to Marathon if you want."

She wrings her hands as she watches Courtney. I can't read Tori at all. I don't know her. But she's acting like she doesn't realize nobody is leaving the island until the boat comes to pick us up at the end of the trip.

"It's okay. It's just that I didn't expect to have a stranger here." Courtney's voice is soft and strained. She sounds exhausted.

Tori closes the distance between them and takes Courtney in a hug. "I'm so sorry. Honestly, I thought you might not love it, and I chose to do it anyway. It was selfish to put that before your needs. I don't know, I just feel so desperate for this to work out with him."

Courtney nods and smiles at her. "I understand."

Interesting. I don't know what to think about this dynamic, but I know Tori has been through hell with losing a husband too, so I chalk it up to them understanding each other in a way I'll never be able to relate to.

15

REESE

Courtney and I have been walking along the beach for a while now, and the dock is way out of sight. We talked a little, but overall we've fallen into an easy silence.

We drank our coffee fast and nestled the mugs into a tuft of seagrass way inland so we can grab them on our way back to the house. That was my idea. I like to have my hands free as much as possible.

I love being with Courtney. Neither of us feels the need to keep up conversation. It was like this over the past year, too. All the hours we logged together watching *The Great British Bake Off* while Bryce rested. The neighborhood walks she joined me on. Sometimes nothing needs to be said when you've gone through what she has. And Courtney is still locked into that place, mentally and emotionally. She might be for quite a while.

I steal glances at the ocean. The morning sun glints off tiny translucent blue waves; the water is lighter where it's shallow, then opaque farther out. The beach is clean, and while it's not manicured or anything, there's a romantic quality to its wildness that I find charming. The humidity is already in full force today, but I don't mind it. I watch herons coast along where the small waves are breaking, hoping to find a morning meal, as the hiss of cicadas grows louder when we approach a twisted green mass of vegetation in the distance.

Maybe my hypervigilance isn't needed here. Maybe there's actually nothing to worry about, and I should relax and enjoy my time in paradise.

"Are you okay?" Courtney asks, and I realize our silence has stretched abnormally long.

"Yeah, of course." I smile. I've tried to hide my apprehension about being in this isolated place, but she's perceptive.

When she first invited me on this trip, I told her I didn't like to travel but that I was happy to make an exception for her. It isn't true—I love to travel. But I knew being on a secluded island would set off my hypervigilance and paranoia. I wanted her to hang anything she noticed about my behavior nicely on the hook of *Reese is nervous about traveling*. Which would be a super normal feeling. Not at all trauma based, and nothing like the reality of why I'm like this. A reality this group of friends can never find out about.

I want to ask if she's truly okay about Rawson being here, but I hesitate to bring him up. What she needs right now is a reprieve from the intensity. From everything. That's what this trip is supposed to be, but it's already churned up its own drama. I want to give her just a few hours' break from the chaos if I can.

"This vacation isn't very relaxing," Courtney says.

I laugh softly.

"Seriously," she goes on, as if I need convincing. "Starting with *a girl died here*. Do you believe Leslie? That it's a rumor?"

Up ahead, the beachy waterline ends in the tangled mass of brush I saw earlier—mangroves. They look pretty dense, and I suddenly wish we had one of those kayaks laying out by the chickee hut near the dock. But we passed those a long time ago.

Courtney keeps glancing at me. She's waiting for my reply.

"I suppose there's no reason *not* to believe him, but something doesn't feel right, and I don't like not having any access to the mainland," I say.

"Right? I didn't expect to have Wi-Fi, but now I wish we did. We're so … isolated. Are you worried?"

It reminds me of how she'd grill me whenever something out of the ordinary happened with Bryce.

"He's sleeping longer than usual. Is that normal?"

"He's not eating as much. What does that mean?"

I've done personalized hospice care for a few years now, and I've learned my role is both to ease the patient's transition out of this life and to help ease their loved ones into saying goodbye. Courtney has looked to me for signals, but this is different. It isn't about Bryce or my nursing expertise.

"Not worried, exactly. But I would like to get some answers."

"Like?"

"Well, I want to know where Leslie is staying on the island. Why isn't he staying in the house? Why did he leave before making us breakfast? I also want to know how we can leave if we need to. You know, if there's an emergency."

I sense a subtle shift in her body. The way she sort of straightens her shoulders.

"What kind of emergency?" she asks.

We've almost reached the point where we'll have to hack through the mangroves to keep going, so I start scanning for an entry point.

"Oh, just in case one of us needs a hospital or if there's a storm. You know, normal emergencies." I try to downplay it, but my words still come out colored with alarm.

"We have a nurse," Courtney says with a smile and a nudge.

I laugh. "Well, yes, but my abilities do have their limits."

"I think it'll be fine," Courtney says. It feels like she's trying to convince herself. "I bet we've seen the last of the weird stuff, and the next few days will be *smooth sailing*, as Bryce would say."

That's totally something Bryce would say. The man could cliche like he was earning royalties.

"I can't imagine what you must be feeling." I reach for her arm and link it with mine at the elbow.

I miss Bryce too. He was a beautiful soul. Such a bright light with a deep well of curiosity about others and endless check-ins about your life even as he knew his own was ending.

She shrugs. "It's hard, but of course, I knew it was coming."

"There's still no way to prepare for losing someone you love so deeply."

She nods and swallows hard, then looks away.

16

REESE

WE COME TO A STOP RIGHT AT THE EDGE OF THE MANGROVE forest. The roots are thin here, where they shoot up from the sand, but they quickly grow dense as the thicket stretches along the shoreline. It looks like it's swallowing up the beach. I can't go around them from behind—the mangrove trees climb inland quite a distance, and if I venture that route, I'd still be bushwhacking. But instead of mangroves, it'd be through a tropical forest.

The appearance of this spot likely changes with the tide, and right now the tide is low, with the water at my ankles. But as long as I make it through in a reasonable amount of time, I'll be fine. I'll turn around before the tide comes in if it looks like a no go.

"Hey, I'm going to keep walking, but I think I'll have to bushwhack through there to get to the other side. Hopefully there's more beach." I point at the thinnest part of the mangrove. "Want to join?"

"Really?" Courtney stops walking, so I do the same. "Why do you want to hike through there?"

"I want to see what the rest of the island looks like."

She squints like she isn't buying it. "It's three square miles. Can you even walk all of that in a day?"

"I won't walk the whole thing. I just want to explore a little."

It'd take a few hours, for sure, even if there were a paved trail. Considering there's not a trail of any kind, and I'd have to use a knife to get through, I probably can't walk it without packing food and water at the very least. That seems extreme. Would I really go through all of that trouble just to ease my nervous system? My heart thumps hard, and I know I would. I will. I need to. But I can't explain it to her. It sounds crazy.

Her eyes stay steady on my face. I have the urge to look away. It's like she can see right through me.

"You're nervous here, huh? Was it the military that made you anxious about traveling?"

I freeze. "Yeah," I say. It isn't *totally* untrue.

"Did you ever travel as a kid?"

"Why?"

I kick myself. I can't sound so defensive. She's already asking a lot of questions, and she's a journalist. So, naturally curious.

Courtney tilts her head to the side. "I'm just realizing there's so much I don't know about you. When we met, you felt familiar, like we'd been friends forever, but then we dove right into Bryce's care and living side by side, and I haven't taken the time to learn about your life. I feel bad."

I made a point of not talking too much about myself over the past year—only when she pressed—but I learned so much about her. I always wondered if it felt like a friendship to her, or if I was merely the person caring for Bryce. I didn't want to get my hopes up that the connection she and I had was real. That it would last beyond Bryce's final day. Then she invited me on this trip.

Even so, I'm not sure how much of myself I'm ready to share. I've always kept my cards close, and I have good reasons for that. But I want this friendship to work, so the last thing I should do is to push her away.

"Sorry. I don't talk much about what I saw overseas. It's mostly stuff I'd rather forget. And then when I started hospice care, I found that I'm better at listening."

"You're a great listener. I really appreciate that about you." Courtney looks out at the water and says, "It's been a long road. I'm just so grateful for our friendship. It feels easy and peaceful."

"Me too." I let down my ponytail, put the hair tie in my mouth, and smooth out the flyaways before pulling my hair up into a high sloppy bun. Just to keep my hands busy while I wrap my mind around the fact that she called me her friend for the first time. She wants to be my friend too. Maybe it's immature, but I'm excited and relieved about it.

"As tempting as it is to hack through the jungle with you, I'm pretty tired. I think I'll head back and let you explore by yourself," she says.

"Sounds good. If I don't return in about an hour, send help," I say and wink.

"That's not funny," Courtney says with a smile.

"You know, what they say about many hands making light work is true for emotional burdens too. You'll find your way through this. You have us to lean on."

"Okay, *Bryce*." Courtney's face lights up. "But for real, thank you for saying that."

She turns and walks back the way we came, her Chacos kicking up sand behind her.

17

REESE

Navigating the mangroves is harder than I imagined. The more dense the twisted branches get, the more difficult it is to fit my body through. I catch glimpses of other vegetation through the thicket to my right. Lots of those hardwood trees and hanging moss. This is such a different place than the serenity of the beach. As if this is the raw version of the island, the true version, and it feels ancient, sprawling, and intent on reclaiming the land.

Claustrophobia squeezes my chest. We don't belong here.

I stop for a breath and glance around, trying to focus. I could move more inland to see if I come across the dirt road, but at this point, it's probably better to bail and return another time to enlist my other idea—kayaking around to wherever the beach picks up again. Assuming it does.

Just then, a stab of pain erupts across my shin. It's enough to leave a small trail of blood down my ankle.

Yep, time to bail.

I retrace my steps as best as I can. It'd be so easy to get lost here.

Is all my obsessing about a second dock really worth this

hassle? If there's an emergency, we can always ask Leslie to bring the boat around and take us into Marathon.

Except the thing is, no part of me wants to ask Leslie for anything. I refuse to depend on someone I don't trust.

Finally, I'm back on the beach where Courtney and I parted, but now the tide is in. The water is up to my knees, so I wade inland. There's still plenty of space to walk on the beach to get back to the house.

As I walk, I keep going back to thoughts about Leslie. What about him makes me so deeply suspicious? I'm not like this about all men. Take Rawson, for example. I don't necessarily like him, but I don't feel this deep need to keep an eye on him, either. He's more like an annoying mosquito that I can't shoo away. Leslie is a snake rearing to strike.

After a long while, I see Tori and Rawson lying in loungers on the beach near the dock. I check my watch. It's already almost 1100 hours, and I'm coming up on the spot where Court and I left our mugs. A hint of green peeks out from the grassy nest in the sand. I can't tell if it's a mug or part of the foliage. Did Courtney forget about them?

I turn to walk up toward higher ground to check it out, and, yep, there sit our empty burgundy and green mugs. I'm sure it's fine. She's been in kind of a fog. Grief does that to a person.

Even so, it feels like something's coming loose inside me. A little nagging sense that something is off.

I stoop to grab the mugs, traipse back down to the wet, packed sand, and beeline for the boardwalk so I can check on her. This pulling feeling inside of me is probably just a result of being in a new place and all the unknowns we've run into.

Paige is in the kitchen when I come inside. Her back is to me, and she's wearing white linen shorts and a teal tank top. Her hair hangs in beachy black curls like she's already showered and diffused it for the day. What's the point of even bringing along a blow dryer? Her hair has more curl than mine, so I bet it'll frizz to high heaven in this humidity. She sort of sways like she has earbuds in and is listening to music. Spread out in front of her are sandwich fixings: lunchmeat, sliced cheese, a head of lettuce, mayo, mustard, and tomatoes.

"Hey, is Court napping?" I ask once I see no earbuds.

She turns and furrows her brows. "No. She went with you."

"She came back early. It would have been about an hour ago, maybe more."

"She's not here. Although I've been focused on the menu since everyone's going to be hungry soon and Leslie won't answer the walkie. I feel like I'm gonna have to hunt him down to cook for us at every damn meal." Paige squirts mustard on a slice of bread. "Speaking of which, it's sandwiches for lunch. What do you want? We have turkey, ham, and roast beef."

"I'm not hungry, thanks."

My stomach is busy doing cartwheels. Maybe Courtney's upstairs napping and Paige didn't hear her come back.

When I get up there, I go directly to her room and open the door. Her duvet is tossed practically off the empty bed.

Her phone is plugged in on the nightstand.

I sprint back down the stairs and into the kitchen.

Paige is waiting for me with her eyebrows raised like she could hear me coming. My words come out charged with alarm.

"Courtney's not here."

18

TORI

I CAN FEEL REESE'S FRANTIC ENERGY APPROACHING WAY BEFORE she actually arrives. God, I hate not knowing what her chart looks like. She has to have some Gemini in there to explain all that sparky nervousness. Or maybe Sagittarius.

She stands next to my chair, blocking my sun. "Did you guys see Courtney walk by at all?"

I set down *Run on Red* and remove my sunglasses. "Not since she was with you." I wondered why Reese came back from the walk alone.

"Fuck," she whispers and turns toward the coastline, tenting a hand over her eyes.

"What's going on?"

"I don't know where she is. We parted ways at the mangroves because I wanted to go through and she wanted to come back to the house."

"Why?"

"She said she was tired."

"No, why did you want to go through the mangroves?"

Reese waves me off. "Just exploring. Anyway, we need to find her."

That's some intense exploring. I know Reese has a military background, but why in the world would you bother with what feels like a drill when there's a beautiful beach to lie on?

"Hey, did you see Court?" I touch Rawson's arm to get his attention. He's deep into sketching something on his drawing pad. I lean over a little and see that it's the Gulf of Mexico, with the Seven Mile Bridge way in the distance. Exactly what's before us. And his rendering of it is amazing.

"Don't think so," he says without looking up.

Worry bleeds through my chest. It seems like we should have seen her walk by, but maybe we were both too engrossed in what we were doing.

"I doubt she's lost. Court has a good sense of direction," I say, more trying to calm myself than anything else.

"When our boat dropped us off here, the captain said something really shady about a girl dying on the island recently. He wouldn't say whether it was from natural causes or if she was killed, but he made it sound like a warning. So that's got me worried about Court," Reese says.

I go cold all over, despite lying in the warm sun. Would have been nice to know that someone died here before we booked the place.

"Will you help me look for her?" Reese folds her arms across her chest. Her eyes are wide and alert. I can sense something more than fear brewing underneath the surface, but I don't know what it is.

"Of course. Come on, Rawson." I shove my book into my beach bag and pick up my empty mimosa glass.

"I'll walk the beach and see if I can find anything," he says, adding his sketch pad to my bag.

"Great. You and I can search around the house and garage," Reese says.

Rawson and I walk with her across the sand in silence. It feels too serious and intense, but I can't think of anything to say. When we get to the boardwalk, Rawson keeps going on the beach and Reese and I peel off toward the house.

"Should we look inside again?" I don't want to make her feel like I don't think her house inspection was good enough. But maybe it wasn't.

"Paige is covering that."

"Covering that." Like this is a mission and we all have assignments. My own energy flickers up a little. I hope it's just in response to Reese's inner typhoon, but even so, a whisper of anxiety climbs up my ribcage.

I take a calming breath. Surely Paige will find Courtney at the house.

"Hey, does Leslie creep you out at all?" Reese asks.

"What do you mean?"

"I don't know. Something about him just ... Never mind."

I want to press her, but instead I check in with myself. Does Leslie creep me out? He's unexpected, and yeah, a little rough around the edges. I don't know that he's veered into *creepy* territory, though. "Let's just focus on finding Court," I say.

She nods and we take the rest of the boardwalk in silence until Paige meets us on the porch. "Anything?"

"No, you?" Reese replies as I set my bag at the bottom of the stairs.

"Nothing. I've looked literally everywhere. Under every bed, and inside every closet. Not like she's hiding from us, but seriously, where is she?"

"You called Leslie on the walkie?" Reese asks.

"I'll do that." She disappears into the house.

Reese and I start calling Courtney's name as we traipse

through the brush on the back side of the house, peering out into the deep vegetation. There's no boardwalk to take us out there, no path at all. I should have changed out of my flip-flops, but I didn't even think of it.

After a while, I stop yelling her name. If she were within shouting distance she'd have heard us.

Reese has gone a little quiet, although she seems on the quieter side in general.

"Remind me, how did you and Courtney meet?" she asks.

"Why?"

It seems like small talk, but there's that energy coming off her, shoving forward. She's after something else, but what is it?

"Just curious. I can't remember."

I explain how I met Courtney through Bryce's connection to Tucker, and through Paige.

"So you met her after you lost Tucker?"

"Mm-hm." I'm glad I'm walking in the brush behind Reese so she can't see my face. Tucker is the last thing I want to talk about right now. It's taking all my focus to dodge palm fronds and duck below the huge spiderwebs suspended between the trees overhead, along with the silver-dollar sized spiders that stand sentinel on them.

Don't look up. Just don't look.

"How long were you and Tucker together?"

Really? She's asking me this right now? Jesus, she might have some Aquarius in there. This unfiltered examination of someone at totally the wrong time is so damn Aquarian.

"I don't want to be rude, but I'm starting to really worry about Courtney, and it's hard to focus on much else," I say.

"Sorry," she says as we break through the foliage. She walks the dirt road toward the garage, and I follow. "Honestly, I feel like I'm at a loss because I've only known Courtney for about a year, and it was the hardest year of her life. I can't help but wonder how well I really know her."

I stop walking. "What?"

"Sorry, that came out wrong. I mean, I'm sure the Courtney I know is a more stressed and sadder version of who she normally is. I can't rely on my knowledge of her right now. For example, has she ever gone off by herself like this before?"

Ah, she's playing detective. This need to prod and investigate, maybe that's the pushy energy I was feeling.

"Court likes to have someone by her side," I say. "She's very capable and independent—her career is proof of that—but when it comes to life, she'd rather have a sidekick. It's her Libra placements. When she met Bryce, they became inseparable, and shortly after that, she clung to Paige whenever Bryce wasn't around. So she's independent, *and* she likes to have someone by her side. She hates conflict, *and* her career is based on putting herself right in the middle of it. Not sure if that answers your question."

"Yeah, it does. Thanks."

Reese keeps periodically scanning behind, like she thinks we're being followed. She's guarded, as if trying to hide her panic. But I'm well acquainted with panic. And underneath it, there's that other thing again—this electricity. She reminds me of a calm sea buzzing with life below. Like there's a lot to her that she doesn't let show.

19

TORI

WE WALK THE DIRT ROAD FOR A BIT, AND I SUDDENLY FEEL LIKE I can't catch my breath, so I sit on the ground.

Courtney is fine. We'll find her. I pull my knees up to my chest and hug them, resting my head on my arms.

"Are you okay?" Reese asks, sitting next to me.

"Sorry, I need to sit for a sec." I focus on slowing my breath. *Calm down.* At least it isn't bad enough to need a Klonopin, not yet. I haven't needed one of those in years, but I still travel with them just in case.

Reese watches me for a minute. It feels like she has her nurse hat on, and right when I'm sure she's going to ask me about the panic attack I'm on the verge of, she says, "So, tell me about astrology. That's what you do at SoulMatch, right?"

I look at her with skepticism, and she nods to show she's serious.

"When's your birthday?" I get the words out evenly, and it's a good sign that I might already be starting to calm down.

"July twelfth. Cancer."

"Do you know any of your other placements?"

"Yeah, I'm a Cancer sun, Gemini moon, and Aquarius rising. At least, that's what Paige told me when I first started working for her. No idea what it all means."

I called that Gemini placement a mile away. And I was even right about Aquarius. I love when I read people accurately. "You want a rundown?"

"Sure. Whatever you want to tell me."

Reese is definitely doing this to distract me, and I'm grateful. It's annoying to have to stop searching, especially right now, but it would be more stressful if she was frustrated with me for this.

I take a deep breath and speak slowly. "You're nurturing and have inner depth and sensitivity. That's your Cancer sun, which is your core identity. The moon is all about who we are when we're most comfortable. It's our emotional world. Geminis are quick-witted and love to learn. They can be restless and nervous though, too. There's a duality to the sign. And our rising is how other people see us. Aquarians are visionaries who see the world as it could be, not only as it is. They're humanitarians at heart, who genuinely want to make things better for everyone. They're unconventional—out-of-the-box thinkers."

"I am *not* nurturing," she says immediately, as if that's all she heard. "I mean, I'm a nurse, so I guess that sounds weird. But I don't really identify with Cancer."

Funny. She's totally a Cancer—look at the way she sensed I needed to calm myself, and she facilitated that without drawing any attention to it or embarrassing me. Very Cancer, just with some real Aquarian flair. "Well, there's a lot more to us than our sun signs. Not just moon and rising, but we also have planet placements that interact with the zodiac too."

"Do you mean literal planets, like in the solar system?"

This is helping. I'm already feeling my body return to normal.

"Yep. There are Neptune influences on certain placements,

which make people more idealistic and dreamy—that's Court. Some of us have a Saturn complex, which makes it feel like life is always against us. That's me." I scoff.

"Hm," she says. "Could you do a reading for me? Maybe when we get back to Idaho?"

"I'd love to!"

Well, that's decided. Also decided is that I definitely like Reese.

"We should head back to the house and see if Paige or Rawson have found Court," Reese says.

When we get inside, Paige is messing with the walkie talkie in the living room, saying, "Leslie, are you there?" over and over.

"Any luck?" Reese asks.

"Nope. Nothing."

Reese closes her eyes and shakes her head. "I think we need to organize a bigger effort now. Pack some supplies and push out to search the island."

This makes my heart thunder again. "Do you guys think she's actually … missing?" I ask quietly. I don't want to know the answer unless it's *Oh, no way, this is all just a precaution.*

"We can't know that yet, but I'm not taking any chances," Reese says. "As soon as Rawson gets back, we can decide on a course of action."

"And maybe by then, we'll get Leslie on the walkie and he can take the boat to the mainland for help," Paige says. "I'll try him again."

"Come in Leslie, are you there?" she speaks into it.

I forgot about the boat, and at the mention of it, my body relaxes. Either Courtney will turn up, or we'll get the police involved. It's going to be fine.

"I'd also like to take a kayak and search along the perimeter of the island," Reese says.

"Let's do that now," Paige says.

"We should wait for Rawson. We've covered all around here. I know it sucks to wait, but it'll put us in a stronger position once we know where he's looked. Maybe he even found her. Plus, I don't want anyone else to get lost."

"I don't want to wait. We're wasting time." Paige's tone is demanding. She picks up the walkie talkie and tries it again. But there's only static.

I look at the clock in the living room. It's two p.m. "Paige, when did you last eat?" I ask.

Paige deals with low blood sugar and is prone to getting very hangry.

"Not sure. I was prepping sandwiches when Reese came back without Court. I'm not hungry."

Yes she is, but I'm not going to push the issue.

"It's been three hours since Courtney and I were together on the beach," Reese says quietly. Then she looks up. "We should eat."

Thank god.

The silence is heavy as we sit in the living room with our sandwiches. I can feel Paige catastrophizing, while Reese's mind seems to be more on a search and rescue. The few words spoken come from Paige, and Reese is quick to shut her hopelessness down and replace it with ideas of where to look.

Surprisingly, Paige doesn't react to being silenced by Reese.

Eventually, the screen door slaps, and all three of us jump. Rawson stands in the entryway.

"What did you find?" Reese asks.

Rawson tries to catch his breath and then runs a hand up his forehead and through his dark hair, clearing sweat. "Not much. Since we're the only ones here, the footprints were easy to follow. Of course, the pair where you and Courtney walked along the beach are now swallowed up by the tide," he says to

Reese. "But I did find another set that veered off toward the brush. Was that you?"

"Was it just before the dock? That's where we walked to set down our mugs."

"No, much closer to the mangroves."

Reese lets out a little gasp. "It wasn't me, then. It must have been her. Where did they lead?"

"Well, that's the thing. It's like she climbed up the little bluff and disappeared."

"She went into the brush?" Reese asks.

Rawson throws his hands up. "Yeah, I mean, she must have. Not only that, but there are no footprints from that spot back to the beach. So it looks like she never came back down. At least not that way."

"Why would she do that?" Reese whispers to herself, then asks, "Did you go into the brush to see where it leads?"

"As far as I could before it seemed ridiculous. Why would she try and Tarzan through all that?"

"It doesn't have to make sense," Reese says, quietly again.

Rawson chews the inside of his cheek. "Well, I went as far as I could without getting turned around. My sense of direction is shit."

Paige rolls her eyes, but I ignore it. Her opinion of him isn't important right now. My stomach is in knots about Courtney.

"Ooh, sandwiches," Rawson says, and disappears into the kitchen.

"I can't believe I let this happen." Paige drops onto the couch. Her normally curly hair is frizzy, and purple bags hang under her eyes. Did she sleep at all last night? I feel a twinge of guilt about my threat to her yesterday.

"Let's try not to overreact," I say. "We'll get a hold of Leslie and use the boat to get help."

"I'm not overreacting!" Paige yells. "I booked this trip. Even if this place wasn't my idea, I went with it. This is my fault."

I grit my teeth. Of course, she's making it about herself.

Reese gently takes Paige's forearm. "None of that matters," she says with authority. "What matters is that Courtney's gone. And we have to find her."

Rawson walks back in with three huge sandwiches piled on his plate. I wince. He took more than his share of dinner last night, too. Maybe this is more than his Aries conjunct Pluto *me-first* energy. Is it actual selfishness?

I should go easy on him. We're all stressed. Maybe he's a stress eater.

Paige, seeming to come back down to earth, nods at Reese. She tries the walkie again, but gets nothing. She exhales and says, "Okay. I don't know how, but I'm going to find Leslie. I guess I'll walk that dirt road until I come across him."

"Perfect. Tori, can you go with Paige? I'll take Rawson back to the footprints he found and see if he missed anything," Reese says. "Here, take this." She produces a decently sized knife from… where? Oh, her waistband. She had a knife in her shorts the whole time? What the hell?

"I'm good. I don't want that," I say, stepping back like she's handing me a tarantula.

"Please take it. I'll feel a lot better."

I look at Paige, but I don't know why. She shrugs, so I take the death stick while Rawson breathes the word "cool," his mouth full of bread and cheese.

Reese shows me how to clip the sheath to my waistband.

"Looks like you got some Florida Man in you, too," Rawson teases her.

"No, just a whole lot of military."

All I can do is stare at this thing in my hand. Why did Reese bring a big-ass knife on vacation? I don't have time to ask before she heads out the front door with Rawson following, complaining that he didn't get to finish eating. But I sit there, Reese's words echoing in my mind: *"What matters is Courtney is gone. And we have to find her."*

20

REESE

RAWSON AND I MAKE IT TO THE SINGLE SET OF FOOTPRINTS ON the beach. They lead to a small bluff, just as he said. The brush is scuffed up so the dirt below shows streaks, as if someone tried to climb it and their footing slipped a few times. He swears it looked like this the first time he came, and that it's not from him climbing up. At least not all of it.

We scramble up until we're almost knee-deep in tropical vegetation with absolutely no path in sight. It's all sawgrass and shrubs with these delicate white flowers, along with green spears —baby palmettos—that shoot directly up from the ground. The palmettos are kind of creepy. Like someone has buried little trees and they're pushing up headfirst from their graves.

"Weird, right?" Rawson says.

Weird is an understatement. Where would Court have gone from here? I scan the bluff, and my eyes find an area that looks more disturbed. It definitely seems flattened, but it's impossible to see any footprints. This spot is directly in front of us, so it makes sense that she might have climbed up and begun walking straight ahead.

I take a step, and Rawson says, "I know it seems like she must have gone that way, but I already looked. It leads nowhere."

He sounds defensive like a schoolboy with a teacher standing at his desk to check his work. But his ego isn't a priority right now.

He follows me, and when I get a dozen or so steps in, all traces of disturbance in the grass and flowers disappear, just like he said. Everything seems untouched.

I exhale loudly. I do know basic tracking, but it's been forever. I'm so used to being overprepared, and I am this time too. I packed extra food, like the ramen noodles, and a first aid kit. I even brought my little Beretta. And god, I hope I don't need it, but thinking about it back at the house puts my mind slightly at ease. So, while I have the training and some supplies to handle myself in most situations, I've never gone looking for a missing person. Nothing could have prepared me for Courtney going AWOL.

"So how do you know this gang of woo-woo chicks?" Rawson asks, breaking my concentration.

"Woo-woo chicks"? What the hell?

"I was Bryce's nurse."

I close my eyes and listen to whatever noises I can pinpoint around me. Sounds carry far in the wild, especially when there's water nearby.

"That's the husband who died?" Rawson asks.

I turn toward him, annoyed. "Why are you here?"

"What do you mean? I'm with Tori."

"No shit, *Raw Dog.* But *why*?"

He and Tori are an odd match. It seems like their only compatibility is that they're both a little wild around the edges. Tori is gorgeous, but not the type I'd think someone like Rawson would go for. She's naturally beautiful. Curvy, freckled, glowing skin, minimal makeup. He strikes me as someone who'd need the high-maintenance type, a woman who enhances his image. Heavy makeup, hair extensions, nails, caterpillar lashes, a curated wardrobe, the works. There's nothing wrong with that, but it isn't Tori. On top of that, I highly doubt he wants to be tied down.

"I love her."

I snort a laugh. "Come on. You've only known her for a couple weeks, and you don't strike me as the type to believe in soulmates. That's the kind of partnership she expects."

I may not know Tori well yet, but Courtney has explained this to me. How Tori has a pattern of seeing the potential in men instead of the reality of who they are. How she's been holding out for a love to rival what she had with Tucker. How, after all these years, she still isn't over him.

He stretches his neck side to side and lands his brown eyes right on me. "I don't give a flying fuck what you think. I love her. She makes me feel alive."

Interesting answer, and it seems sincere.

I make my way down the bank and Rawson clambers after me. If Courtney came through here, I have no clue where she went next. As much as I hate it, our best bet might still be getting that boat and going to Marathon for help.

"I have an idea," Rawson says. "I'll draw a map of the island. We can use it to keep notes and make sure we're covering everywhere."

I nod and look at my watch to see it's about 1700 hours now. Five p.m.

Courtney's been missing for six hours.

21

PAIGE

Tori's threat from yesterday reverberates inside me.

"I'm done keeping your secrets."

Despite what's going on with Courtney, despite all the crazy shit on this island, despite the fact that I'm only on this trip because I owe it to Bryce, my brain can't let go of those words. Tori has caused problems in the past, at least on a smaller scale by griping about how the company was her idea, but this is on a different plane altogether.

Tori and I walk the narrow dirt road in silence. I have no patience for small talk. Not while I'm split between worrying about Court and worrying that Tori will burn my life to the ground.

Speaking of burning, god, it's hot. I love the heat when I'm in a bikini on the beach, but this humidity is killing me. It's like I can't breathe very well. Almost as if the air is liquid. Thick soup in my lungs.

Just then, a slightly cool gust of wind swishes my hair, and I look up. A wall of clouds edged with aluminum gray moves across the sky. It had better not rain on us.

Tori is a few steps ahead of me, her red hair in a ponytail, swiping side to side against the green tube top she's wearing over her cheetah-print bikini. For a split second, I'm pulled back to when we were kids. When life was simple. Before Tucker died and she lost her fucking mind. She could make me laugh like nobody on the planet. Is that version of her still in there somewhere? I miss her.

But is agreeing to let Rawson stay really going to keep her—this version of her—silent?

I sigh. Right now, I need to focus on Courtney. I'll deal with the Tori thing when we're back in Boise. That's a tomorrow problem.

The silence is growing awkward between Tori and me, but I don't trust what will come out of my mouth if I start talking to her. Even if I could keep it off that topic, I'm sure she'll find some way to accuse me of being selfish again. Of not caring about Courtney. *"How dare you try to chat about the weather when our best friend is missing."* Selfishness is her main complaint about me, but for someone who claims to understand me so well, she never takes a breath to consider things from my perspective.

I gave her a prominent spot in the company to try to make up for her feeling like I stole her idea, even though she didn't come up with it. We talked about it together. One of those joint-inspiration moments. You wouldn't know it by the simple way she lives, but I pay her a solid six figures a year, and the work isn't stressful at all. She owns a home in Boise's historic and expensive North End, but of course she never talks about that. I don't know what else she wants from me.

Whatever. I'm not a rookie at being hated.

"I'm really worried about Court." Tori's voice jolts me back to reality.

"I'm sure she's fine. We'll find Leslie and get the police out here to help search in no time."

I can't show Tori that I'm worried sick about Courtney. She's constantly looking for opportunities to knock me down. I have to keep my mask firmly in place around her, all vulnerabilities armored up, because I never know what will set her off.

"Don't you even care?" Tori stops in her tracks and turns toward me. "How are you so calm?"

Calm? I practically had a breakdown a few minutes ago in the house. I couldn't keep it together with Reese around because something about her makes me want to lean on her for everything. I assume it's her role as a caregiver. She's so mature and solid for thirty-one. I'm tempted to break around her, and it's uncomfortable since I'm used to signing her paychecks, not going to her for support. Plus, being around Reese and Tori together is brutal. Tori triggers me, and Reese makes me want to melt into her like she's my mommy.

"What are you talking about? I—" I'm about to say something I'll probably regret when Leslie comes into view on the ATV.

I wave my arms furiously as if he's going to somehow miss us even though we're standing smack dab in his way, and he'd have to plow through us to get by. Dust kicks up behind the vehicle, and he slows as he gets closer.

"Let me do the talking," I say.

"You always do," Tori mutters.

I ignore the jab, wondering if someday I'll crack and finally lose my shit all over her because I'm stuffing down so much anger. But that's another tomorrow problem.

Leslie stops about ten feet in front of us, but he doesn't kill the engine or get off the ATV. He just stares like he's waiting for us to get out of his way.

"Hey, we can't find Courtney and we're worried she might

have gotten hurt or lost. Can we take the boat back to Marathon for help?" I yell over the engine noise.

He finally turns the ATV off.

"Who's Courtney?"

I explain the situation to him as calmly as I can.

"She's probably down at the beach, or maybe she took one of the kayaks out," he says.

His super unhelpful suggestions stoke the fire of anger in me. He's doing the man thing. Acting like my concerns are no big deal while suggesting the most basic solutions that I've already tried. Men get in their own way constantly, living like they're still stuck in 1953 even if they were born in 1993. They see women as helpers, not as leaders or equal partners, or even independent thinkers. Despite this, I soften my voice and approach him less directly, like I would with an animal I don't trust. Like we're in 1953.

"Those are such great suggestions, and I appreciate it. But she's been missing since this morning, so we'd like to go into town and get some help. What do you think?"

I'm trying to make him feel like taking the boat to Marathon is his idea. I should have gone with that initially, but I never would have guessed he'd say no. Of course he'd want to help us find a missing guest.

Right?

Tori folds her arms, probably thinking about all the ways I'm botching this. Maybe she's right. We both keep our eyes on Leslie. Why's he taking so long to reply?

"It's almost dinnertime. You said she's been missing since this morning?"

I nod. I want to ask if he's planning to cook us dinner. Maybe that's why he's heading toward the house. But dinner doesn't matter right now.

"I've got a guy on the mainland already. He took the boat this morning. Not sure when he'll be back."

My jaw drops. Are there more people on this island? Where are they all staying?

"Why don't you know when he'll be back?" My tone is icy and I don't even care.

"He had a family emergency."

I want to say, *What if* we *have an emergency and need the boat? You know, like our friend going missing*? But instead I say, "Then can we take the ATV and look around the island?"

"I can't let you drive it, but one of you can hop on and I'll take you for a spin," Leslie says.

"Hop on"? It's an old ATV—a four-wheeler, not the fancy kind that looks more like a golf cart. I'll have to sit behind this man, hugging him in order to not fly off. I shove my dread down.

"We'll find her. She probably fell asleep somewhere," he adds.

"Fell asleep somewhere"? What's with this guy? Does he think she's some tropical Snow White? Did she find a cabin and decide to clean it up, too? Then, a dark thought snakes around my mind: Snow White fell asleep because she was poisoned.

I turn to Tori. "You can find your way back, right?"

"Maybe *I* want to go with Leslie," she protests, because of course she does.

"I need you to update Reese and see if they've found anything."

"Found anything where?" Leslie asks, suddenly interested.

"Oh, they went out to look … " I stop talking and watch as he hangs on my words. "Well, we've all just been looking for her." Something makes me nervous about telling him. It's irrational—Leslie obviously wants to help now that I've nudged him toward that—but I learned a long time ago that the only person I can really trust is myself.

22

PAIGE

Leslie is driving too fast for this bumpy road. I'm hanging on to him for dear life so I don't bounce right off the ATV. I don't have a free hand to hold my hair, so it's whipping all around my face, and I can't see a damn thing. The sun is below the palm trees, so at least my vision isn't also accosted by sunshine.

My nose, however, is quite accosted. Leslie smells like stale cigarettes and unwashed hair, so I'm suffering at every moment.

"Can we stop so I can look around?" I ask, my voice choppy from the ATV bouncing.

He doesn't respond. It's like he didn't hear me at all, but my mouth is right next to his ear.

This isn't as helpful as I thought it would be. It's a wild green tropical forest as far as I can see. If he had just let us take the vehicle, I could stop and search. Not that I know how to drive this thing, but surely one of us would. Rawson, at least.

I groan at my sexist assumption. It popped into my brain before I could think it through. I have to admit it's probably true, though. Don't all rednecks drive four-wheelers?

Ugh. Another assumption.

Never mind Rawson. We have Reese, and I'd put money on her ability to drive one. She seems to know everything.

I twist my hair quickly and shove it under the collar of my shirt, risking my life by holding on to Leslie with just one arm. It works for a few seconds, but then my hair's out again, lashing my face in the wind. Fuck this. How am I supposed to look for signs of Courtney under these conditions?

I have an idea. "Please stop! I need to pee."

"Not here," he tosses over his shoulder.

I knew he could hear me.

Not even a minute later, he slows to a stop. It feels like one of those things people do to assert dominance.

"I won't stop where you tell me to, but I'll stop fifty feet away because it's my idea."

Whatever. I fling myself off as soon as it's safe to, but before the damn thing has stopped rolling completely.

"What the fuck?" I'm yelling at him before I think about my words. Before I consider that I'm out here in the middle of a secluded island with a man I don't know.

He laughs.

"Our friend is missing and you're driving like this is a Formula 1 race. We need to find her, not take the road at record speed."

"That stretch was particularly dangerous. Needed to get through it quick."

What the hell does that mean? How can a stretch of dirt road be dangerous?

He cuts the engine and adds, "There's a few things about the island you don't know. As long as you keep your ass at the house or on the beach, you don't need to know 'em. But obviously, we have to venture into these other parts to look for your friend.

And I don't want something to happen to any of you guests on my watch."

Keep my ass at the house?

Why does he think he can talk to me like that? Also, something *has* happened to one of us on his watch. Not to mention he should have told me about these potential dangers when I booked the place.

Leslie gestures toward the brush on the coastal side of the road. "Be fast. We don't want to linger here."

"Why?" I ask.

But again, he acts like he doesn't hear me.

Well, I have to at least pretend to take care of my business or I'll show my hand, and his tone just now increased that fear of making him angry while we're out here alone.

He goes to start up the ATV, but the engine doesn't turn over.

"What are you doing?" I ask.

He groans like I'm an annoying kid. "I'm not going to leave you, if that's what you're worried about. Go over there." He points again to the left side, where the forest turns into those mangroves that stretch out into the water. Why doesn't he want me to go inland? It would be much easier to find a tree to pee behind.

The ATV still won't start. He curses and gets off the vehicle, then lifts the seat to inspect the engine.

Twice now he's told me to go left to find a place to pee. It makes me want to do the exact opposite. It isn't like I'll wander far out into the brush.

Not like Courtney did.

The intrusive thought makes me gasp quietly. We really need to find Courtney. Then a burst of frustration takes over. Why the hell did she venture out into this tropical wilderness?

But, no. I don't know what happened, but I doubt she just wandered off. My gut says she's in danger, and I'm scared to death at the prospect of losing her after losing Bryce. She's more than a connection to him. She's my best friend.

While Leslie's engrossed with the ATV's motor, I slip off to the right.

Walking into the vegetation, I still have a view of Leslie's bright-red tee shirt between breaks in palm trees, but that's all. No way he can see me if he even cares to look.

It's probably a good idea to pee even though it isn't urgent.

I squat, facing into the brush opposite Leslie, and something grabs my attention. It's way out in the distance and to the right, parallel to the stretch of road Leslie rushed through.

It's a small building. Faded turquoise so light that it's almost white. It might be made out of painted cinder blocks? A shed, maybe.

Perhaps that's where Leslie is staying. I could ask him about it. See if I can look for Courtney there. But there's something off about this. He seemed to purposefully rush past it. He doesn't want me to see it.

Which means I absolutely need to see it, and without him finding out.

23

PAIGE

THE ATV ENGINE REVIVES WITH A RUMBLE, AND I GLANCE BACK.

"Come on!" Leslie shouts.

I need to hurry, but I should document this so I can find it again. I reach into my pocket and pull out my phone. The little building is barely visible, but I zoom in as much as I can to capture it and snap away. Then I start taking pictures of this area all around me as I move closer to the road.

I don't know for sure whether Leslie is involved with Courtney's disappearance—it's a huge leap—but I'm not taking any chances.

"Paige!" Leslie calls out from the road, his voice muffled a little even though I can hear it over the engine. His back is probably to me. Of course, he thinks I listened to him and went into the brush on the other side of the road.

I move closer, not wanting to call out and give away that I'm inland.

I glance around quickly for something—anything—to use as a marker so I can find this spot again.

It's taking too long, but everything here looks the same—all shades of green. I need something that'll stand out.

"Hurry up!" His voice splits with anger like a hungry lion peeking out of its cage, and this little slip of his seals it for me. I absolutely cannot trust him. We're guests here, yet he's treated us like an inconvenience from the start. Now, one of us is missing, and he's angry with *me*?

I don't want to get on that ATV with him again, but it's growing dark, and I need to get back to the house. I can't be out here alone on foot.

"Sorry, I'm finishing up. Be right there!" I call back, trying to keep my voice sweet and even. My eyes scan wildly but there's nothing to mark this spot.

When Leslie comes into view through palm trees, he's leaning against the seat of the ATV, staring directly at me, glaring. He shouts, "Why the fuck didn't you go the direction I told you to?"

I swallow hard. My body buzzes with alerts. *Danger, danger.*

I move fast toward the road, scanning around with desperation. I can't lose this spot, and his patience is running out.

Shit, shit, shit ...

I know what to do.

Once I reach the dirt road, I throw myself to the ground like I've tripped. Then I use my feet to really scuff up the dirt on the side. It probably looks comical, like I'm flailing, but I don't care. I need to make this area look different from the rest of the road.

He watches me. Doesn't ask if I'm okay, doesn't offer to help me up. I stand and brush off my shorts, noticing my knee is bleeding a little.

"I told you to go on that side." He throws a finger toward it.

"Oh, you did?" I cock my head, playing dumb. Dumb and cute. Works every time. "I'm so sorry, I had to go so bad that I bolted." Hands up with a shrug. Innocent, no mockery, just a clumsy girl who didn't hear a thing.

He gets on the ATV and I straddle behind, gripping his waist. "I need to go back to the house," I announce in Leslie's ear while he accelerates.

"What? Why?"

Why? Great question. Why don't I have a believable answer lined up and ready to go?

"I … started my period."

He groans loudly and I smile behind his back, because it's the perfect excuse. No way for him to argue.

24

COURTNEY
EIGHT HOURS EARLIER

IT'S NOT EVEN NOON YET, BUT IT'S ALREADY GETTING SO HOT. As soon as I turn my back to leave Reese at the mangroves, my mind is whirling. The fact that she's concerned about us being isolated here doesn't help. Yesterday on the boat, when I could feel her anxiety, I dismissed it as apprehension about travel. But now it's shifted to match my own. The dead girl. No service. A house manager who is shady, to say the least.

My feet sink slightly into the wet sand as I walk toward the dock and the house. Worries about this trip are only overcome by thoughts of Bryce. I picture him walking next to me, and if he were, I'd reach for his bicep and gently trace my fingers down the inside of his arm until they landed against his warm, wide palm. Thick fingers entwining mine. He loved to hold hands, maybe more than I did. Why didn't I hold his hand every single day? Bryce would know how to comfort me if he were here. He knew how to manage grief, how to live with it as a constant presence, something he'd been doing since the day I met him.

It was back when I was in my twenties, living in Spokane, Washington, and I'd recently left my job at *The Spokesman-*

Review so I could do more freelance and investigative pieces. On this particular day, I saw on Twitter that shots had been fired at a cabin in Boundary County, located in the isolated panhandle of Idaho, near the Canadian border. It was the perfect chance to flex my freelance muscles.

I reached out to my mentor, Don Hart, who had established a lot of contacts in North Idaho, mostly from covering Aryan Nations activity during the 80s and 90s. He was retired, but agreed to use his connections to find exactly where this cabin was located. He said we could meet up and try to get close enough to cover it.

I drove almost three hours to the site.

It turned out that federal agents had set up there days prior. There was a barricade about a mile away, so tensions were high, but nothing had *actually* happened yet.

Until the gunfire that day.

Initially, it was routine. The U.S. Marshals were there to serve a bench warrant for the cabin owner's arrest—he'd failed to appear in court for a previous firearms charge. It quickly escalated into more: a cabin in the woods, surrounded by feds, soaked in knife-edge silence for days. Neither side was budging. The cabin owners weren't coming out, and the feds weren't leaving.

I remember seeing a plane doing these aggressive figure eights over the cabin, which was surrounded by police cruisers and a couple federal Humvees. It confirmed what a huge, possibly career-making opportunity this was for me, but my excitement was quickly followed by guilt for thinking about myself while the situation was putting people at risk. Namely, the children the police believed were inside the cabin.

If I could get close enough, my story angle would be about the children—child protection was my passion. What had these kids gone through growing up with a nut job for a father? How many other kids, especially in rural areas, were victims of their parents' ideology?

It wasn't like I was personally in danger. I was a mile away from the scene and would probably be fine. Only problem was, Don and I were two among dozens of other members of the press who were a mile out as well. How would we get anything close to a story?

Don had no patience. "Maybe that whack job will talk to us since we aren't the law." He glanced around. When the police had their backs turned, he leaned over the construction roadblock they had set up. "Maybe he'll want to get his side of the story out."

"You're gonna try to approach the cabin?" I whispered. We hadn't spoken with any of the feds, but the local police said the owner was threatening to shoot on sight anyone who got too close.

Don pulled back and looked at me like I was crazy. "Stories that shift the cultural consciousness don't write themselves."

These words embedded deep inside me, but in the moment I didn't have a response.

"It's a mile to the cabin along the road." He pointed beyond the barricade. "But my contact says it's about half that distance if you cut straight through the forest."

It was this sort of risk-taking that made Don such a successful journalist. But no way was I going to breach the barricade. It was the beginning of my career, and the last thing I needed was to land in jail or get a black mark on my professional record because I had been reckless. Or, even worse, I could end up dead.

"Don, that's crazy. You could get arrested. Or shot! Don't do it."

He waved me off and slipped into the woods adjacent to the police roadblock.

I stood there, stunned. What should I do? Inform the police?

Yes, I decided. Don getting arrested was better than him getting shot.

Right then, an unmarked SUV came up the road headed toward the cabin. I got in front of it and waved them down before they went through the barricade. The passenger window lowered.

I started talking immediately. "My friend went through the forest to get to the cabin. I don't want him to get hurt."

It was Bryce. He looked back at me with his kind eyes, and instead of making a comment about what an idiot my friend was, he just smiled and said, "I'll check it out and update you as soon as I can." His voice was calm and measured.

I nodded and got out of the way.

Minutes later, gunfire broke out, and I imagined the worst. It sounded like a warzone.

Finally, there was silence. I saw that unmarked car coming back toward me. Bryce was alone. His face was red, I thought from exertion, but when I looked into his eyes I saw that they were damp like he'd been crying.

"We got him to safety," he said.

"Thank you so much." I saw his hands shaking on the steering wheel. "Are you okay?"

"An agent was shot in the process of trying to locate your friend."

"Jesus, I'm so sorry."

I didn't know what else to say. I hated that Don had caused a death, but saying so felt thin. Bryce seemed suddenly uncomfortable and said goodbye before he drove back toward the cabin.

The guilt weighed on me, and after a couple months, I tracked Bryce down to say how much I regretted my role in bringing Don to the scene because it had led to that agent's death.

When we started talking, I learned that it wasn't just any agent. It was Bryce's best friend, Tucker, who died that day.

And Tucker was always somewhere on Bryce's mind the entire time I knew him. Maybe that's just how grief operates. Maybe you don't ever get past it, but rather, you absorb it. Make it part of who you are.

A buzzing sound breaks through my heavy thoughts. It's not the constant buzzing of cicadas, which got louder the closer Reese and I got to the mangroves.

This hum has a different quality. More mechanical, and coming from the sky. What the hell is that?

25

COURTNEY

I FINALLY SEE IT. A DRONE. HUGE, BLACK, WITH FOUR propellers that make me think of an overgrown insect. It flies over the beach, then hovers where the vegetation meets the sand. This isn't your average hobby drone. I can tell by looking at it that this thing is expensive. The kind with thermal imaging features they use during search and rescue operations. Not that I've covered a lot of those. My experience with drones is mostly limited to documenting rural housing and school conditions. Still, I know this one is fancy.

What's it doing? And who is operating it? I turn and look out at the water. Could it be someone from Marathon? I don't have drone ranges memorized, but Marathon isn't *that* far away. This drone could probably do it.

It's carrying a tiny message capsule, which makes me think of a bomb, but I know it's not.

The payload drops into the brush, and the machine immediately dips, makes a turn, and whirs out to sea until I can't hear it anymore.

"Well hello, old friend," I whisper to that inner nudge that there could be a story here, and maybe a story is exactly what I need right now if it'll slice through this numb fog I've been living in.

I walk toward where I saw the item drop and climb up a couple feet of dirt and brush until I'm standing in lush, green vegetation.

I glance back at the beach, hesitating. This isn't very far inland. Is it dumb to explore alone? I still have about a forty-five minute walk back to the house.

Maybe I should wait for Reese—she'd certainly be eager to join me. But also, I'm just gathering preliminary information. It's not like I need someone with me for that.

I make my way into the tropical forest where I'm greeted by more of those trees with low branches and Spanish moss.

I'm pretty sure I remember where the capsule fell, but I can't see anything through all the wide leaves. So I keep my eyes on the spot, slowly stepping forward, each time being careful not to stumble. I wonder how often people walk through this brush. It's anything but easy.

Finally, I reach the spot and bend over to move leaves aside and feel around for the capsule. When my fingers touch it, anticipation grips me. That feeling of being on the cusp of something —a secret, a break. It's intoxicating.

Something rustles in the brush nearby, and I duck to hide without thinking about it, but there's nowhere to go. Like quickly looking away when you accidentally make awkward eye contact with a stranger even though they already saw you.

Leslie appears through the brush about thirty feet away and stops suddenly when he sees me. I reach down and grab the capsule.

"Hey," I say. "There was this drone, and it dropped something." I hold it up.

"Did you open it?" His voice is uncharacteristically flat. It's not like he's been overly cordial to us, but there's this tinge of anger now.

"Not yet," I say, and start to pull the top off.

"I wouldn't do that," Leslie barks, and normally I would listen, but I've almost got it unrolled, and I'm so damn curious.

He walks fast toward me, covering ground comfortably, like he marches through dense vegetation all the time and isn't worried about making a wrong step and twisting an ankle.

But he isn't fast enough, because in seconds, I'm reading what's on the piece of paper.

Before I have time to look up, a blow connects with my temple, and it's lights out.

26

TORI

Earlier, after Paige left with Leslie on the ATV, I made my way back to the house, trying so hard to stay present in my body as I walked the dirt path. It was either that or allow my mind to twirl into orbit. Fear and anxiety over Courtney are the only things there, and I can't let myself think that way. It's hard, especially when I return and find that Reese and Rawson aren't back yet. I'm alone with my thoughts looping.

Courtney's missing.

It's been too long.

I manage to keep myself calm, but I'm only narrowly avoiding tipping over into panic.

When Reese and Rawson show up about forty-five minutes later, it's almost dark, and Rawson is zinging with energy. He doesn't even greet me, just runs up the stairs, taking them two at a time.

I look at Reese for an explanation while handing her the knife she gave me earlier.

"He wants to make a map of the area," she says with a shrug.

"That's smart. He's an artist." I imagine my words batting her skepticism out of the air.

"Yeah, that's what he said." Reese goes into the kitchen, and I follow her.

"You don't think he can do it?"

"It's not that. He said he had an idea, so I guess I got my hopes up. You know, that it'd be a good one."

She fills a glass with water and chugs it.

"It is a good idea." I fold my arms across my chest. Reese doesn't strike me as a judgmental person, but her reaction to this is giving big Paige vibes.

"Well, it could be a good idea if we knew what the rest of the island looked like. At this point it'll only be what we've already covered." She furrows her brow and looks around. "Where's Paige? Did you guys find anything?"

I tell her about meeting Leslie on the road, and how someone has already taken the boat to Marathon for the day.

"Jesus, the boat is gone?" Reese says. "And he doesn't know when this guy'll return?"

"Yeah."

"Okay, well at least Paige may be able to help round out Rawson's map when she gets back," Reese says.

Rawson comes downstairs, but before he can say anything, Paige is there, in the entryway, announcing, "I found something!"

She tells us about the building she glimpsed, and how we need to hurry to get back out there, and how she doesn't trust Leslie at all.

Reese latches on to this. "We absolutely cannot trust him. I felt his aggression the first time he showed up here."

"Wait," Rawson interrupts. "You guys don't trust him because … why?"

"Did you not hear anything Paige just said?" Reese turns to him.

We're all standing. Nobody has bothered to sit down since Paige got back.

I don't tend toward paranoia, but even I feel something is off with Leslie. Maybe I didn't sense it when he first showed up with our food, but he didn't even seem to care when Paige told him Courtney was missing.

"Maybe he's grumpy about toting you all over the island," Rawson says to Paige.

Is he serious? It's not like we're doing this for fun. Our friend is *missing*.

I stare at him, and even though we're soulmates, that little doubt pushes through again: I've only known him for two weeks.

"We don't have time to explain to you the nuances of a woman's highly evolved gut instinct when it comes to knowing whether a man is safe. You'll have to trust us," Paige says.

Rawson's cheeks and the tips of his ears grow red. I hope it's embarrassment, but it seems more like frustration. He glances over as if he expects me to stand up for him, and I want to because I love him, but he has his man glasses on and can't see the situation clearly.

"She's right," I say. "You don't have to agree with us. But don't waste our time trying to convince us Leslie isn't a threat."

I feel Paige's gaze on me, but I don't meet it. I don't want to give her the satisfaction of my agreement. I'm only taking her side because it's the goddamn truth and too many men share this blind spot.

"I think it's time we start considering the possibility that Courtney is in real danger," Reese says quietly.

My insides recoil and I grasp for other possibilities. "Maybe she's just lost."

Paige glares at me. "Wake up. She's not lost. Leslie is acting weird, and we can't trust him. Courtney isn't safe out there."

"I sketched a quick map," Rawson interrupts, holding out the piece of paper. "Maybe you can help fill in some of these details, Paige?"

I hate how real it's becoming—Courtney actually being in danger. I go quiet and focus on my breath so my growing anxiety doesn't spiral.

Paige takes the map and glances over it quickly. "Maybe. But I don't know how accurate it would be. Here, I took some pictures."

We move to the living room and she sits on the couch, and I go for the seat right next to her. I have to sit. My head is starting to feel floaty.

"How long were you guys driving?" Reese asks.

I rub one eye.

"I don't know. Ten, maybe fifteen minutes?" Paige says.

"How fast do you think he was going?"

"Not sure, but I almost bounced off a couple times."

"Those old four-wheelers can get up to sixty miles an hour or so, but that one isn't in great shape," Reese says.

"How do you know that?" Paige asks.

"The frame has a shit ton of chipped paint, so it's likely been in an accident or two—probably bad enough to affect performance."

"A few of the cables and wires looked super worn—frayed," Rawson adds.

It feels like he's trying to redeem himself by offering something useful. We look at him, mostly out of surprise at the way he jumps into the conversation, but he takes it like he needs to explain his expertise.

"'Florida Man Gets Reckless Driving Citation After Racing Jet Ski Through Swamp.'"

"What?" Paige says.

"I know four-wheelers, I'll just say that." He puts his hands up in surrender.

There's a beat of silence and I can feel everyone trying to figure out where to go from here.

"I think we have to get back out there and see the shed for ourselves," Reese says.

"We should go now. Court could be in danger," Paige says.

Reese shakes her head. "If Leslie is sleeping in that shed, we have to go during the day when he's less likely to be there. You and I will go first thing in the morning."

DAY 3

27

REESE

THE SHED PAIGE SAW WAS ALL I COULD THINK ABOUT LAST
night while I took a shower and then as I fell asleep. Paige tried
to reach Leslie on the walkie over and over as the night
progressed, but there was no answer. We don't even know if the
boat has returned to the second dock.

Now that night is finally receding into a powder-blue morning, I can't wait any longer. I pull on the only pair of pants I
brought—cargos—along with a white tank top. I look like a military cliche, but at least the cargos aren't camo. They're gray. I
comb fingers through my hair, mindlessly sectioning it off to
create a French braid.

Courtney has to be in that shed.

If she's alive.

No. Not helpful.

It's 0600 hours, which means Courtney has been missing for
about nineteen hours.

I dump the contents of my duffle bag onto the bed and
cringe. Of course, there are clothes, a swimsuit, and a few

toiletries. But that's nothing compared to all the other stuff I packed out of paranoia. My little Beretta 30X, for example. Small, but semi-automatic. I check the chamber even though I know there's nothing in there. Then I toss a few items of clothing aside while trying to locate my ammo. I grab a magazine, shove it into the gun, and drop a second mag into one of my pants pockets. After flipping on the safety, I put the small gun into a long pocket and survey myself in the mirror to make sure it's not visible. It would raise questions I don't want to answer.

I shove my fully charged phone into my sports bra and notice my hunting knife on the bed. I clip it to my waistband and pick up the little canvas knapsack I brought along to shove the travel-size first aid kit inside. I brought my medical kit, too, but that's too big. And that's almost as suspicious as a gun if the others find out I've brought it. Who packs an entire medicine cabinet for a tropical vacation?

Me, that's who.

Downstairs, Paige sips a cup of coffee on the patio that connects to the kitchen, and I add a few bottles of water to my knapsack.

"Morning," I say. "Did you get any sleep?

"Not really. You?"

"Nah, I never really do."

"That sucks." She sets her mug down on a side table. "I'm anxious to get moving. What's your plan?"

I turn around and pop a K-Cup into the machine. "Simple. We'll start on that dirt road and keep going until we find the shed."

"I've already tried to reach Leslie, and of course, there's no reply."

"Of course," I say.

I wonder why she even bothered, but it doesn't matter. All I can think about is getting to the shed. If that's a bust, we need to find the second dock and hope the boat is back so we can take it out on our own to get help.

Tori and Rawson saunter into the kitchen, looking as exhausted as we are.

"Paige and I are heading out," I say. "Rawson, I want you to find Leslie and get him to tell you when the boat is coming back. If it's back already, you two go with him to Marathon for help."

"And if it's not back?" Paige asks.

I look at Rawson, but answer her. "Do whatever you can to keep Leslie busy here. We need time to search the island without him knowing."

"Why me?" Rawson asks.

"Because I think he'll be more willing to help if he knows another man considers this a big deal. And he'll have a harder time telling you to fuck off."

"You obviously don't know men very well."

When I don't respond, he asks, "How do I find him?"

"No idea. That's your job," I say.

"How do we keep him here?"

"Again, your job."

Paige stands and rinses her coffee mug, then sets it in the sink while I blow across the top of mine to cool the coffee.

"I packed water and a first aid kit, but we need some food," I say.

"Why the hell do you have a first aid kit?" Paige asks.

"I'm a nurse, remember? Hey, can you put together some food that's easy to pack? Protein bars, muffins, jerky, anything. We'll put it in my knapsack."

"Your military training sure makes you prepared," she says.

She has no idea all the ways my life has shaped me into this.

I look at the clock on the microwave. It's already past 0700 hours. We have to get going.

"Do you hear that?" Tori says, walking to the front door.

It's the familiar sound of a motor.

Leslie.

28

TORI

Paige and Reese go upstairs to sneak out from the back balcony—the one we had dinner on only two days ago. Rawson immediately disappears upstairs.

"Rawson?" I call out. "It's showtime."

"Coming." He rushes down the stairs, taking big strides toward the front door. I follow, praying this will be easy—that the boat is back and we can go to Marathon for help.

We stand on the front porch and watch Leslie park the ATV in front of the garage. We have to get him into the house because he's exactly where Paige and Reese need to pass by to get on the dirt road.

Leslie turns off the engine.

"Hey," Rawson calls out. "We need to take the boat to Marathon."

"No can do. My guy's not back." He stops and leans against the ATV.

"Well, when do you expect him back?"

Leslie shrugs. "Thought he'd be here last night, so your guess is as good as mine."

"Plan B," Rawson whispers to me. Leslie is too far away to hear.

"Do you have a way to contact your guy?" I ask as a last-ditch effort to get the boat.

Leslie ignores my question, but comes toward us, and when he reaches the porch, he offers Rawson a handshake, like I'm fully invisible. Maybe Reese was right about letting Rawson take the lead.

"Where is everyone?" Leslie asks, leaning to peek inside the house.

I watch him—the way his eyes dart and how he seems to avoid eye contact—and I can't help but wonder what his chart looks like. Immediately, I think of Scorpio. Scorpio gets a bad rap because of its shadow side—paranoia, jealousy, and manipulation—and they can be volatile, too. But they're also insanely intuitive, resilient, and magnetic.

Scorpio has a way of dominating a chart whenever it's present, even if it's not a person's sun sign. I adore Scorpios. They tend to know what they want and how to not give a fuck, and we can all use a little more of that in our lives.

As for Leslie, I have this inkling he's something else.

"Still sleeping," Rawson says, answering his question.

Leslie squints like he's trying to determine whether Rawson is lying.

"Did your other friend turn up?"

My heart hammers.

"No," Rawson says. "She probably twisted an ankle or something and can't find her way back. You know how women are."

Wait. Rawson is supposed to bring credibility to our concern, not play into what we believe Leslie already thinks: that we're overreacting.

I stiffen.

"Hm," Leslie says, and shoves his hands into the pockets of his khaki cargo pants.

It suddenly occurs to me that if he's involved with Courtney's disappearance, he would know we're bluffing.

"Sorry to hear that. I've been looking and haven't found anything either. Maybe she took a kayak to the mainland," Leslie says. There's a glint in his eye like he's holding back a smirk.

He's playing with us, and Rawson is fumbling this. My breathing has become shallow, so I take a deep inhale. I have to make this better.

When Rawson clears his throat like he's about to speak, I jump in. "There's still two kayaks on the shore, just like when we got here. So, no, she didn't take a kayak."

He smiles, and it makes me feel like I have spiders skittering up my spine. It's horribly insincere and slightly amused. "You've seen the whole island? And you know there are only two?"

"Of course not," Rawson says in a flustered tone. "It's just unlikely she went searching for a third kayak when there are two on the beach."

Courtney didn't take a kayak. That's totally beside the point, and we're standing out here arguing about it while Paige and Reese are waiting for us to get Leslie inside.

But how do we do that?

I bite the inside of my cheek. I don't want to say anything when I have no clue what will help our situation and what will hurt it.

Rawson clears his throat again. Maybe it's a nervous tic. "Hey, while you're here, can you come in and take a look at one of the bathrooms? The toilet's overflowing. I tried to plunge it, but that made it worse."

What? Why didn't he lead with that?

"Damn it," Leslie says under his breath. Then, louder: "You can't put shit down the toilets! The plumbing here is tricky."

Rawson chuckles. "Shit is literally what goes in a toilet."

Normally, I would laugh, but I'm so wound up right now.

Leslie walks between us and up the stairs to the house. When he passes by, I catch Rawson's eye, and he winks at me. So, that's what he was doing upstairs before we came outside—clogging the toilet.

Once Leslie is inside, I whisper, "Why didn't you ask him to fix the toilet right away?"

"The whole point is to stall him."

"Yeah, stall *inside* the house."

"Well, I got him in there, didn't I? Tell me if you see him coming." Then he runs down the stairs and toward the ATV.

From where I'm standing on the porch, I can see through the screen door into the house, and I have a front row seat to whatever Rawson is doing with the ATV. He squats down as if to inspect the vehicle, then goes into the garage.

29

PAIGE

REESE AND I SLIP OUT OF THE HOUSE BEFORE LESLIE PULLS UP.
It's weird he came so early in the morning since he's apparently
not making us any meals, but then again, he did check in early
yesterday too. The morning of the Border Patrol visit.

Was that really only yesterday?

Fuck this trip. I should have told Bryce that taking Courtney
away so soon after his funeral was an insane idea, my guilt be
damned. I want to laugh at two-days-ago me, who imagined this
would be all tanning and getting in some work when Courtney
wasn't looking.

Reese and I hide behind the house. We have to wait for Tori
and Rawson to get Leslie inside so we can sneak away.

When Leslie says his guy hasn't returned with the boat,
Reese and I exchange an alarmed glance. "Do you think he's
lying?" I whisper.

Reese shrugs. "Honestly? Yes. But even if he's not lying,
he's not going to help us. We're on our own."

I nod. I can do this. Depending on myself is second nature.

Finally, when Rawson mentions the toilet, we hear hard footfalls on the porch stairs, so we scramble out to the road and sprint. After a few minutes, we're still booking it even when we're probably safe from immediate view.

"Do we have to keep running?" I ask. I'm already winded even though I do yoga regularly and try to hit the elliptical at least three times a week. Maybe in reality it's less than that, though. And maybe it's been a while since I've actually done it.

"We need to get to that shed before Leslie is done at the house. If he gets on the ATV and we're still on the road, he'll see us."

I know all of this, but my body is revolting against this much exertion. I feel like I'm dying. My knees ache—dumb soccer injuries from way back in the day, which is part of why I never run. I'm wearing the wrong bra too, so my boobs hurt. Sweat drenches my hair at the roots and rolls down the nape of my neck, but I keep going.

Eventually, I say, "I can't keep up." I'm annoyed with myself for being more out of shape than her, and because she's right. We need to bust ass.

"Can you keep pushing? Once we get there we'll slow down." She speaks clearly as she jogs, without even breaking to gasp for air. CrossFit seems to be paying off for her.

I don't reply, but I keep running and focus on pacing myself, breathing, and trying not to think about how much I want to stop. How much I want water. How my lungs are going to explode.

The minutes pass so damn slowly until I truly can't run anymore. "I need to walk." I pause to breathe. "We'll hear the ATV when it starts up, and we can jump into the brush to hide."

"Fair. Any of this look familiar?" Reese says over her shoulder because, of course, she's ahead of me.

"What?" The word falls out of my mouth. Of course it looks familiar. I was just here.

She comes to an abrupt stop and spins. I almost crash into her. "Does it seem like we're getting close?"

I wipe the sweat off my forehead with my hand and shrug. "No … idea."

It's hard to speak, so I try to catch my breath while she looks at her watch. "We've been jogging for about fifteen minutes."

I walk behind her and dig into her backpack for water. "I scuffed up the dirt on the right side of the road as a marker. I don't think we've gone far enough yet, though."

"I bet we're running about six miles an hour, and you said you were on the ATV for about ten minutes, right? I wish I knew what speed so I could figure out how much farther we have."

"We'll just have to keep going." I take a few huge gulps and hand the bottle to her. "How do you know we were going six miles an hour?" I've never, ever thought about what speed I could run at.

She reaches for the water, takes a few sips, and then smiles. "I know a lot of random shit. Did you think I was only good at bathing your brother?"

A flash of heat courses through me. I'm not offended, but her comment does catch me off guard.

She immediately turns to face me and says, "I'm so sorry, Paige. That was insensitive. Please forgive me?"

"Of course. It's just still so strange to me that he's gone. You gave him the best care imaginable. You've earned the right to joke about him."

I want to tell her that she's one of the few people who have shown up to support me in my life. I'm always the one doing the supporting. But I feel mixed about it; does it count as support if you're paying someone?

Reese looks to the side, like she can't make eye contact. "I tried. I feel like I failed at the end."

"The end."

She's talking about how Bryce died. How it wasn't a slow fade into a quiet passing, surrounded by everyone who loved him. It was unexpected, which sounds impossible, but it happened when nobody was home. He was totally alone.

Guilt churns inside me. I can't stay in this mental space. "Let's keep going. We've got to be close."

"You good to keep running?" she asks, putting the water bottle back in her bag.

"Do I have a choice?"

She smiles. "We always have choices."

The words land like a ton of bricks. It reminds me of something Bryce used to say during those last weeks when he no longer had use of his voice or hands, and had to communicate through a device that tracked his eye movements as he crafted his words visually.

"I should have a choice about how I go, Paige."

That's where the conversation always ended.

30

REESE

PAIGE IS RIGHT, WE PROBABLY DON'T NEED TO RUN. BUT IT'S like there's a hook in my bones, pulling me toward finding Courtney. It's hard to slow myself down, and we've stopped so many times for false alarms when Paige swore she saw the spot. Turns out scuffing up the road isn't the best choice for leaving a mark.

I'm kicking myself for what I said about Bryce. It's all I can think about. Courtney and I can talk like that, but Paige has always been more distant.

When I first took the job with Bryce, it was in response to an ad Paige had placed on Care.com. She wanted someone who could be a live-in, and I needed somewhere to live. It was a niche of care I'd fallen into after my military career and getting my RN license. Taking care of terminally ill—usually elderly— people. My first hospice care job had offered me room and board too, and that was such a good setup that I started only taking on patients who fit that bill.

I tried to connect on a deeper level with Paige over the past year, tried to offer her the support I knew she'd need when Bryce finally passed on. But she's always been a little arm's-length with me. This trip is the closest I've gotten to seeing past the employer-slash-big-sister persona she's always projected. And I shouldn't push it. If she doesn't want to be open with me, I respect that.

"This is it!" Paige calls out from behind. I can barely hear her over the growing noise of the cicadas coming from the mangroves we're approaching. It isn't like the road runs perfectly parallel to the shore, but this spot is about where the mangroves pick up on the beach. The same ones I tried to hike through the morning Court went missing. I wonder how far they stretch until the Gulf. When I was fighting my way through them yesterday, I couldn't see the road because they were so dense.

I stop and turn to face her. She's bent over again, hands on her knees with her head hanging so the tip of her dark ponytail almost touches the dirt. I intertwine my fingers and cradle the back of my head with my hands. Open the lungs.

"Are you sure?" I ask.

"Yeah … see? I … did that." Paige points to some scuffing in the dirt that looks to me like evidence of a struggle. She leaves the road and ventures into the brush. As I follow her, I realize how much I've been banking on finding Court in that shed. But what if she isn't even on the island anymore?

This thought slices through my hopes, so I shake it off.

No more what-ifs. Focus on right now. Searching the island.

"There it is," Paige says, pointing through the palm trees toward what might pass as a meadow in Florida. It's all sawgrass and seems easier to navigate than this brush. And standing out in the open is a little square shed, exactly like she described.

31

TORI

Leslie has only been inside the house a few minutes when I hear the upstairs floor creaking, and I know he's heading for the stairs.

"He's coming," I shout-whisper.

We go to the bottom porch steps and quickly sit, acting like we've been there the whole time Leslie was in the house.

"He can't be leaving already," I whisper.

"Oh, he's not. I shoved one of your hair thingies down the toilet. It'll take more than plunging to fix it."

"The tortoiseshell one?"

"What?"

"The brown one with black spots? My clip!"

"Oh yeah. That one. Sorry."

Leslie stomps past us, mumbling under his breath.

He doesn't even look at the ATV when he passes it to go into the garage. Within seconds, he comes back out with this skinny metal thing. It looks like a whip.

"Shit. He has a toilet snake," Rawson whispers.

Leslie stomps past us into the house without saying anything.

"I just need a few more minutes. I've almost got it," Rawson says, standing.

"What are you doing?"

"Making it so the four-wheeler won't start."

"What do we do if he figures it out?"

"It'll take him a while to do that."

I hope this works. If Leslie maintains this property, he's probably a passable mechanic. What if Rawson is overestimating his idea? Worse, what if Leslie figures out we sabotaged the ATV?

When Rawson is done, we both go inside the house, puttering around downstairs while we wait for Leslie.

He comes down holding the toilet snake in one hand and my hair clip in the other.

"Oh wow, thank you!" I say. "It must have fallen in."

He tosses the clip at me—super aggressive. I try to dodge it, and it skips across the white tile floor like a flat rock on a glassy lake.

Leslie goes out the front door without saying a thing and Rawson and I stare at each other for a beat. Then I chase after Leslie and shout, "Hey! Have you ever had an astrological reading?"

Maybe Rawson's idea will work and this isn't necessary, but the longer we can keep him here, the better.

"I don't believe in that horoscope shit," Leslie grumbles.

He isn't even pretending to be nice to us anymore. His black-hole energy makes me want to shrink and hide, but I can't give up. Keeping him here for hours is more what we had in mind, and it hasn't even been one hour.

"Oh, definitely, horoscopes are total shit. I agree," I say, and I mean it. I don't believe in predictive astrology. I think natal charts are what's useful about the system.

He stops at the bottom of the stairs and turns around. "My mom was into all that. She died when I was eleven," he says.

Whoa, I can't believe he opened up like that. I need to tread carefully, so I say, "I'm sorry to hear that."

He narrows his eyes, spins back around, and blazes toward the garage.

I run down the stairs, calling out, "Wait, when's your birthday?"

Rawson scoffs from behind, and I can't totally blame him. I know it's a little ridiculous to keep trying to pursue this. It's not like I can't tell when someone isn't interested in my zodiac obsession, but we have to keep Leslie here, and this is one thing I know I can talk about for hours.

Leslie waves me off instead of answering.

"Sometime in late April to late May," I shout. I just have this feeling he's a Taurus. He has this vibe that reminds me of one of my foster dads. Taureans are some of the most loyal and grounded people you'd ever meet, and they build lives worth living. That's the side my foster dad showed everyone else. But I got the shadow side of him. Stubborn and emotionally repressed. Cold, detached.

That's the energy I'm getting from Leslie more than a manipulative Scorpio vibe. Taurus is ruled by Venus, and it's one of the only signs that exists to receive. So there's this sensuality and a craving for comfort and pleasure, but when those aspects are focused inward, greed, callousness, and self-interest will dominate. Plus, there can be a tendency to use control as self-preservation.

Leslie turns again, this time more slowly.

"May eighth, actually. How the hell did you know that?"

I enjoy a quiet, smug celebration for a second. There's no way for me to look up his whole chart, but I can work with his sun sign.

"You're a Taurus. Hardworking, practical, and committed to your values. You're loyal, and once you set your mind on something, you'll see it through. I bet you're super self-reliant, and since your mom died when you were young, that trait probably defines you."

He takes a few steps toward me, closing what little space there is, and I lean back. I try to find Rawson in my periphery, but he's still on the porch. Then I hear the stairs creak from behind—he's on his way down.

"And you're a fucking pain in the ass. My mom always said she had a 'sacred calling.' That she was a 'healer,' here to 'help people.'" He repeatedly makes finger quotes. "She was a Virgo rising. I probably know more about this shit than you do. But guess what? She didn't help a single person. Not even herself. Drank herself to death instead. So how's that for the truth of the fucking stars?"

My heart is beating frantically and my mouth goes dry. I don't know what to say. Something in his eyes terrifies me.

He walks to the four-wheeler and gets on, then tries to start it up.

Nothing happens.

Rawson comes to stand by my side and takes my hand. "I think you met your match, zodiac lady."

Yeah, total plot twist that this asshole house manager knows what a rising sign even is, let alone the archetype of a Virgo.

We watch Leslie try to start the ATV and fail a second time.

"Looks like your tinkering worked," I whisper to Rawson.

"Should take him a while to figure it out."

"What did you do?"

"Reversed the kill switch. So it looks like the rig is on when it's actually off."

"You're a goddamn genius, Raw Dog."

32

REESE

Staring across the meadow, I'm thinking there's no way Leslie is living in that shed. It's tiny. Maybe he'd stay there if he had no other options, but he did: at the house with us.

My heart hammers with adrenaline. The shed is so out in the open, and it seems likely Courtney could have stumbled upon it.

But it doesn't explain why the hell she wouldn't just walk home. I suppose she could be injured and unable to walk.

That's not what happened.

My gut says she was taken.

"Let's go," Paige says. Her eyes are wide and sweat beads at her hairline, so she wipes it with her palm. Her lavender Lululemon tank top has dark spots where the sweat has broken through.

I'd say the shed is about seventy yards away, and I take off for it without another thought.

"Should we leave more markers as we go? You know, so we don't get lost too?" Paige asks.

I don't want to tell her my new theory yet. That Courtney

didn't, in fact, get lost. "I think we'll be able to find the road from here."

"If you say so."

I appreciate her caution, but we don't have time for it. I glance behind to see what the scene looks like from the angle we'll take to get back to the road.

As we approach the shed, I start stepping more carefully. I wasn't afraid before—maybe because I've been so worried about Courtney. But that worry has bloomed into a little flower of uneasiness, and when we're steps away, it becomes a flash of dread.

We shouldn't be here.

It takes everything in me not to turn and run back to the road. I swallow the urge down and try to hide my fear.

"This place is fucking creepy," Paige whispers.

I nod. It's about the size of a single bedroom and made of painted cinder blocks, the light blue color peeling off. It has these weird windows—I've never seen anything like them before. They look like blinds, but they're made of actual glass panes. As if you can crank them open and closed and they'd never fully seal. I bet it's some ventilation system from a time before air conditioning. The windows are high up on the structure, narrow, taking up the top portion of the building. If I stood, I'd barely be able to see inside.

I look at Paige and put a finger against my lips. *Don't say a word.* I point to myself, then make an upward motion with the same finger.

I'm going to look.

She nods fast. Her face is scrunched up, her eyebrows are practically at her hairline. I'm not used to seeing her afraid. It makes my heart go out to her.

I slowly stand to my full height.

The section of window on the other side of the building is

missing a lot of slats, creating a large hole. Big enough that I could crawl through it if I needed to.

Inside the room, there's a bed, a rifle standing next to it, a bucket, and a roll of toilet paper. The door is on the other side.

Then I see a woman lying on the ground. She's in the shadows, facing the wall in the fetal position, but I can see black-sandal-clad feet and bound ankles.

This is bad. I suddenly feel like I could vomit.

I drop below the window and squat, leaning my back carefully against the building. I squeeze my eyes shut.

"What? What did you see?" Paige whispers, and before I can answer, she pops up to look. I pull her by the wrist, but it's too late. She's seen inside.

"Oh my god. Oh my god," she repeats over and over. Tears form in her eyes. "Is it her?"

"Just breathe. I need you to calm down so I can think."

I don't know for sure, but the sandals do look like Court's. Paige nods fast, like a child obeying a parent, trying to comply no matter what they're feeling inside. No matter what the situation is. Lord knows I've been there.

"Stay here."

She nods again, swiping under her eyes with a finger to catch unruly tears.

The only other time I've seen her cry was at Bryce's funeral.

I slink along the perimeter of the building and peek out. All clear.

I move to the side with the door and there's a slide lock on the outside. My mouth goes totally dry, but I slide the lock open, then gently grab the handle and turn it.

The door is locked.

33

PAIGE

My body is freaking out. I try to silence the sobs while I sit here, under the window, waiting for Reese to tell me what to do next. I'm not used to being the one taking orders, but I have no choice right now. I can't keep my shit together. My breath comes in rapid, shallow bursts. Tears stream faster than I can wipe them away, and my nose is running. I need to blow it but I have nothing to use, so instead I wipe it with the bottom of my tank top.

Is that Courtney? Do I want it to be her? If that woman's not hurt, then I hope it is. But if she's hurt, or worse, then I pray to god it's not Court.

I'm small and helpless, and only one other situation has ever made me feel this way: When I was a kid, and my mom would come home strung out.

The anticipation, the fighting sleep to stay awake waiting for her even though it was usually well past midnight. Knowing what was coming. The slaps. The hair-pulling. Guiding her tweaker ass to her bed so I could finally go to sleep in mine. Her demanding she didn't need sleep. And sometimes she didn't for days, but I would stay with her until she settled down enough that I could sleep. All so she wouldn't go after Bryce.

"Hey, come on." Reese breaks me out of my panicked reverie, waving me toward her.

I'm frozen, but I think of Court and manage to get to my feet and make my way over to Reese.

"The door is locked," she says. "But this window has missing slats. I think I can fit through if you give me a boost."

Even with all the noise we're making, the woman inside doesn't move. Not even a flinch.

Shit.

"Hurry," I say, cradling my hands to boost her.

She steps up and uses my shoulder to brace herself as she reaches for the window ledge.

Her boots have some massive tread and they hurt my hands, but in a moment, she's up and snaking through the window.

I stand and watch the woman, who still doesn't stir.

Reese slips inside and I hear her move to the front door. In seconds, it's unlocked and I'm inside too.

We both go right for the woman.

"Court?" Reese whispers as she touches her back.

Something about her hair looks different. It's longer, pulled into a loose ponytail. And her build, it's curvier and much shorter than Court's.

Reese takes her shoulder and gently turns her toward us.

And that's when I know for sure. Whoever this is, it's not Courtney.

34

COURTNEY

I wake up in water. Warm wind cools my face as if I'm drenched in sweat. The sound of gentle waves lapping from behind.

"Open your eyes." I hear Bryce's voice in my mind.

I'm on my ass, knees bent. There's no room to stretch them out because I'm surrounded by all these spindly trees coming out of the water. Mangroves. I'm in the mangroves and the water is up to my waist. The cicadas are so loud I want to cry. It's a maddening and ear-splitting cacophony. I can't move. My hands are behind my back, bound to something. I spider my fingers along to figure out what, and I feel a few smooth and slender branches—or roots? I don't know, but then I touch plastic and my heart sinks. Zip ties.

A wave of panic hits. What the hell is going on?

Then I remember Leslie. He knocked me out after I read the note the drone dropped. It was a time and a location—some kind of meeting here on the island. That's all I saw.

I look around and take in more of this place. Masses of branches, so tight together. No way to know how far they go, and

I'm tucked into what seems to be the only space a person could fit, as if someone cleared out a few of these tangled trees to make a tiny mangrove cage.

The mangroves Reese tried to explore ... I whip my head around as if Reese is here somewhere, but a bolt of pain charges through my neck and into my skull, sending a louder-than-I-mean-it groan into the hot, damp air.

"Reese! Help!" I scream, but it's muted by those damned cicadas. Even if Reese was nearby, she wouldn't hear me over them.

My ragged breaths start to speed up as I realize I'm trapped here.

I wrench, twisting and pulling as hard as I can to try to break the thick plastic at my wrists.

"Ow!" I yell.

I've cut myself right where the zip ties dig into skin.

My throat is tight from crying. And now there's an open wound right where the plastic presses against my wrist. I take a deep breath and shimmy my hands so the tie isn't digging directly into the wound, but it still hurts like hell.

My head throbs. I'm so damn thirsty. All this moisture around me, in the air, in the water, and I can't use any of it.

The side of my face feels tight—I think it's covered in dried blood. Has to be since it's only on my left side. Where Leslie pistol-whipped me.

Why the hell did he do that?

The note. Something is going to happen on the island, but what? My brain stalls.

How long have I been out?

The beach walk with Reese, the drone, all of that happened during the late morning. My stomach roils with hunger. I look up, and the sun is overhead. It seems like it's only been a few hours, but the hunger and thirst is maddening, and my body is sore like it's been in this position a while. I try to stretch my legs a bit, but I can't fully extend them.

A large ripple of water pushes against my back, and I gasp. Is the tide in or out? How high will the water rise?

How long was I out? I keep going back to that. My brain is looping. If I was unconscious for longer than a few minutes, I'd be in serious danger of brain injury. Did he drug me, too?

I rest my head against the tree behind me and stare at the clouds scattered across the blue sky. If I wasn't in this situation, I'd be in awe of how beautiful it is. I guess I am anyway—it looks like a calendar shot.

I wish Bryce were here.

It's not over 'til it's over, I imagine him saying. He believed this deeply. Down to his very last breath, when it became a cold, hard fact that he was dying and I could do nothing about it.

35

REESE

Who is this woman? Where did she come from?

A stone drops in my gut: And where the hell is Courtney?

I turn the woman around, but she still isn't awake. Her hair is light and curly—wildly tangled as if she's been in a struggle—and there's a dried blood smear on her forehead. She's wearing a gray tank top with a very dirty pair of jean shorts. Her left shin is covered in blood, and she's bound at the ankles and wrists.

I jostle her gently, saying, "Hey, wake up. Are you okay?" But she doesn't respond.

"Is she dead?" Paige whispers from behind me.

"No, but maybe drugged."

The woman's skin is warm to the touch, and I can see her chest moving up and down with each breath. I start inspecting her leg and notice her knee is twice the size it should be, and there's a gaping wound. It's not actively bleeding, but it doesn't make the cut any less nasty.

"Leslie did this. I guarantee it. We have to hurry," Paige says.

I think she's right, but Leslie said another man had been on the island, too. The man who took the boat to Marathon. So we can't know for sure who did it. Not yet.

We have to get off this island.

I shake all of that off. Again, I'm racing ahead when I need to slow down and simplify things, make a plan based on priorities. First, is this woman okay? Second, get out of this shed. Third, find Courtney. Then, get the fuck off this island.

I shake the woman's shoulder with more force. "Hey," I say. "Wake up. We have to get out of here."

Her eyelids flutter, then open and immediately widen. She groans and I reach for my knife so I can take care of her zip ties.

"Water," she croaks.

I slip the knapsack off my back and hand it to Paige. She gets a bottle of water out, cracks open the top, and hands it to the woman as she moves slowly to sit up. The woman cries out in pain when she tries to bring her knee around to sit. Then she gulps the water when Paige puts it to her lips.

She moans, touching the spot on her head where blood is smeared.

"Who are you? How long have you been here? Who took you? Was it Leslie?" Paige rapid-fires.

"What?" the woman whispers, groggy.

"Leslie. The house manager. Is he the one who did this to you?" Paige repeats.

The woman squints her eyes and groans again as she tries to stand.

"I'm … Leslie."

36

TORI

Rawson's little switcheroo on the ATV works for a solid hour and a half before Leslie finds the reversed kill-switch wires and fixes them. Now Leslie's pissed.

"Clogged toilet, huh?" he shouts from the garage.

We're sitting on the porch stairs again.

Rawson shrugs, channeling his Libra moon to come off as charming and polite. There isn't a hint of a smirk in it, either. I'm impressed.

Leslie's energy is a gathering storm, and he charges fast toward Rawson, who stands.

I stand, too, but move a bit away from Rawson just in case this gets ugly.

Leslie shoves him so hard Rawson almost falls on his ass, but he recovers.

"You have no idea who you're fucking with," Leslie shouts, spit spraying.

"It was a joke, man."

"You better fucking stay out of my way or you're dead."

Ice runs through my veins. I keep my gaze down as I will myself to be invisible, but I can still see Leslie in my periphery.

"And you." He's in my face, shoving a finger at me. I don't look up, and instead stare at the dirt caked below his nails. "Tell your friends if I catch them wandering around the island, they're dead too."

Then he marches back to the ATV and drives off.

My body shakes and I exhale a cry.

Rawson hugs me, saying, "He's full of shit. It's just a flex, that's all."

I don't believe him. Not for one second.

We go inside and Rawson suggests I take a bath, which does not sound nice right now because it's like five hundred degrees out, but I have to admit it's a good idea for relaxation. I take my time, only getting out when the water has grown lukewarm. By then, an hour has passed, and when I go downstairs, Paige and Reese still aren't back.

Rawson is on the porch, sketching, but I can feel his energy. He's a live wire. He finally says, "I can't just sit here. Surely this place has a marine radio," and he disappears into the garage.

My mind spins with Leslie's threat. What has he done to Courtney?

I resort to chewing my fingernails and staring out the front window, hoping to catch sight of one of my friends. It's been hours now, and they should be back, but there's no sight of them. My stomach rumbles, so I walk toward the kitchen to make myself a peanut butter and jelly sandwich. Distraction plus sustenance.

Rawson barges into the house. "We need to go."

"Whoa. Go where?" I ask, setting down the butter knife and turning around. A black space grows inside my gut. I know my intuition is trying to prepare me for bad-becoming-worse, but I can't acknowledge it or I'll fall apart.

"Marathon. We'll take a kayak."

"What?" I practically shriek. "I'm not leaving my friends here."

I don't know what's taking them so long, but I'm not abandoning them.

"We have to get help."

"There's no fucking way I'm kayaking across the Gulf of Mexico. Marathon is two miles away," I say. It may be doable for some people, but not for me. I'm not even in the same galaxy as sporty.

"We can do it."

I look at the clock on the microwave. It's a little after one p.m.

"Let's give them more time. See if they're back by this evening."

Surely everyone will be here by then, and there'll be no need to kayak across the Gulf. They'll have Courtney, and we can drink margaritas, and I'll even wear the stupid kaftan Paige bought. I told Rawson I left it in Boise, but I didn't. I brought it. Then we'll go home to Boise and I'll tell Paige her secret is safe with me. That I'll carry what she did to the grave.

I just want everything to be normal. And everyone to be safe.

"It shouldn't take Reese and Paige hours to get to that shed. I … I think they're missing now, too." Rawson's voice is soft, like he's explaining something to a toddler.

My heart palpitates and my breaths come fast.

"No, they're not. They'll be back any minute." I press the two slices of bread together and cut the sandwich in half. My hand trembles and starts to tingle, so I drop the knife. A burst of heat courses through my body, making my upper lip sweaty.

No. Not this. Breathe.

I groan and brace my hand against the kitchen counter when a wave of nausea hits.

I start muttering under my breath fast. "Aries in the first house of self. Taurus in the second—material possessions. Gemini in the third house of communication. Cancer in the fourth—"

"Are you okay?" Rawson rushes to my side.

"—house of family. Leo in the—"

"Tori, what's happening?" he asks, leading me to the couch.

"Panic attack. My pills … upstairs in my purse."

It's hard to catch a full breath, and breaking my self-talk ritual makes me feel even more dizzy. I blink, trying to keep my vision clear. Keep it from darkening around the edges.

He runs up the stairs and I whisper to myself. "Leo in the fifth house of creativity. Virgo in the sixth—work ethic. Libra in the seventh house of relationships."

"Found them! Hang on," he shouts while careening down the stairs. He stops with a jolt. "Fuck, water."

"Don't need it," I say and open the bottle, taking two instead of my usual one pill. The Klonopin won't take effect immediately, but knowing it's in my system calms me down enough to hold steady while I wait for it to work. Rawson leads me to the couch and I lie down, closing my eyes, thinking the words instead of saying them out loud.

Scorpio in the eighth house of deep connections. Sagittarius in the ninth—expanding horizons.

"Does this happen a lot?" Rawson asks.

"Not as much as it used to. I think it's just everything piling up … " I don't open my eyes, and I'm grateful I can string a few words together. He sits by my feet and puts a hand on my leg. The gesture is so tender it makes me want to cry.

He doesn't know about my childhood yet. About how my parents died when I was young and I was tossed around foster homes until I was an adult. About what happened to Tucker. About how the panic attacks are triggered by a certain quality of loneliness. When I feel trapped by it, like it's a cage. Like a guarantee that I'll always be alone, locked up. I can't get into any of that with him right now. "It's just everything. Courtney, my past —our average childhood sob story."

I feel myself disassociating, hovering outside of my body as I speak.

Capricorn in the tenth house of career.

I open my eyes to find a visual detail to fixate on, and they land on Paige's red-and-white striped towel, draped over the back of an armchair across the room.

What if I never see her again? What if I can't tell her I'm sorry for all the drama I've caused? That she's the only person who has stuck with me throughout my life. That I do really love her.

"Don't leave me," I say.

"I won't. I swear."

I clench and release my fists. Can't check out right now, and I can't give in to my fears. It would be an invitation to the black-hole monster that's never far, taunting me that I'll always be abandoned. That I'll forever be completely and utterly alone.

It isn't long before I feel the Klonopin tugging me toward sleep, and the last thing I remember is Rawson tucking a strand of my hair behind my ear.

37

PAIGE

I hate that I didn't listen to my gut. That I didn't trust myself, because I know better.

Reese looks right at me, but she doesn't say anything. Her expression tells me she's thinking the same thing. But we went along with things because we needed food, and wanted to keep the peace.

No time to discuss it, though. We have to get out of here.

"I doubt she can walk with that knee," Reese says, reaching for the rifle standing in the corner and slinging it crosswise over her body.

That, and she's barely awake, so we have to pull her to her feet. Reese hands me the knapsack to carry and ducks below one of Leslie's arms, holding her in support. I pick up the half-empty water bottle and put it back into the bag. Then we move out the door, starting through the patch of open brush toward the road.

"No! No … road." Leslie pushes the words out with effort.

"We have to get back and warn our friends," I say.

"There." Leslie points in the opposite direction.

"But that's not the way to the house."

"Hit … the beach … opposite," she says, swaying a bit. Whatever she's gone through must have been hell. Her face is dirt-smeared and she has bruises and blood on her left temple.

"At this point, it's just as urgent to avoid whoever the hell that man is," Reese says to me. Then, to Leslie: "You want to get across to where the beach is on the other side?"

She nods. "Keith."

"What?" Reese asks.

"His name."

This whole situation is so bizarre. So, the man we thought was Leslie is actually named Keith.

"Okay, avoid *Keith*, then. So, we cut through to the opposite side and follow the beach to the house?" Reese clarifies.

Leslie nods again.

Tori is at the house. If this guy is capable of drugging a woman, tying her up, and holding her in a dirty shed, what else is he capable of?

Courtney. What did he do to you?

The thought is pure devastation.

My instinct is to pull into myself, lock up, distrust everyone. When the two of them start moving, I hesitate, and Reese groans in annoyance.

"Paige, come on! We're out in the open."

I've never seen her like this. She's strong, in charge, and not afraid of hurting anyone's feelings. She's intimidating. People say I'm intimidating. Is this what they see?

My feet are moving, but my brain is stuck trying to make sense of our situation. Why did that man—Keith—take Leslie and then pose as her?

It's honestly horrifying.

We're almost to the trees with hanging moss, and my mind is spinning out. We don't know this area at all. Does Leslie? How can we be sure that asshole Keith won't find us? We still need to look for Courtney, but how long until Keith figures out the real Leslie has escaped? Then what?

The ATV engine growls in the distance, echoing all around, so I can't tell where it's coming from.

"Run!" Reese shouts over her shoulder and picks up her pace while supporting Leslie, who is crying out in pain as her bad knee gets bumped and jostled while they move.

We run to the trees—they should provide some cover.

When we get there, we crouch and move to our stomachs to get completely out of sight. Reese has to lower Leslie slowly, supporting her at every point.

"You think … he'll check … the shed?" I get the words out between breaths.

"No idea, but we'll rest here until we know for sure," Reese says.

The engine grows quieter. He isn't stopping and he isn't getting closer, either. He was just driving by. I close my eyes and feel some tension leave my body.

Reese and I are lying on our stomachs in the palm fronds and sawgrass, and Leslie is on her side to protect her hurt knee. At least we're hidden by the trees.

"Why did he kidnap you?" Reese asks Leslie, wiping sweat from her forehead. It's so fucking humid.

"Drugs," Leslie whispers. Her eyes droop like she's sleepy, or drugged. "Wash-ups … "

"He gave a brick to Border Patrol. You're saying there are more?"

"Dozens."

"So *you* were the one who called Border Patrol," I say. The pieces are starting to fit together.

She nods slowly.

Smart of Keith to give Border Patrol one brick but hold on to the rest, I have to hand it to him. That asshole knew Leslie had already called them. If he told them it was a mistake, it might have only piqued their curiosity and caused them to investigate.

"That means Keith blocked the Wi-Fi too," Reese says to me. She's right. There must have been a Wi-Fi signal for Leslie to call them.

"He did this to you so he could have the wash-ups," Reese says.

She nods.

"We should keep moving." Reese reaches for the knapsack I've been carrying and hands Leslie the bottle of water. "But we'll go slow. You're dehydrated."

Leslie nods again. It seems like all she can do, as if talking has taken any last ounce of energy out of her. I have more questions, but they'll have to wait.

Reese pulls Leslie to her feet, then goes to support her weight again. I stand too, and try to brush the dirt off my clothes. The two of them move in front of me, and Reese struggles to use her knife to clear a path, so I step in front of them. "Let me help Leslie while you do that," I say.

Reese nods and I duck under Leslie's arm, but I can't support her. She falls to the ground, and the cry that comes out of her is sheer agony.

"I'm so sorry!" I rush to help her up, but Reese is the one to bend down and pull Leslie upright.

She hands me the knife and I start cutting back the brush as they follow behind me. I'm much slower at this than she was—I need to get my ass back to the gym when I get home. If it were only Leslie and me out here, I'd have to leave her to get help.

Reese asks, "How far to the beach?"

Leslie doesn't answer. Her eyes are barely open, and it looks like Reese is practically carrying her.

"Will she be okay?" I ask Reese.

"Yeah, I think so. She needs fluids and rest. Moderate dehydration can make you seem drugged. But she might also be drugged; I'm not sure."

I turn back around so we can continue our slow trek through the scrub and sawgrass.

"How … long?" Leslie whispers, suddenly awake again.

"How long what?" Reese asks.

"Was I … out?"

"We've been here for three days. So that long, at least. Once we find our friend, we'll get the fuck out of here."

"He … has a gun. Ex … military," Leslie's words are strained. They're quiet, but laced with panic.

Reese grips her tighter around the waist to offer more support as they walk. "Same," she grunts.

"No … " She looks right at Reese with wide eyes. "More men … are coming."

38

COURTNEY

I THINK I'VE SUCCESSFULLY STAYED AWAKE MOST OF THE DAY. To distract myself from how damn thirsty I am, I focus on how the sun moves, trying to orient myself. I'm facing it right now, so I know that's west, which means Marathon and the Gulf are behind me.

The tide is highest in the morning, and even then, it only comes up to my waist, so at least I won't die by drowning. Is it better to die by thirst, though? Considering there's no way to get out of these zip ties, and no way anyone will find me, dying is very much on the table. This spot where I'm at is maybe three feet in diameter, and then it's a sea of branches jutting up from shallow water. How in the hell did Leslie even get me into the mangroves this deep? I still can't see a way in. I close my eyes and try to remember what I observed from the boat while we were coming in the other day. The mangroves grow directly out into the Gulf of Mexico, so perhaps that's the only way into this spot—by water.

And the only way out.

The sea lowers as the day goes on, but my legs and feet are

still submerged. I wiggle my toes and feel the tender, pruney skin. Soon they'll get a break from the water. For a while at least, until the tide starts to rise again.

A headache grows—a different pain than the one from being clocked with a gun. It's more like nausea.

Movement on a branch right by my shoulder startles me. My eyes wildly try to find whatever it is until a small, black crab comes into view.

I exhale. I can think of a handful of worse things to run across here. The crab spirals the branch and marches higher, and my eye catches another one nearby.

There's no room to stretch my legs out, so they're cramping from having my knees up. I try to drop my legs into a crossed position to get relief, but the cut on my wrist screams. It hurts so much worse than it did yesterday, and for some reason, the zip ties feel tighter, making the tiniest movement excruciating.

I use my fingers to try to feel the wound, and the skin of the cut wrist is warmer than the other one. *Infection*. But the wound has been submerged in salt water a lot of the time. That's good, right? The salinity will help keep infection away. No idea if that's true, but I'm going with it. I wish Reese was here to ask.

A white bird with a curved beak lands on a branch across from me, then steps into the water with its long, stick legs. It's unlike anything I've ever seen in Idaho. So beautiful, yet strange looking. It stares as if I'm the oddity here. I suppose I am. It begins poking around in the water, looking for food.

I wonder how successful Reese was in navigating this place. There's no way on earth she could tromp through. A heaviness settles in my chest. My friends will come looking for me, but there's barely anywhere to step in this minefield of branches. They won't make it this far.

Will Leslie ever come back for me? Will I get anything to drink?

A pit digs deep into my stomach. Leslie has a gun. He's involved in something bad enough to knock me out and tie me up just because I read a message.

A drug deal.

It feels obvious the moment it lands in my mind. That has to be what the meeting is for.

A sloshing noise comes from behind me.

Could it be Reese? I imagine her wading through the water, and a spark of hope makes my breath hitch. I want to look, but my head and neck cry in protest if I even move toward turning. Caution tells me not to call out. It could be Leslie, too.

I shut my eyes and let my chin drop to my chest. My back is to this person, so it's not like they can tell if I'm awake, but it feels like the right thing to do.

After a minute of silence, I open my eyes and try to turn, but again, it hurts way too much. Do I have whiplash?

Then something cuts through the water behind me in a way that makes my brain scream: *shark.* I have blood on my face. Possibly at my wrists, too, although maybe not anymore.

I have to see whatever this is. I tuck my legs closer and swivel my body the best I can, even if it hurts my neck. At least my feet are free so I can kick if I need to defend myself.

It swims nearer to me. So close I can feel the brush of scales as the tail grazes my right hip.

I hold my breath, willing myself to be invisible.

It isn't a shark. It's a crocodile.

39

REESE

AFTER SOME TIME, LESLIE AND I FIND A WALKING PACE THAT works. It's slower than I'd like, and I think she'd need less support if she wasn't so damn dehydrated and sick on top of her injured knee.

Out of nowhere, she turns her face away and vomits.

"You okay?" I ask, and she lifts a hand. I'm not sure if that's a *yes* or what, but she throws up again, then wipes her mouth with the bottom of her sweat-soaked tank top. "I feel so shitty."

Fuck. Vomiting will only make dehydration worse. But on the other hand, she's talking more normally now, so that's good. She needs a hospital and IV fluids. And I need to check out her head wound and wrap that knee. I lift her chin and look more closely at her forehead. The cut isn't deep. And since it's not bleeding, I think we're okay for now.

"Here, use my shirt to wrap her knee," Paige says, removing the knapsack and peeling her purple tank off. She hands it to me.

I quickly wrap it around Leslie's bad knee. I don't have an ACE bandage in the first-aid kit I brought. It's in my larger medical kit back at the rental.

"You're definitely dehydrated," I say. "Are you sure this is still the best way to get back to the house?"

Leslie looks around and says, "Yeah. The beach is through that patch of sawgrass, and then if we turn right, there's a path that goes to the house."

"And where's the second dock?" I ask.

Leslie narrows her eyes, as if she's confused, and I get a sinking feeling.

"There's only one dock, isn't there?"

"Yeah, why did you think there were two?"

"Keith told us he used it when he arrived on the first day. But I guess he only said that so we wouldn't be suspicious about how he suddenly showed up without a boat coming in," I say.

"He was already here. He attacked me almost immediately after I returned from Marathon on the day you were supposed to come. The boat had left and I was moving all the groceries up to the house."

No second dock. No boat until the one we chartered arrives tomorrow. More men are coming. Maybe ex-military, same as Keith. I need a new plan. We might have to fight, but right now, I have to get Leslie back to the house so I can keep searching for Courtney.

"Why is Keith even here?" Paige asks. "I don't remember you saying anything about him in our emails."

"I hired him to help with some hurricane cleanup, and it turned out he was handy, too, so I asked him to stay a few weeks longer to tackle some other projects. I didn't expect him to be very visible during your stay, just working on repairs elsewhere. But then he found the wash-ups and went rogue. This is absolutely batshit," Leslie says.

"God, that's scary," Paige says.

"Good news is there's a VHF radio in the garage. Once we're at the house, we can call the police," Leslie says.

"Amazing. They'll help us find Court," I say.

"Find her?" Leslie asks.

"She's missing," Paige says.

Leslie's eyes widen. "What do you mean *missing*?"

"She disappeared. No rhyme or reason, and we've been looking nonstop," Paige says.

Leslie's face blanches. "Oh my god. Keith said something to me the other day about a hidden spot he found on the island. I bet that's where he's holding her."

40

COURTNEY

I DON'T EVEN HAVE TIME TO FREAK OUT BEFORE THE CROCODILE swims away, and I'm shocked to realize I feel a little disappointed.

Being eaten by a crocodile would be a horrible way to go, but in those split seconds when I felt sure I was going to die, I think I was relieved.

What do I have to live for, anyway? Why am I fighting? I'm tired and alone. For years I haven't been able to see beyond Bryce's impending death. And now, with all of that behind me, my future feels like an abyss.

I'm not sure what happens after you die, but I won't see Bryce again while alive. That's a fact. So my odds of seeing him in some sort of afterlife are higher.

Maybe it's crazy talk. But it's also true.

When I hear the crocodile coming back, I exhale and let go, closing my eyes and releasing myself to whatever happens next.

Adrenaline pounds in my veins as if it didn't get the memo that I'm not going to fight or flee. I'm going to forfeit.

I conjure a mental image of Bryce's smile. The dimple on his right cheek, and the way it darkened his five-o'clock shadow in that one spot. His teeth that weren't crooked, but never braces-perfect either, and that kissable bottom lip. I think about how it felt to be held by him. He was my home. And if he isn't here, why the fuck am I?

The water sloshes around me, but nothing else happens. Soon, it settles back into place at my hips, and all I can do is cry.

I'm so thirsty. So exhausted. So broken that the only thing left is to crumple into myself.

For the next few hours, I watch the water recede with the tide, going in and out of consciousness. Each time, I wonder if I'll wake up again, and when I do, I feel a deeper squeeze of thirst and despair, followed by more dizziness and fatigue.

My mouth is completely dry and I think about Sour Patch kids to get my salivary glands going. That gives me temporary relief for my dry mouth, but I need water.

Laughter rings distantly. It sounds like a child's based on the squeal at the tail end of each giggle.

Then it's gone.

Is there a kid on the island?

Then she's in front of me. Her face is so close to mine that if my hands were free, I could reach out and tuck the mousy brown strand hanging alongside her cheek. She doesn't say anything, but she doesn't need to. Those topaz-blue eyes lock onto me, searching my face, then meeting my own eyes.

Which are the exact same color as hers.

I recognize the sadness she's hiding in that seven-year-old face, the driving curiosity behind the tilt of her head. She's me.

Am I seeing things? I squeeze my eyes closed and open them again.

I'm so lightheaded that I'm spinning, nausea growing. The

illusion of her fades and comes back. She isn't real. She's in my mind. But it feels so damn real.

Am I going crazy?

She watches me, and I feel how lost she is. As a kid, I was really good at masking the emptiness and my longing to be seen. Bryce was the first person who truly saw me.

I feel this intense urge to tell her about Bryce. That he'll come into her life eventually, and he'll light her up and make her who she's meant to be.

My throat tightens and I let out a small sob. Maybe he's still in her future, but he isn't in mine.

And even for her, sure, Bryce is coming, but Bryce will also be leaving. She has that whole heartache ahead of her. I open my mouth to speak. To say something—anything, but she puts a finger to my lips.

"It was always you," she whispers.

"What?"

"It wasn't Bryce who made you whole. It was you, and you miss the version of yourself you got to be with him."

My mind scrambles to make sense of this. What the hell is she talking about? Bryce brought out the best in me. He did that. If I was capable of doing it, I would have done it decades before I met him.

"I don't understand," I whisper.

"Your life with Bryce. The joy. The fulfillment. You can have that without him because what you're really in love with is your own spark. It's inside of you. Bryce illuminated it, and you loved him deeply, but that spark isn't attached to him, and he didn't take it away when he died. It's inside of you, and you can awaken it anytime."

"I don't want to. I don't want to live without him." I start blubbering.

"Do it for me, then."

I close my eyes and consider this. It's a lifeline. A second chance if I want to take it.

I'm just not sure I do.

41

REESE

Those damned mangroves.

That's where Leslie said Keith is holding Courtney—assuming she's still alive.

It's all I can think about the whole way back to the house, and it takes everything in me not to immediately run there.

That's not an option, I keep reminding myself.

Paige can't support Leslie enough to keep her from further injuring herself. If I get us back to the house faster, we could use the radio to call the police and then I'll make a beeline for the mangroves. And Court.

But between the bushwhacking, our slow pace, and frequent stops so Leslie can hydrate, it takes us hours. My exhaustion is bone-deep. Nobody has spoken, as if we made a silent agreement to conserve energy. Paige drags behind Leslie and me, no longer bushwhacking, but it's fine because the vegetation has thinned out.

Leslie's head keeps nodding as if she's falling asleep—or worse, passing out.

"Hey, stay awake," I say periodically, stopping to get her attention while ignoring the intense urge to sit and fully rest.

The only time we stop is to hydrate, and even that's getting critical. The last bottle of water is only half full.

"I have to stop," Paige says from behind. "I'm sorry."

I find a somewhat clear spot in the palm fronds to set Leslie down and pull the last of the water out, unscrewing the cap. "Have some," I move the bottle toward her mouth, cupping her chin gently.

Paige catches up to us and stares at the water bottle. When she sees me watching her, she looks away quickly.

"How much longer?" I ask Leslie, who is momentarily revived by the hydration.

"We're almost to the beach. It's just through there." She points ahead and I think I can see blue water through the thick stand of palm trees.

"Here, take the last of it." I hand the almost-empty bottle to Paige.

"No, you're thirsty too. We need you to be strong."

I scoff. "No way in hell I'm drinking the last of our water. If you don't drink it, I'm sure Leslie will."

"Go ahead," Leslie mutters.

Paige keeps her eyes on me, not moving toward the bottle I'm holding out to her. Then her head drops in defeat and she steps toward it, taking it with a tired smile. "You're a really good human, you know that?" she says to me, then downs the water.

If she only knew how untrue that statement is.

We continue walking until the thick foliage finally opens to a small beach. The sand is minimal, and instead there are these light-colored boulders and flat rocks mixed in with a few solo mangrove trees. Nothing like the forest on the other side, though. These look drowned, like they've been through a flood. The water is so light in color and riddled with seagrass that I'm certain it's quite shallow.

"Which way to the house?" Paige asks.

I sit Leslie on a rock and move closer to the sea.

"Just up there." I imagine Leslie pointing as she says it, but my back is to them as I stare out at the water, tenting a hand over my eyes. I think I see something.

"Is that a kayak?" I turn to ask the others. It's not too far out, but its blue color blends in with the water so it's not immediately obvious.

Paige gasps, and I step carefully through the water so I don't slip and cut my feet on what I assume is coral.

When I get to the kayak, I notice a huge gash on the side, as if it hit one of these rocks too hard.

I grab the short piece of rope on the nose and pull it behind me to shore.

"I think it's from our beach," Paige says when I pull it up onto the spit of sand.

"Yeah, it's definitely ours," Leslie says. "Those limestone rock formations can really fuck a kayak up."

"And you're sure Courtney's in the mangroves?" Paige turns to ask Leslie. "What if she took a kayak out?"

"Not possible," I say. "I distinctly remember walking past two kayaks on the beach, and that was after Court went missing. Come on, we have to get to the house and call the police."

42

TORI

My eyes open, but everything is blurry. Perfect silence surrounds me, and I sense that I'm alone. I just know I am.

I rub my eyes and find that I'm lying on the couch with a throw blanket over me. It's still bright out, but the sun isn't pouring in from the living room window like it was when I fell asleep.

I look at my phone and gasp. It's already almost seven p.m. Fucking Klonopin.

"Rawson?" I call out hesitantly.

If Paige and Reese had returned, surely they would have tried to wake me up to tell me they found Courtney—or didn't.

I sit up and look around. There's a note on the coffee table in front of me. It's written on a small pad of paper with green palm trees lining the top.

Went to Marathon for help. Sorry, I don't think it can wait.
I'll be back for you.
—Rawson

But he said he wouldn't leave.

My throat constricts and that spot behind my nose prickles

like I might cry, but instead, I tear the note off the pad and crumple it, then chuck it across the room. "Paige? Reese?" I call out. If they're upstairs, they should be able to hear me.

Menacing silence is the only answer.

Why aren't Paige and Reese back yet?

"I think they're missing now, too." Rawson's words soar into my mind.

And just like that, my worst fear has come true: I'm completely and totally alone. But instead of freaking out or panicking, a cold numbness moves over me. Not really acceptance—more like surrender. I knew this would happen someday. That I'd find myself alone.

I run down to the beach, I don't know why, maybe to see whether Rawson actually took one of the kayaks and left.

When I get down there, a lonely two-person kayak sits on the sand by the small tiki hut.

My eyes fill with tears. I can't believe he left me after promising not to. He *chose* to leave me totally alone. I would never do that to him.

My logical brain knows this isn't the full truth. He didn't *leave me*. He went to get help, but still, all I can see is that he abandoned me. Left me alone on a strange island with my missing friends.

Maybe they left you too.

I look around and wipe the tears. What if the others left the island like Rawson? What if they found Courtney and the other dock and took off, and now I'm the only one here? Just me on this island with scary Leslie.

I sit in the sand and stare out at the Gulf. It's still hot as fuck, and the sun is beating against my back. I don't know what to do, so I stay there and sweat, zoning out. I wish I had my Tarot deck, but it's back in my room and I don't have the energy to go get it.

"Tori!"

I turn around. Paige is running down the boardwalk. They're back.

Thank god. My knees go soft so it's hard to stand up.

"Did you find Court?" I call out.

When she gets to me, Paige stops and bends over, putting her hands on her knees to catch her breath. Her dark hair falls toward the sand as she shakes her head no.

"What?"

She stands. "Not yet. Keith kidnapped Leslie. He was holding her in the shed. Still no Court."

"What?" I practically shriek this time. "Who's Keith?"

She repeats it more slowly, connecting a few more dots, then adds: "I was right the whole time. Leslie's a woman."

It feels like a jab, but I'm too baffled by the news to take issue with it.

"Shit," I say.

"Come back to the house and we'll explain everything. Leslie knows where Courtney is. And she says there's a radio in the garage."

"I don't think there's a radio. Rawson looked for one in there earlier."

"Where is Rawson?" she asks, looking around.

"He took a kayak to Marathon." I point to the single red kayak like it's indisputable proof.

"What?" Paige whispers slowly.

Is she about to rub this in too? *"See? That dickhead wasn't really into you after all."*

"He left to get help."

He left you.

Paige's eyes wander behind me toward the hut where the kayak is, then she finds my eyes.

I don't like the way her face falls, how the flush in her

cheeks melts away and she goes white. This isn't her planning to rub something in. It's something else. Something worse.

"What is it?" I ask.

She winces and then breaks eye contact to look out at the water. It's a moment of hesitation. Pity. She feels bad for me for some reason. My chest tightens.

"When did he take the kayak out?" she asks.

"Paige, just tell me."

"I saw the blue one … " She turns and points to the shoreline in the opposite direction from the kayaks. "Leslie—you know, the real Leslie—brought us back a different way so we could avoid the road. When we got to the beach, there were all these rocks. And Reese found the blue kayak. It was empty so she pulled it in. There was a crack on the side like it had hit something … "

She trails off, and her brown eyes search my face for under-standing, like she hopes she doesn't have to say it out loud.

"All these rocks."

A crack in the kayak.

The empty *kayak.*

I clench my jaw to keep from crying, but my mouth goes dry. I feel like I'm standing outside myself.

"When did Rawson take it out?" she repeats.

I squeeze my eyes closed. Because I don't know. I wasn't awake. I tell her I took a nap and leave out the part about my panic attack.

"Hey, don't assume the worst. There's no reason he would be way over there"—she points to where she saw the kayak—"when Marathon is that way." She points out to the sea in the opposite direction. "And the one I saw was old, maybe a third one leftover from other guests. Rawson probably made it across okay."

This wishful thinking isn't Paige. She's trying to spare my

feelings, and even if her attempts are lame, it means something. It really does.

"He must have gotten away. If he didn't, I would have seen his body." The moment she says it, her eyes widen. "I'm sorry."

The last thing I need is to visualize Rawson's dead body. My throat constricts and tears fill my eyes. He's gone. Just like Tucker.

43

REESE

It's late evening when we get to the house. Paige searches inside quickly before running down the boardwalk to look for Tori.

Leslie tugs me toward the garage. I readjust my arm around her waist, and when we get inside, she directs me to a small, rickety workstation in the corner. Tackle boxes, spools of fishing line, and various metal cans litter the surface.

She gasps. "It's gone."

"Are you sure? Could it be somewhere else?" I look around.

"I'm positive. The radio's been in this exact spot for as long as I can remember." She keeps staring at the empty space as if she can make it materialize.

"Do you think Keith has it?" I ask.

Leslie huffs a sigh and shakes her head. "I don't know. But in the meantime, we have no way to contact the mainland."

Courtney's name pounds like a drumbeat inside me.

She can't wait for us to figure out what's going on with the radio or to make a contingency plan. I have to go after her myself—and now.

I bring Leslie into the house and lead her to the couch, then I toss some ice cubes into a plastic bag and take it to her, placing it on her elevated knee. I grab the small pad of paper on the coffee table and write down the recipe for a DIY electrolyte drink that I affectionately call Gross Gatorade. Paige or Tori can make it for her.

I go upstairs to find the ACE bandage in my medical kit. When I return with it, Leslie eyes me suspiciously. "Did you bring that?"

"Yeah, my wrist acts up sometimes. Carpal tunnel," I lie as I move the ice pack to the side and start wrapping her knee.

I suddenly realize that Keith might have been lying about that girl who died here a year ago.

"Hey, our boat captain mentioned that a girl died on the island. Keith said it was a rumor?"

Leslie rolls her eyes. "Yeah, he's right. Nasty rumor. People love to scare the tourists."

Well, that's one thing I can put out of my mind. No dead girl.

It's only been a few minutes, but by the time I'm done with her knee, my body is zinging with adrenaline.

Slow the fuck down, Reese.

I exhale and take in a long breath, then hand Leslie a fresh bottle of water. "Can you give me directions to that spot inside the mangroves?"

"Sure. Take a kayak and paddle down the shore toward them. You know the spot?"

I nod.

"Okay, there are two mangrove tunnels you can paddle through. They look like openings in the forest. Pass by the first one and keep going maybe a hundred feet. You'll take the second one. It's wider and goes all the way through to the beach on the other side, although you won't go that far."

"Mangrove *tunnels*? Like there's brush overhead?"

"Sometimes, but not always. They're just channels of water that you kayak through."

Should I be writing this down?

Rawson's map!

"Just a sec," I say, rushing over to my knapsack by the doorway and rummaging around until I find the map.

I draw a line from the house to the beach and then to the start of the mangroves, which thankfully, Rawson has noted, then add the mangrove openings. I say, "Okay, I'm ready. Keep going."

"At some point, you'll see a third, smaller mangrove tunnel that branches off to the right and dead-ends in this tiny clearing." She makes a circle with a flat palm. "It almost looks man-made, like someone cut down some of the trees. I'd bet my life that's where she's at."

"How can you be so sure?"

"Keith made a comment a few days after he got here. Some wisecrack about how if he had to hide a body, that's where he'd do it."

My blood turns to ice.

Leslie seems to notice how I've stiffened and says, "I'm so sorry. I don't think he killed her. I bet he's holding her there like he was holding me at the shed."

I nod and take a deep breath. My insides feel like bottle rockets. I have to get to that mangrove clearing.

44

COURTNEY

I STARTLE AWAKE. THE WATER IS STILL AT MY ANKLES, WHICH means I didn't sleep all day, but I keep going in and out. My vision is starting to blur, and the placement of the sun confirms what I thought—that Marathon is behind me—but this matters very little compared to the thirst, my dry mouth, my pounding head, and the torturous throbbing pain at my wrist.

It has to be infected. The ties feel too tight. It's swollen. And I think I was hallucinating.

I try the Sour Patch Kids trick again, but nothing happens. I think of biting into a lemon slice, and I feel a tingle, but I'm so dehydrated that I can't even produce saliva anymore.

Water's all around me. Sea water. I shouldn't drink it because that will make the dehydration worse. But does it really matter at this point? Even if I don't die from infection or dehydration, it'll be something else. Leslie isn't going to release me. He hasn't even been back to check on me, and maybe that's his plan— leave me here to die.

"Leave me here to die."

These words linger and echo in my mind as the chirping cicadas pound in my ears.

"It was always you."

"You miss the version of yourself you got to be with him."

It always seemed like Bryce was responsible for my happiness. I leaned into it. He was my sun.

But what if it wasn't him and I was just experiencing a freer version of myself that whole time? Bryce held space for me to be who I really am at the core. Can I experience that even if he's gone?

A little flicker of something lights up inside of me. If I survive this and get to go back to my life in Boise, I can pick my journalism career up where I left it when Bryce was diagnosed.

"Stories that shift the cultural consciousness don't write themselves."

Stories don't need me to write them. They have a way of finding exposure through anyone who is paying attention. But maybe *I* need *them*. Maybe they're a part of this spark inside me.

But that's not what's most important right now. What matters is my friends. They're not going to find me, but I need to find them. They may not know they're in danger.

I groan. None of this matters if I don't get out of these fucking mangroves, and I have no idea how I'm going to free myself.

But I have to try.

45

PAIGE

AFTER OUR CONVERSATION ON THE BEACH, TORI LEAVES ME AND runs up the boardwalk and toward the house. I follow, but there's no rush, so I walk. I can't believe everything that's already happened in the span of a few days, and now Rawson … I didn't like him, but it guts me to think that he's dead.

Reese stands in the doorway of the house, rifle slung over her shoulder and knapsack in her hand as if she's on her way out. Tori brushes right past her and goes inside.

"Is she okay?" Reese asks.

"Rawson's gone. He tried to take a kayak to Marathon last night."

Her face falls. "The blue kayak … He's dead?" she whispers.

I shrug. "We think so."

Reese drops her gaze momentarily, and when she looks up, her eyes are full of determination.

"I wrote down the recipe for an electrolyte drink. Can you make it and give it to Leslie in small sips, as often as she can handle it?"

"Sure. Are you going after Court?"

She nods and reaches into one of her cargo pants pockets. She pulls out a little gun.

"Take this," she says.

"You brought a gun?" I shriek.

"Pretty sure I already told you that."

"No, you said, 'same' when Leslie mentioned Keith was ex-military."

"Ex-military *and has a gun*," Reese corrects me.

"I thought you meant the rifle you grabbed out of the shed."

"Nope."

I cross my arms. "I don't know how to work it."

Instead of saying, "Oh, never mind, then," like I hoped she would, Reese steps closer and gives me a quick tutorial. Check the chamber. Turn off the safety. Aim. Squeeze the trigger.

"I don't do guns. My husband is a fanatic and it almost ended our marriage a couple times."

She watches my face and says, "You can do this. You're strong." She tries again to hand it to me, but my arms stay crossed. "Paige, Keith kidnapped Leslie. He has Courtney. We're a threat to him if we get off this island and talk to the authorities. Not only that, but any minute more men could show up for the drug deal—men who want us silent and out of the picture. You must protect yourself, Tori, and Leslie while I'm gone. You're the only one who can do it, and you're more than able."

I clench my jaw and slowly reach out to take the gun because I know she's right. Leslie is wounded and Tori just lost her boyfriend. It has to be me.

The gun feels lighter than I expected. I tell myself I won't have to use it, that there won't be a reason to. But I'm not sure that I believe it.

Reese runs down the stairs and toward the beach. Then she disappears from sight.

I go to the couch to check on Leslie. She's clearly wiped out.

I see the recipe Reese scrawled on a notepad. It says "Gross Gatorade" at the top, and it's a mixture of water, salt, sugar, and a little apple juice. I go into the kitchen, make it quickly, and give some to Leslie. Her knee looks expertly wrapped with real bandages. Leslie takes a few sips then closes her eyes to rest.

I stand in the living room in silence. I feel so useless. I'm not equipped to lead under these circumstances. It's all so … physical. Sure, I can manage and distract people and get them to see things my way when I need to. But actually, physically fight? The thought of it makes my stomach turn.

It also reminds me to get the gun I set down in the kitchen when I was making the drink. I hate it, but holding it does make me feel better.

My husband is an alcoholic whose favorite thing to do when he comes home after a night of drinking is get into his gun safe and play around. He isn't violent or angry when he does this. Just careless. He accidentally shot our ceiling one time, and after that, I got him to tell me the password to the safe while he was sloshed, and I changed it. So, now he has to go through me to get access to his firearms.

I stand up straighter and take a deep breath. Even if I hate this, I have to be strong.

I can do it. I navigated Bryce's drug addiction. I kept our mom from hurting him. And now I run a million-dollar corporation.

I look down at what I'm wearing and laugh. I might be a badass, but I'm not rocking this bralette-and-shorts look as well as Reese would. I go upstairs to my room and quickly pull on a black quarter-zip tank top.

Now it's time to pull Tori from her pouting to help me stand guard.

Familiar anger floods me as I make my way to her room. Tori, selfish and fixated on stuff that doesn't matter. I shake my head. No, she just lost her boyfriend. And sure, she only knew him for a couple weeks, so he was basically a stranger, but that's beside the point. I need patience. Whatever happened between her and Rawson was real to her. Tori and I have a lot of shit between us, but right now, I need to be her friend.

I knock gently on her door.

"Come in," she says, her voice cracking.

"You okay?" I ask, pushing my way in slowly.

She's sitting on the edge of her bed, so I sit down next to her.

"I'm trying not to freak out again. I don't want to have another panic attack and get in the way." She doesn't look up, just keeps her eyes on a spot in front of her feet.

I don't know what to say to that. It's a level of self-awareness I rarely see in her.

"You're surprised, huh? That I'm trying to stay out of the way. It doesn't fit your mold of me as a selfish diva."

I don't take the bait and instead ask, "What do you mean *another* panic attack?"

"I had one earlier." She looks down at her clasped hands in her lap. "That's why I don't know when Rawson left. I wasn't napping, I was out thanks to my meds. Not that I could have stopped him. I asked him to stay. He wanted me to go too, but I wasn't leaving without you guys." She wrings her hands. "Anyway, if I have another attack, I'll need to take my meds, and that'll make me groggy at best, sleepy at worst. I don't want to be a burden, so I'm hiding out up here."

I feel something for her that I haven't felt in a long time. Compassion. She's dealt with periodic panic attacks since Tucker died. They're truly debilitating for her. I remember the very first one. It happened in a car wash, and she had to wait to get out until I could exit. She hasn't had one in years.

Even though I feel that compassion inside of me, I'm blocked from offering her any of the softness that comes with it.

It's like I can't let her see me show weakness even though I want to.

"You stole my idea," she says gently. "You know you did, and you're afraid to admit it because you don't want to lose your company or the high-class life you've built for yourself. You think I'd actually come after you for it because that's what you'd do to me."

Instead of pissing me off, this squeaks through the sliver of sympathy I feel toward her and unlocks something. My face quivers a little with the start of tears.

The silence expands until she breaks it.

"When we get home, I'm going to the police about Soul-Match's involvement in that murder."

46

PAIGE

My body goes numb. It's like I'm standing outside of myself watching this conversation. I can't formulate any words.

"You know that woman was using our app," Tori says. "That's how he found her, and when she tried to block him, he made new profiles and found her again. And again. Our algorithm allowed him to keep getting back into her carousel of potential matches. If she'd been able to block him completely, she'd still be alive. It's our fault she's dead."

"You said if I let Rawson stay, you'd … " I can't bring myself to finish the sentence. It seems so shallow, so stupid to try to convince her not to go to the police. I look away as tears stream down my cheeks.

"That was before Courtney went missing. And before Rawson … " Tori doesn't finish her thought, either.

"We don't know for sure that it was SoulMatch. Just that it was a dating app," I say.

It started with escalating complaints through customer service. We had a blocking feature, of course, but it wasn't savvy enough to detect the same person if they used a new phone number or email address to sign up.

"I needed more time to fix it," I say when Tori doesn't respond. "I was working on it."

"She wasn't the first woman to complain about not being able to block an abusive ex or a creep, Paige. You know that."

I look at the ceiling. She's right. I was reluctant to launch a full blocking feature. Allowing users to block each other for good would reduce the dating pool, which we couldn't afford since we were already competing with bigger, more popular dating apps.

This woman in particular had only exchanged a few messages with the man, got creeped out, and unmatched. He popped up again for her under a new profile, and she denied his match request. He started addressing her directly in his profile, writing to her in the section reserved for his bio, begging her to match. The whole thing only went on for two weeks. During that time, she'd reached out to our help desk about blocking him, and we advised her to stop using the app if she felt unsafe.

I remember Tori asking me how this could be happening since the app was matching them based on their natal charts. As if their astrological compatibility was infallible. As if it was a scientific predictor of behavioral outcomes. I had laughed at her naivety and religious devotion to astrology.

And astrology aside, this guy was evil. Evil *and* stupid. The police caught him within days of the murder because he'd left DNA at the scene. He's currently serving life in prison without parole. The only reason the police didn't look into her dating apps was because they caught him so easily. Open and closed case.

After the news of the murder broke, one of my employees recognized the woman's name. He'd tried to help her block the man. I asked our tech team to dig into it, hoping for information to exonerate SoulMatch. It was a delusional Hail Mary, but I had to try.

What they found was ... bad.

There was a backdoor into our app. Anyone with the know-how—and it was some serious computer shit know-how—could access critical user information. The data they put in when they set up their profiles—full name and birth date, along with their current location even if they opted out of that feature in-app.

I lost my shit and put the IT director who'd found it on a solo sprint to patch the vulnerability and add an ironclad blocking feature. Who fucking cared if male users complained? Who cared about the narrowing dating pool or whether we lost out to competing apps anymore? I couldn't believe her death was our fault, but that was very likely the case, and I hated myself for it.

I made everyone who knew about the leak sign a nondisclosure agreement to protect the company against any defamation lawsuits that might follow in the wake of the murder. I didn't truly believe they'd hold up at a legal level, but maybe they'd keep employees from speaking out. A couple customer service employees and this IT director all signed, and I gave them each a six-figure bonus.

Tori was the last to comply. She felt it was our fault, and said we needed to take responsibility for it. But I explained that even knowing about the privacy leak wasn't proof that the man had accessed that data or that he'd used it to find the victim. It wasn't like we were covering up a crime. And by this time, they'd charged the murderer.

Tori finally signed.

I spiraled hard after the dust settled. I hated that that motherfucker had taken advantage of my company. I hated that an innocent woman had died. I hated that I hadn't taken the complaint seriously while she was still alive. That I'd treated Tori the way I did. But it wasn't like I could go back and fix any of it. I could only move forward.

"You already lost Bryce," Tori whispers, cutting the silence again. "I lost Tucker. Now I've lost Rawson too. We've both likely lost Courtney. I can't keep going on like this. I have to dig myself out or I'll die under the grief and regret."

Something about this steels me up again and I'm back to my hardened self. Except this time, it's not directed at Tori. "We didn't lose Courtney. Not yet. We're going to find her."

I have no idea what to do about Tori wanting to go to the police. Maybe it's time to turn over all the rocks and take on whatever the fuck crawls out. And as for Courtney, I'm determined. We aren't losing her.

Tori nods, but it's a defeated gesture.

"If you need to take your meds and they make you sleepy, I'll take care of you," I say.

She looks at me suspiciously, and I wrap my arm around her shoulders. "I mean it."

I pick up the little gun that I set down on the bed next to me, and Tori and I go downstairs.

But when we get there, the living room is empty.

"Leslie?" I call out. I walk out the door and onto the porch to look for her.

She's nowhere in sight.

47

REESE

WHEN I GET TO THE BEACH, THE SUN IS SINKING LOW ON THE other side of the island, painting the sky with swaths of orange and yellow that remind me of flames. Before me is the red kayak —a tandem.

I climb the short ladder up to the door of the chickee hut to look for a paddle. Luckily, it's unlocked.

The hut is small, about the size of a backyard garden shed. Inside, life jackets hang on the wall, and there are fishing poles and tackle boxes, snorkeling gear, folding chairs and beach umbrellas, along with what looks like an inflatable-paddleboard bag. Next to that, a few kayak paddles. Two, to be exact.

This stops me for a minute. Did Rawson take out a kayak without a paddle? I unzip the paddleboard bag to see if maybe he took that one, but why would he go searching for a single-blade paddle when there are two double-bladed ones in front of his face? Sure enough, the extendable two-piece paddle is still inside the bag. Maybe there were more than two kayak paddles to begin with.

I grab the paddleboard leash from the bag in case I need it to stabilize the kayak to load Courtney in. Then I go back down the ladder to the sand and lodge my bag into the front hammock of the red kayak. I'll paddle from the rear for better control.

I add a life jacket and Keith's rifle to the kayak. Hopefully the weight of my bag and this stuff will help balance it a bit. It's dark now, and when I shove the boat into the water, I remember how warm it is—probably close to eighty degrees. Small favors.

The kayak slides in easily, and I'm grateful we're on the Gulf side—no big ocean waves. This is absolutely navigable. I dip the paddle into the water, pushing through the dark as fast as I can.

I wonder why we haven't seen more of Keith today? Surely he knows by now that Leslie escaped. That she'd have told us he kidnapped her, and that we have his gun. He must know that we suspect he has Courtney, and that we know about the spot in the mangroves—if he's smart, he has to realize that anything Leslie knows, we know too.

So why isn't he trying to stop us?

Stop us from what, though? What can we do? Turn him in?

No way to do that without a boat or a radio, so as long as we're on the island, he's fine.

Adrenaline courses through me, and I glance over my left shoulder. In theory, I could take this kayak to Marathon. The lights of Seven Mile Bridge are low across the expanse of water, and suddenly, I'm second-guessing my initial impulse to go after Courtney. I could abandon this mission right now and make for the mainland. Maybe even return with help tonight.

But if Courtney's alive, the worst-case scenario is she's gone days without water. Almost thirty-six hours, actually. With the saltwater all around, and the humidity, I don't know if she'd even make it three days.

Of course, Keith could be giving her water, but I don't know that for sure, and in the mangroves, she's been exposed to the weather and god knows what else. What if she's wounded?

Would Courtney get the medical help she needs more quickly if I resist the urge to be a hero and go for the police instead?

I look over my shoulder at that faint line of lights again.

It would take me hours to paddle across to Marathon, and Courtney might not have time to wait for the police to get here.

If I go after her now, at the very least I can administer first aid and give her water. I'll still have the option to take her directly to Marathon in the kayak if I need to.

I fix my eyes ahead and try to shut my mind off so it doesn't second-guess what my gut is telling me. I have to get Courtney.

The dark tangle of mangroves is ahead, and soon, I pass the edge of it. I flick on my headlamp to search for the first tunnel opening.

An explosion rings out, and in the basement of my mind, I recognize the sound. It's the crack of a gun.

A little ping of something hits the water about ten feet from my kayak.

Someone is shooting at me.

48

REESE

I turn off my headlamp, and even though my eyes aren't adjusted to the dark, I paddle faster than before.

The gun goes off again, followed by another bullet hitting the water. This time a bit farther away.

I duck and put all my strength into paddling in this crouched position. Whoever is shooting at me isn't on the beach; the shots are coming from the water, even though I don't see a boat. After two misses, I still can't find them, so returning fire isn't an option.

I keep paddling until I finally pass one of the little openings into the mangroves.

"Take the second one."

It isn't too much farther before I enter the second little stream through tall branches—a mangrove tunnel. I have to go slower by moonlight than I would if I used a lamp, but I can't risk giving away my location.

Once I'm sure I'm hidden from view, or at least an impossible target thanks to the maze of branches around me, I turn the headlamp back on. I expect the light to be a relief, but it only makes this place scarier. I move through the shallow water, my single beam of light slicing through darkness. The water is surprisingly clear, and I can see things swimming, but not what they are. I don't want to look too closely. There's movement near me, and my light is on it in a breath: little black crabs crawling up the branches like spiders. I shudder.

I want to call out for Courtney, but the shooting has stopped, and I can't draw attention to myself.

They saw you go into the mangroves. They know where you are.

The shooter is probably waiting for me to come back out. This thought gnaws at me, but I have to focus on finding Court.

When I come to a fork in the water, I follow Leslie's instructions and go right. This tunnel is narrower, with mangrove branches hanging so low I practically have to touch my forehead to my knees while paddling.

I hear something as I get farther down the tunnel—whispering? I can't make out the words at first, but I keep moving toward the sound.

"I didn't want to … "

It's a woman's voice—Court. Is she alone? My heart beats faster.

Again, I fight the urge to call out to her. I'm almost there.

I carefully dip my paddle as I go, trying not to make any sloshing sounds when it hits the water. I just have to stay straight and keep my head low.

"He made me. He did … "

She keeps rambling. It doesn't sound like a conversation; I only hear one voice.

Then Courtney comes into view, cradled in the mangroves. Her back is to me, but I see the blue tank top she wore that first day, and her hair falling out of its spout of a ponytail.

Nobody else is here.

"Court!" I shout-whisper.

Her face turns so I see her profile.

"Reese? Is that you? Are you real?" The words are raspy.

"Yes! I'm almost there. Hang on."

I can't get the kayak to her because the water is getting too shallow, so I go as far as I can and then tie up the kayak with the paddle leash. The water comes up to my ankles as I wade over to her. I pull out my knife when I see the zip ties, and when I get the blade up to the plastic, she cries out.

I wince but work the knife anyway.

Courtney screams and her hands come free. She draws them in front of her and turns toward me.

I take her hands and my headlamp shines on her wrist. I suck my teeth.

"It's bad, huh?" She moans.

It's beyond bad. Courtney has what appears to be only a small cut, but the whole area around it is swollen and red. There's yellowish pus under the surface of her skin. I press my palm gently on her face.

She's fiery hot.

"You have an infection."

"I need water."

I stop to retrieve a plastic bottle of water from my bag and hold it to her mouth. Most of it runs down her chin.

My chest tightens as dread builds from deep within me. I could take her directly across the Gulf to a hospital, but I don't think she can make it in this state. Plus, I don't know what the tide or currents are like right now, and I'd be paddling twice my weight.

I look closer. It's hard to tell in the dark how severe the infection is, but a bacterial infection from the wound being submerged in water makes me think of sepsis.

I want to say fuck it all, I'm paddling her to Marathon.

But there's the issue of whoever was shooting at me. Even if we elude them, what about our friends back at the house?

I shine the light in Court's face to check out her skin color. I'll let the presence of sepsis determine my next move. She's a little pale, but that's all. I inspect her lips and nail beds.

"What are you doing?" she asks.

"Checking you for sepsis."

She doesn't freak out. She must know it's a possibility.

Her nail beds and lips aren't blue—a good sign that her blood still has decent oxygen levels. I'll take her back to the house and treat her there. I have antibiotics and syringes full of saline in my medical kit. I'll irrigate and dress the wound myself.

I look at my watch. It's almost 2100 hours. Eleven hours until the boat gets here.

"Hang tight a sec," I say, and loosen the straps on the rear hammock seat where I've been sitting. I need to lay her down as flat as possible so she isn't a target. Having her in the back might cause some drag, but I'm pretty sure we weigh about the same, so it should balance out. I'm not nosing this kayak out of the mangroves with her in the front seat, even if she's lying low.

I pull Court to her feet and support her while I put the life jacket on her. She cries out in pain.

"I know, I'm sorry."

I move her into the kayak. That takes a couple attempts, but eventually we do it. Then I get into the front seat and make sure the rifle is within arm's reach.

For the first time in years, I feel out of my depth in a survival situation. My body starts trembling as I move back through the mangrove tunnel.

I ground myself by thinking through how I'll dress Courtney's wound and treat her infection while also trying to keep everyone else safe until morning.

My heart jackhammers as I get closer to where the tunnel

opens up into the Gulf. I'll have no cover from the shooter as I paddle back to the beach. My mind moves slower than usual. Spinning like a computer trying to load software.

Just before the mangrove tunnel ends, I lean back and whisper to Courtney, "No matter what happens or what you hear, don't move, and stay low."

49

TORI

The past twenty-four hours have felt like Whac-A-Mole, and I'm exhausted.

Find a shed, but Courtney's not inside and a different kidnapped woman is.

That woman is Leslie, which means this other guy isn't.

There's a radio in the garage—*psych!* There's not.

Bring the real Leslie back to the house, help her rehydrate, and she disappears.

Reese went after Courtney, but what if it follows the same pattern? What if Courtney returns and Reese goes missing?

And Rawson—

I swallow a hard lump.

No. Don't think about him.

I shove it down. Lock it up in the same spot where I put Tucker. It's the only way through.

"Where the hell did Leslie go?" I ask Paige as I go to stand beside her on the porch. She's staring out at the dark island, as if searching.

She shrugs. "No clue. I'm going to look."

"I'm coming with you."

"No, you stay here."

"Wow. Have you never seen a single horror movie? You don't split up unless you want to die."

She smiles. It's tiny, but I made her smile. My Sagittarius placements rejoice.

"Fine, let's go," she says.

A light flashes in the garage. Someone's in there.

Paige marches quickly toward it, and I can feel her energy is in *you're busted* mode, wanting to charge in. I pull her tank top to stop her and whisper, "Wait, we don't know who that is."

She nods quickly, sort of rolling her eyes, but not at me. It's more like she's annoyed she didn't think of it. My eyes fall on the gun in her hand and my heart beats a little faster. For some reason, she seems really off-kilter. We're all tired, but I don't like how wired she is all of a sudden. Jumpy.

"Let me have the gun," I whisper as we sneak toward the garage.

She stops and turns to me. "Why?"

"Just thought you might be uncomfortable with it. I know how you feel about them."

"I'm fine."

Her tone is sharp—she's telling me this is the end of the discussion. I wish I hadn't made it a power struggle because she shouldn't be the one with the gun right now.

Whoever is in the garage is searching for something. I hear things being moved around.

When we're about five feet away, I trip over my own damn feet and it sends a shuffling noise through the night.

Fuck.

Paige cocks the gun and I put my hand over hers. "Not yet," I whisper.

"I don't know how to undo it," she says softly.

I reach over and uncock it for her. She looks at me, surprised. I want to remind her I used to be married to a U.S. Marshal who regularly sat at my kitchen table, cleaning his firearm.

"Who's in there?" Paige asks. Her voice is commanding.

No answer.

"I have a gun. Come out with your hands up."

I feel the urge to laugh. Did she get that line from *NYPD Blue* reruns or something?

She reaches into her back pocket with her free hand and gives me her phone.

I take it and tap the flashlight button, pointing it at the opening of the garage.

"It's just me. Leslie."

I feel Paige's energy relax for a moment, but then it revs up again. "Get out here."

Leslie hops out of the garage. She's moving around better than she was before, even if she can't put any weight on her leg. She extends an arm to brace herself against the opening of the garage, clearly exhausted from the effort.

"What the fuck are you doing? And why did you try to hide?"

Leslie's face is expressionless. "I haven't been totally honest with you."

50

REESE

I'M AT THE OPENING OF THE MANGROVE TUNNEL, BUT NOT exposed yet. I stare across the Gulf at the lights of Seven Mile Bridge again. It's like they're taunting me. So close, but so far away. I can't believe this is my play, but it's the only thing I can think of.

I paddle the nose of the kayak out so the boat is just barely exposed, but we're still hidden well behind the mangrove branches. Then I wait.

Nothing happens. My heart surges, thinking maybe they left.

But it's dark enough that it's possible the shooter can't see the boat. I need to be sure.

I retreat into the mangroves and stretch my paddle out in front of the boat to slap the water. Maybe they can't see, but I bet they can hear.

A bullet zings into the water. It came from the left, the exact way we need to go to get to the beach. But at least I know they don't have night-vision goggles or some insane military-grade tool to see in the dark.

I use the paddleboard leash to attach the boat to a few of

the mangrove branches, then grab my hunting knife and slip out of the kayak and into the warm water as quietly as I can. It's deeper than it was in the mangroves, but it's still only up to my waist. I duck down to swim—I need to stay as low as possible.

"Where you going?" Courtney moans.

"Shh," I whisper. "Remember what I said. Hold still and be very quiet. I'll be back."

I place the knife between my teeth and do an almost-silent breaststroke, practically brushing against the mangroves. As long as he doesn't hear me, my plan might work.

I keep swimming, focusing on silence over speed, trying not to think about how I could be shot at any moment.

Soon, paddling sounds come from somewhere in front of me.

It's him. He's moving in from the Gulf.

I cut through the water and can make out the broad shoulders of a man silhouetted by the moon. He's in a small boat about thirty feet ahead. I duck even lower in the water until it hits just below my eyes, only coming up for air as needed.

I hug the mangroves as much as I can without stirring them. And I get closer.

The barrel of his gun is aimed at exactly where Courtney and the kayak are hiding. I can't help but smile to myself. He's so sure I'll come out in a boat that he doesn't even suspect I'm almost within arm's reach.

I use my foot to test where the sea floor is. If I stand here, the water will probably hit right below my chest.

Then I creep up behind his small metal rowboat, now noticing his face is obscured by the hood of a sweatshirt pulled low. When I'm at the stern where all his weight is concentrated, I wrap my fingers around the edge, and in one motion, I jump on it, pulling it down with all my might.

The boat wobbles hard but doesn't capsize, and because he

isn't expecting it, he flails right into the water, dropping his gun in the boat. I lunge after him with my knife.

It's only a couple feet farther from shore, but it's deeper here than I anticipated, and the water is up to my chin. My fingers close around fabric. His sweatshirt, maybe.

A fist connects with my face, sending me underwater again. I swim to the surface, but I must have gotten turned around because I feel the wall of his chest against my back, followed by his arm wrapped around my neck. I'm stuck in the crook of his elbow. He squeezes, and my throat constricts.

I grip my knife and send it up with all my strength, aiming for his neck behind me. I land the blow somewhere, but he twists and I lose my knife.

"Fucking cunt!" he shouts as his grip loosens. I push off him to free myself and swim for his boat, glancing back to gauge how badly I've wounded him. He's still moving.

I jump up on the side of his boat and clock his rifle at the bottom. I swipe for it but miss. I'll have to actually get in.

His chaotic splashing behind me says I have little to no time.

I crouch down and push off the sea floor, kicking my legs furiously while grabbing for one of the boat's handles and pulling myself up. Just as I can feel the boat tipping toward me, I tuck and roll into it. A bench seat cracks against my back as I land.

I wrap my fingers around the gun and sit up, immediately aiming it.

He isn't there.

I scan the water's surface, but it's quiet. Nobody in sight.

He's using my own trick on me, quietly getting close. He must be underwater.

Just then, he surfaces about three feet away, gasping for air. I take the shot.

He falls back into the water.

I don't know if I got him for good or if I only wounded him again.

I hold the gun at the ready and slow my breath.

He floats to the surface, face down.

I row over to him and poke at his body with the paddle to pull it close. I have to know if this is Keith.

I carefully reach out of the boat and roll him over. It's too dark to make out details, but I can tell it isn't Keith.

I've never seen this man before.

51

PAIGE

Anger floods my senses, but it's not aimed at Tori. It's aimed at this shitshow we're in. I have this fresh determination to get us all on that boat in the morning, and then we're flying home to Boise. Period.

Leslie, however, cannot be trusted. That comes into clear focus right now as I stand a few feet away, not pointing the gun at her, but ready to do so at any moment.

"You're coming back inside, and then you're telling us everything," I say.

She nods fast but doesn't move.

"Do I need to walk behind you and hold this at your back?" I lift the gun.

"No! No. Please, I'll do what you say." She puts her hands up until she needs them to brace herself against the railing to move up the porch stairs.

Once we're inside, Tori locks the door behind us and I direct Leslie to sit against the wall in the living room. She tries to lower herself, but she can't do it without help. Tori goes over to support her as she slides her ass to the floor.

"Talk," I say.

She lifts her face to us. "I'm not the house manager. I'm the owner."

"And?"

"And this place has been in my family for a couple generations."

"Okay?" I say, drawing the word out. This doesn't seem like a secret worthy of *I haven't been totally honest with you.*

"That's it."

I scoff. "That doesn't explain what you were doing in the garage just now."

"Fine!" Leslie raises her hands. "I was looking for a weapon. Sue me. I told your friend that it was a rumor—that a girl wasn't really killed on the island—but I lied, and I'm scared shitless."

"More lies. If you wanted a weapon, you could have taken a knife from the kitchen."

"Paige—" Tori starts, and I whirl around to face her.

"Don't tell me to calm down. She's lying to us."

Tori leans back, keeping her face neutral. It's an expression I know well. It's her *you're wrong, but you're also the boss* face.

But I'm not wrong. And there's no way I'm ignoring my gut again. "There's more. Spill it."

"That's all, I swear," Leslie says. "I'm so grateful you guys found me when you did. Thank you."

Oh, please. She's fawning. I've done it a million times in my life, and my employees do it to me all the time.

"I don't believe you," I say.

Leslie's eyes flick to the gun in my hand. I'm gripping it tight, but it's still hanging by my side. I understand her fear, but I'm not putting it down.

"I promise." Tears spring to her eyes. "Please believe me. I'm sorry I didn't tell you I'm the owner. I didn't think it mattered while we were emailing, and then everything has been so crazy since then."

"Why did you lie to Reese about the girl who died?" I ask.

"I don't know. I was still pretty out of it."

"It was only a few hours ago, at most."

"Please, I'm sorry. I'm just scared. Same as you guys."

I narrow my eyes at her. There's no reason to keep pressing her. She's made it clear she isn't saying anything else. But she's hiding something, and I don't like how easily she lies.

52

TORI

I AGREE WITH PAIGE ABOUT LESLIE, BUT I DON'T LIKE HOW unhinged Paige's energy is, especially when she has that gun.

It's been forever since any of us have eaten, so I go into the kitchen and make microwave quesadillas. It's fast and it's better than cold cereal.

We eat in silence, and as we're finishing, I hear hard footfalls on the porch.

I shoot a look at Paige. It could be Reese, but what if it's not? We have to be prepared for the worst, and I'd rather be the one with the gun.

Paige nods at me. She's in the process of passing it over, and as I take it, there's a light rapping on the door.

"Tori? It's me."

Rawson.

I shove the gun back at Paige and run to fling the door open.

I can't believe he's standing there, right before my eyes. But his face—it's all beaten up. Bruised on his left side, with a big cut. The blood has dried, but it doesn't seem like he's taken any time to clean it up.

"Are you okay?" I pull him in for a hug once we're in the living room, and he winces. "Where have you been? What happened?"

"I crashed the kayak." He touches his face gently where the huge shiner's at.

"Oh, baby!" I say, leading him to the couch.

"Where have you been all day?" Paige asks, that gun still in her grip. "What took you so long to get back here?"

"Paige! Look at him. He needs some pain meds and a glass of water, not the third degree."

"We're doing this my way. Period."

"Water would be great. Or actually, give me something harder," Rawson says.

"No alcohol," Paige says. "We need to keep our heads clear, and you don't get anything until you explain yourself."

She's redirecting her anger toward Leslie at Rawson. She does this at the office. Whatever gets into her line of sight is a target, even if it has nothing to do with why she's mad.

"Who is that?" Rawson asks, pointing at Leslie.

I bring him up to speed on everything—the real Leslie, Keith, Courtney, and Reese—then say, "I'm getting him water."

When I stand up, Paige blocks me.

"Sit your ass down."

My eyes travel to the gun in her hand. At least she's not pointing it at anyone.

"Paige, hand me the gun."

She shakes her head.

"Holy shit, where'd you get that?" Rawson asks, eyes wide.

"Answer my questions first," she says.

"Okay, shoot." He puts his hands up. "I mean your questions, not that thing."

It's hard to stifle my laugh, but I do it. Even I know now isn't the time for a joke.

Paige doesn't miss a beat. "Where have you *actually* been?"

"Just woke up on the beach and came here."

My stomach drops. Either he's hiding something, or Paige is lying to me about not seeing him at that beach this morning. I face her, waiting for her response.

"Try again," she says.

"It's the truth! I crashed the kayak and was lucky enough to wake up on land instead of waking up … in heaven. Or maybe hell. Not sure I'd make it to heaven."

He's still treating this situation too lightly, and it makes my stomach turn.

"You weren't on the beach," Leslie breaks in. "We were there. We saw the kayak."

True. All three of them came that way. A wave of relief that Paige isn't the one lying here, followed by unease. That means Rawson is lying.

I stand and walk over to Paige. She watches me the whole way, her face skeptical. I imagine she thinks I'm going to demand the gun again. But when I get there, I touch her arm and nod.

I'm with you.

Here's the thing: My sun, rising, and Mercury are all in Sagittarius, and that sign is obsessed with truth, even when it's uncomfortable. *Especially* then.

I swear to god I see tears glistening in her eyes. She gets it.

"There are zip ties in the garage," Leslie says. "I unlocked the dock box. They're in a clear baggie in there."

"Take my phone as a flashlight," Paige says to me, nodding toward the entryway table.

"What's happening?" Rawson asks, standing.

"Sit," Paige demands, pointing the gun at him.

"Fine, Jesus."

I run out of the house, but I'm barely out of earshot when I burst into tears.

53

PAIGE

TORI BROUGHT BACK THE ZIP TIES AND A SPOOL OF FISHING LINE. I made Leslie restrain Rawson; it felt like too much to ask of Tori, especially after she chose to trust me over him.

Now Leslie is back at her spot on the floor, adjacent to Rawson, who is bound at the wrists and ankles. We used the fishing line to tie him to the stair banister. We're not taking any chances.

"Now, for the third time, where were you all day?" I ask him.

He ignores me and zeroes in on Tori. "You believe me, right? She's just using you like she always does."

Tori stands still beside me, but her expression is hard. She crosses the living room and goes to look out the front window in silence.

"I crashed the fucking kayak and took a hit to the head. Look at me!" he yells. "Maybe I woke up on the beach, maybe it was back farther in the brush and that's why you didn't see me. I don't know. I don't remember much. I need water and Tylenol."

"Are you working with Keith?" I ask.

"What? No!"

Before I can press this, Tori turns to face him and crosses her arms. "What about your student loans? Your dream of being *free to practice your art* like Hemingway?"

Okay, random. But I let her keep going.

"What about it?" he asks.

"Getting a big drug deal payout could be the solution to all your problems."

"What drug deal?"

He knows what drug deal. Tori just told him when she caught him up to speed.

"We know you're in on this with Keith, *Raw Dog*," I say. "Cut the shit and tell us. You can't get a payday if you're dead." I still have the gun trained on him, but my hand is shaky.

"Fine! Yeah. I'm broke, and I'll never dig myself out of the hole I'm in unless something changes. I have too many DUIs and student loans, and I'm living with my mom. When Border Patrol came for the wash-up, I started to wonder if there was more than one, so I went to talk to Keith last night. Took me so damn long to find him that by the time I finally did, I was exhausted and starving. He's camping out on the other side of the island. Anyway, I threatened him. Told him if he didn't cut me in, I'd go to the cops."

"And?" I ask.

"And he beat the shit out of me."

I want to laugh. I look over at Tori, and her face is stone. Her jaw clenches.

"So then he … what? Let you go?" I ask.

"Yeah."

I sigh. "You're a child if you think we believe that. Why did he send you back here?"

"He didn't send me back. I came on my own. Where else am I supposed to go?"

Then Tori is at my side, stripping the gun from my hand. I'm too surprised to resist.

She points it at him and steps closer. "Did you know Keith before you met me? Did you target me? Was that your play the whole time?"

"No!" he shouts. "Hell no. I swear to god. I didn't meet him until that night he showed up, same as you guys."

"You betrayed me." Tori's voice catches on the last word, but her hands are steady. "You never even cared about me."

"What? That's crazy. I love you!"

"He's lying," I whisper.

"I know," she says. "Tie Leslie up."

"Why?" I glance at Leslie who is cowering on the floor.

"Because next to the zip ties in the dock box was a fucking serial killer's Home Depot haul. Duct tape, rope, bleach, rubber gloves, the works."

I gasp and step over to Leslie. I can't believe this is happening.

"That stuff's not mine!" Leslie protests. "One of them must have put it there."

"Tori, look at me. You're overreacting," Rawson says.

She doesn't even glance at him.

I reach for Leslie's hands to tie her up, and I notice a small tattoo on the inside of one of her wrists. It looks like a bushy tree with a root system underwater. A mangrove?

Then the blast of a gun makes me jump out of my skin.

54

COURTNEY

I'M DYING. PAIN AND HEAT WRACK MY BODY. MY VISION'S blurred.

I'm in a boat with Reese.

Then I see sand.

I'm floating over it.

No. Not floating. Someone's carrying me. My chest and stomach are against their shoulders. They have a tight grip on my good wrist and one leg.

Holy shit. I knew Reese was strong, but this is insane. How is she doing this?

I lift my head to make sure it's her, but I see Bryce's profile. His angled nose, his thick brows.

I close my eyes. Tired. Too tired to think.

You did the right thing, Bryce says.

"I didn't want to," I say.

"What?" Reese asks, the single word clearly a lot to manage.

I don't respond to her. I'm talking to Bryce.

I know you didn't want to, but you did it anyway, and that's love, he says.

I clench my jaw so I won't speak out loud. I can't tell what I'm thinking and what I'm saying.

It was murder, I reply in my mind. *I'm a killer.*

Then I'm at Bryce's bedside on his very last day.

I'd given Reese the morning off even though she'd protested. She couldn't say no when I also asked her to run a bunch of errands for me. I told her I was going to an appointment, and I ignored Paige's calls for once.

I took Bryce's hand and started the playlist that I'd been working on for days, ever since I agreed to do what he'd been asking me to.

"Thank you," he said, but the words were in the generic voice of the eye-gaze device. I missed his voice, but at least this way I could watch him while he spoke instead of looking at a screen.

The device represented how far gone Bryce was. He was almost totally paralyzed—unable to move, yes, but also so many of his involuntary functions had shut down. He was dependent on ventilators and breathing and feeding tubes. But the device also showed me how very *himself* he still was. His mind was completely intact. That fact made everything so much harder.

I pulled my hand back and looked down, pretending to fiddle with my phone while Percy Sledge sang "When a Man Loves a Woman."

"I'm killing the one person who gives my life meaning. No reason to thank me," I whispered.

I hated the edge of anger in my voice. I blinked through tears and looked up at the hand I had just released. Once so strong, it was now limp and shriveled. It looked cold and alone there against the red-and-black fleece blanket. I swallowed hard and reached for it again. No matter what I felt about the thing I was doing, I wouldn't let him feel alone.

"You are saving me. I know you cannot see it clearly and you are just trusting that it is true, but you are my rock. You always have been and I have never felt more loved by anyone than I do right now," he said.

I looked up toward the ceiling and tried to swallow the sobs pushing against my throat. I wanted to argue. To tell him he was wrong and that he'd always been the strong one. I wanted to ask how I was supposed to go on after this. But I refused to burden him.

"You will get back to your career. You will fall in love again," he said.

"Stop," I demanded, now looking directly at him.

This was a new thing he'd started doing. Talking about my future and finding someone else. Not only did it hurt to think of him imagining that, but it felt so far beyond impossible to even entertain the idea. He was the only person I'd ever fallen for. My once in a lifetime.

"You will find happiness again. You have a lot of life ahead and I want you to keep living."

Without me.

He didn't say it, but he didn't have to. That fact had swollen so large that it was all I could see. My eyes were down, fixed on our clasped hands. It was hard to tell where his fingers ended and mine began. This was us. One soul. One flesh.

When I didn't respond, he said, "Promise you will."

I wanted to say no. I wanted to scream it. But when I saw his weak and watery eyes, I knew I couldn't do that to him. And so I nodded. "I promise."

The music switched to "Bring It On Home to Me" by Sam Cooke, and we sat in silence for a minute until Bryce said, "It is time."

I shook my head. "I'm not ready."

"Baby, you will never be ready, but I have waited long enough. I am ready."

He didn't mean he was ready to leave me. We'd already had those arguments, and I knew deep in my bones that what he was experiencing was bigger than that. He needed to go out on his own terms.

I nodded and forced a smile. It took all my strength to stand. To lift my arms and add the solution I'd made from sleeping pills to his feeding tube. It went against everything in me, and I forced down the thoughts clamoring for attention.

You're pulling the trigger.

You're killing him.

When I returned to my seat next to his bed, he said, "Come here," and I climbed onto the bed with him. His frame had grown so small that I could fit fine.

I nuzzled next to him and let my hot tears drench his gown. We probably only had about ten more minutes together.

When "These Arms of Mine" came on, I started sobbing. I couldn't control it. All the resolve to be strong for Bryce that I'd built over the past years shattered. Maybe it was wrong to do that, to let him see how broken I was in those last minutes, but I had no choice. My body took over.

"You are the best thing that has ever happened to me," Bryce said, and my brain cut through the sadness with a thought about how of course he would bust out a cliche at that moment.

But then I noticed his breathing stopped. His heart was still.

I wrapped my arms around him and squeezed tight, much tighter than I normally would have, typically worried that I was hurting him. And then I truly let myself go. I cried so hard that I must have fallen asleep, because when I woke up, it was to songs that I knew I hadn't added to the playlist.

But I still didn't move from that spot.

I marveled at how right and normal it felt to be this close to his body, even though he wasn't in it. It had been his soul's house, and I loved it. There was nothing morbid about being here. Nothing grotesque, only memories of love.

55

REESE

I GASP FOR AIR WHILE STAGGERING ON THE LAST LITTLE STRETCH of beach. I imagine my heart driving me. My willpower is strong. That, I fucking know about myself after everything life has thrown at me.

I thought I could carry Court all the way to the house, but I'm totally spent. My legs and arms were jelly after the fight with that asshole, then I paddled the kayak until we reached the tiki hut on the beach, where I pulled it ashore. Now my muscles scream as if they're tearing apart, and my lungs are blazing with every gasp for air.

Slow down. Be methodical. Stay present.

I know I have to keep moving, but I need a quick rest, so I set Courtney gently on her feet.

The air is warm, but less humid than it's been during the day. The sky is an explosion of stars, no light pollution to erase them from view.

I hold Courtney upright so her arm drapes over my shoulders. Her height works in our favor, and she's able to lean against me. I don't like how out of it she is. All the muttering about Bryce. But we're almost to the house. I keep my eyes fixed on the boardwalk, which is lit up like a runway.

My brain shuffles through options.

Charge forward. Get her there now.

Leave Courtney here and make sure the house is safe.

No. I'm not leaving her on the beach after that ambush from the rowboat guy.

"More men are coming."

Maybe they're all converging tonight for the drug deal.

We move forward toward the house, all stumbles and shuffles, but I'm keeping her with me, and soon our feet touch the boardwalk.

"Leslie. He took me," she mumbles.

Keith. She isn't even up to speed on the fact that Keith is his real name and the real Leslie was kidnapped. There isn't time for that now, though.

"I know. But that's over. I'm getting you to the house and I'll patch you up."

Courtney isn't really walking, but she must be supporting herself somehow because when she suddenly stops, it wrenches my momentum backward. I lose my footing, but catch myself before skidding on to the boardwalk.

"I killed him," she says.

"What?"

"I killed Bryce."

She breaks down, and her body shakes with ragged sobs.

I take her into a hug, holding her up. "I know."

"You … what?"

"I know about the sedatives."

She pulls back. Her face, lit by the moonlight, is gaunt. Her mouth gapes open and her knees sort of wobble. "You knew?"

I help her sit down on the wood slats and guide her to lean against a tree that's so close to the boardwalk it's almost growing up through it. She holds her own hand, babying the wound on her wrist. I sit down next to her.

"Of course. Between the missing meds, the long list of stupid errands that you demanded be done before lunch time, and the claim that nobody was there when he died, I made the leap."

She covers her face with her hands and cries harder. "I hate myself for it. I miss him so much."

If anyone understands what it feels like to hate themselves for something they've done, it's me. There's a lot I could say right now, but I don't want to move the focus to myself, and I have to convince her we need to get back to the house. But the truth is, you can't control when the waves of grief decide to pummel you. They're in charge. Always.

"I know. I can only imagine how hard it must be to face life without him. But the truth is you did the right thing. We all know he wanted to go *months* before he did."

She doesn't respond, so I continue. "It's so hard to see clearly when your mind is clouded by sadness. Add fear and shame to the mix, and it can be impossible. But you did for him what he couldn't do for himself. I don't know shit about romance, but to me, that's the whole game. You sacrificed your own feelings, your own comfort, your own desires, for him."

I glance over, studying her profile. Her jaw ripples; I can tell she's still unmoved. This isn't working, and I can't just stand up and say, *Alright, good talk, let's get to the house.*

"I killed someone too," I whisper. What I did is night and day from what she did, but I have to meet her on her level, and unfortunately, she feels like she killed Bryce even though she actually assisted his death.

She gasps and says, "What?"

I've never told anyone about this, and Courtney isn't the

person who should hear it first, but I have to give her something. "When we get through this, I'll tell you the whole thing. But I want you to know that I understand the weight you carry, and you aren't alone."

Right then, the sound of a gunshot cuts through the night, coming from the direction of the house.

56

PAIGE

"Tell us fucking everything, Rawson!" Tori screams. She's shaking and her face is wet with either sweat or tears. Probably both.

He's looking at his bleeding shoulder in disbelief. "You shot me!"

"Oh, please. The bullet just grazed your shoulder. I could have done a lot worse. Now, out with it. Everything. Where the fuck were you all day?"

"I need a doctor!"

Tori lifts the little gun, aiming it at him again.

I had no idea she was this good with guns. As much as I hate to admit it, the fact that she's so calm and knowledgeable with one makes me respect her in a new way.

"Okay! Jesus! Fine. He told me if I made sure y'all stayed at the house until morning, I'd get half."

Jesus fuck. What an absolute bottom dweller. "What, like 'Florida Man Turns His Soulmate over to a Killer So He Can Pay off His Student Loans'?" I scoff.

He glares at me.

"What's happening in the morning?" Tori asks.

"You go home on the boat," he says, like she's an idiot.

Tori laughs. "And you believed that? That he'd let us get on the boat and go back to our lives?"

"Of course. He's not a murderer. He just wants the deal to go through. I get some cash, you guys get home safely. Wins all around."

"Actually, he might be a murderer," Leslie pipes up.

I want to be shocked at this, but I'm not. I turn to her and say, "What do you mean?"

"I just have a feeling he's got a past," she says.

I look at Tori. Our dynamic is flipping.

"Thoughts?" I ask her.

"What's your zodiac sign?" Tori asks Leslie, and my hope deflates. Right when I think we're understanding each other, she pulls this. Why the hell does it matter?

Leslie sighs. "Capricorn."

Tori looks surprised. "Interesting. Capricorns are badass. Disciplined, protective. Their shadow side, though, can be calculating. What were you planning, Leslie?"

"Nothing! In fact, my lack of planning may be what got us all into this. I needed someone to help me clean up the place and a friend recommended Keith. They vouched for him, and he was dirt cheap, so I didn't do a background check."

"God, that was a stupid business decision," I mutter.

"I know. Lesson learned."

"She could be lying," Tori says. "All of this could be a strategy. And it doesn't explain what I found in the dock box."

A thumping right outside the door jolts our attention to the entrance.

The door handle jiggles, but it's locked. Tori turns the gun toward it, and then someone starts banging.

"Let us in!"

It's Reese.

"Oh my god," I say, and immediately feel the prickle of tears.

I rush to the door, unlock it, and tear it open. Standing before me is the most beautiful sight in the world: a haggard Reese with two rifles slung crosswise over her chest.

Her arm is wrapped around the waist of my dearest Courtney, who looks sick as hell.

"Court!" Tori cries out, rushing to my side.

Reese scans the room. "I heard a gunshot." Her eyes fix on Rawson, and she leads Court to the couch and runs into the kitchen, as if seeing two people tied up in the living room is an everyday affair.

I sit with Court, but she's really out of it. I brush her hair away from her sweaty face, trying not to look at her wrist. It's a swollen, gory horror show. I hope Reese knows what to do.

Courtney is moaning, but that means she's awake. I can't think of anything to say except: "You're going to be okay. Reese is a nurse." As if she doesn't know that.

Please let her be okay, please. I repeat the words in my mind as some sort of prayer.

"Lock the door and turn off the lights," Reese says, situating a headlamp and flicking it on. "Paige, can you boil a pot of water and bring it to me? Along with a clean washcloth and some soap."

Tori turns off the lights, and I spring to my feet and navigate my way toward the kitchen in the dark.

"Here," Tori says, handing me my phone.

I thank her and turn on the faucet so the water can run hot while I point the flashlight at cabinets, opening them one by one until I find a pot, then put it under the faucet.

Reese runs up the stairs, and I flick on the stove, setting down the pot of water. I stand there, waiting.

Bryce would say, *A watched pot never boils.*

God, I miss him, and I don't know if it's the heightened emotional state I'm in right now or what, but tears fill my eyes. I've cried more these past days than I have in years.

Reese comes back downstairs with a bag in her hand. "She has a bad infection. I need to irrigate the wound."

I can't see through the kitchen into the living room now that it's dark, but I hear pills shaking in a bottle.

When I see the first bubbles float to the surface, I say, "It's boiling."

"Needs to boil for a few minutes. Keep watching it," Reese says, then to Court, "Here. Antibiotics. And Tylenol for the fever."

"You have antibiotics on hand?" Rawson asks. "Nobody thinks that's weird? Who brings that shit on vacation when they're not sick?"

I shake my head in annoyance. He's still trying to point fingers at other people.

"Okay, Paige, I think the water's probably good. Bring it over, along with a couple bottles of water."

I shove two under each arm, then snatch up the soap and a washcloth with one hand while carrying the pot as quickly as I can in the other without spilling it.

"I think they're coming," Reese says, pulling on a pair of surgical gloves and taking the pot from me. She pours the bottled water into it—cooling it down. Then she adds soap and starts cleaning around Courtney's wrist. "I had a run in with one of them."

Courtney moans and sucks her teeth.

I sit next to her again and put my hand on her knee. Surely the soap stings.

"I know it hurts, Court, and it's gonna get worse, but this just might save your life," Reese says, working fast.

"Hey! I've got some coke in my pocket. Give her a bump to help with the pain," Rawson says.

"Jesus, you are a Swamp Rat. That could kill her!" Tori says.

"Just trying to help."

"Actually, hand it over," Reese says. "It could numb the surrounding skin if we apply it topically."

"Seriously?" I ask.

"Dead," she says. "Can you bring me the coke?"

I dig around in Rawson's pocket while he makes a sex joke, and I avoid eye contact with Tori in case she's stifling a laugh. It would only piss me off.

I hand the little baggie of white powder to Reese, and after she's rinsed all the soap away, she dabs the cocaine on Courtney's wrist with a gloved hand. "We'll give it a minute and then irrigate it, along with all the bacteria and shit in there."

I hate drugs with all my heart, but if this can ease Courtney's pain, I'm all for it.

"Why's she tied up?" Reese asks, nodding toward Leslie.

I fill her in while she fishes around in her kit and brings out what look like syringes.

"What are those?" I ask.

"Sterile saline flushes."

She's like a medical Mary Poppins, and for a second I wonder why she brought all of that with her.

A quiet moment passes in the dark, and then Reese says, "Paige, how the fuck did Bryce find this place?"

I guess it's fine to come clean about that now. Bryce is gone, and the situation is a little different than it was when I promised him total secrecy.

"I don't know. He emailed me the details, and when I replied asking why, he said, 'Don't ask why.' I remember it clearly because it felt kind of aggressive for Bryce. But I was so busy navigating some stuff with SoulMatch, and honestly, I was eager to do whatever he asked me to do because … well, never mind. I did what he asked. Swore not to say another thing about it to him or anyone else while he was alive."

Reese looks up. "What? That doesn't sound like him at all."

"I know, right? God, I've been keeping that secret for months for Bryce's sake, but I thought it was so strange."

"What email?" Courtney mumbles.

"What do you mean?" I ask.

"What address?" Her breathing is labored. It's like she's barely coherent.

"God, I don't know. Just a sec." I go into the kitchen where I left my phone.

I scroll through old emails and stop when I find it.

"Bryce072624@gmail.com."

"That's not him," Court whispers.

"What?"

"That's not his email address."

57

TORI

THOSE NUMBERS. MY STOMACH DROPS AND I ALMOST RETCH when Paige reads them aloud.

My vision narrows and I feel a panic attack coming on.

No. No. No!

"Paige." It comes out as a whine. "The email address. Those numbers. 072624. It's a date. July 26, 2024."

Paige reaches for support against the doorway to the kitchen.

"What's happening?" Reese asks.

By the faint light, I see Paige breathing erratically. She's about to hyperventilate.

"It's the date a girl was murdered," I say.

"A Miami girl who was targeted by a stalker. A stalker who found her through our app," Paige adds, and tears warm my eyes. She's finally taking responsibility.

"She was my sister." Leslie's voice cracks.

Total silence fills the room. Nobody moves.

"Janie Alvarez. She was my everything. I fucking put the date in there, half hoping you'd catch me, but you didn't," she says to Paige. "It only proved I was right about you. You don't give a shit."

"What did you say?" Paige whispers.

"I sent you the email." Leslie's tone is strong, defiant. "I brought you here. I was going to force you to confess your part in Janie's murder. I tried to come after you through legal channels first, but the lawyers said I didn't have a case, and of course the cops were no help, just like they were useless to my sister. It was a good plan. I just had to get you here, where it's secluded. Nobody would know, and if you refused to go public within twenty-four hours, I would release the footage. I hired Keith to help me film your confession. His military background made him intimidating, and I was fine with him roughing you up until you confessed. It would still be nothing compared to what Janie experienced in her final moments."

She clears her throat, then laughs gently and says, "Janie was always unlucky in love. When she found your app, she was certain she'd match with her *Twin Star*. She always was a sucker for that woo-woo shit. But she was smart too. She had a PhD in environmental science, and her research was focused on saving the mangroves. Since we grew up coming here, they've always been special to us—our hiding place as children. Our version of a fairy forest. Janie and I played for endless hours in that exact spot where Keith held Courtney. He found it one day before you guys came and suggested we put Paige there instead of in the shed. That's how I knew he'd put Courtney there."

She tries to adjust her body, get more comfortable. She suddenly looks small, vulnerable.

Reese goes back to irrigating Courtney's wrist, and Courtney has stopped making as much noise. The coke must be doing something.

My eyes travel between Leslie and Paige, and I can't read

Paige. She's staring at Leslie, not looking down or away, but not crying, either. Her face is blank.

"Anyway, that motherfucker followed Janie here, to our island, and attacked her while I was asleep at the house. Right under my nose. I didn't hear a thing."

The pull to feel sorry for her is strong, but an ember of anger burns in my chest. *She's* the reason we're in this situation.

"My understanding is that Janie was on a couple dating apps," Paige says. Her voice is calm and measured. Businesslike. "What makes you think mine was to blame?" She glances at me.

Maybe she's worried I'll think she's trying to skirt responsibility, but no. Paige is right. Leslie wouldn't know about the security breach, only that SoulMatch was one of a few apps Janie was using. The hot stone inside me burns, and I clench my teeth to keep from saying anything.

"She told me it was SoulMatch," Leslie says.

"But he'd found her on other apps too," Paige counters.

"It was *your* app!" Leslie yells.

"Our friend almost *died*!" I scream. This bitch lured four women here under false pretenses—using Bryce's death, for god's sake!—just to get back at Paige for something she can't even be sure we did.

"I didn't mean for that to happen, but it still doesn't compare to what Janie went through," Leslie says. Her tone is surprisingly soft. "She told me a guy was bothering her on your app, and I believed her. I took it seriously. The police brushed her off since she hadn't even been on a date with him. They'd only chatted for an afternoon when she got creeped out and unmatched. It wasn't like he was an abusive ex, or had stalked her for months. And then, just weeks later, she was dead. So yeah, I never planned to hurt any of you, but Keith went totally off script when we found the fucking drug wash-ups."

Paige sinks to the floor and leans against the doorway, her

face in her hands. Her body is shuddering. It's been years since I've seen her cry that hard.

But my cheeks burn hot. She shouldn't get off this easy. "So you were going to make Paige confess, and then what? Just let her go? And what about us? What was your plan for the three friends you knew she was bringing along?"

"Keith was going to isolate Paige in the island shed for a few hours. However long it took to get a confession. We had a boat coming to take us from here to the Bahamas at a moment's notice, then we'd go our separate ways long before you guys could even get off the island. I have enough money to stay overseas. My husband left me. I'm selling the island. I have nothing to live for. Not anymore."

She's still trying to get us to feel sorry for her. She's still convinced it was *a good plan*.

"And what if Paige had refused to confess to something she's not positive she even did?" I ask.

Paige shoots me a look. We both know it was SoulMatch, but Leslie doesn't have proof.

Leslie shrugs. "She would have. Keith would have made sure. Three friends within arm's reach of us would have been good motivation, too."

"How did you know Bryce used to plan trips for Court?" Paige asks. "How did you know we'd fall for that?"

"Because that one"—she throws a finger at me—"puts everything on social media. Not just her own damn life, but both of yours too." She indicates Courtney and Paige.

"No I don't," I say.

"You kind of do," Reese adds, bandaging Courtney's wrist.

Fury reaches a breaking point, and I shout, "This isn't my fault. You're the one who hired Keith. You're the one who tricked us into coming here." Before I can think about it, I lunge at Leslie.

"Wait," Paige says, catching my elbow before I can get to her. Then, to Leslie: "Janie was found in Miami, not here."

Paige is still trying to find cracks in the story, but I just want to punish Leslie for what she's done.

"That monster abducted her here, then took her to Miami to kill her."

My heartbeat thrums loud in my ears, but I breathe and force myself to calm down. Finally, something makes sense. When Janie was murdered, the news said she was abducted from a family vacation spot and killed in Miami. There were no other details.

But it was here. This is where she was abducted from. "So the rumor about a dead girl, that was Janie?" I ask.

"Yeah. She was taken from here, but not killed here. So it's a half truth," Leslie says.

"Why did he take her all the way to Miami?" Reese asks.

"My guess is power. Control. The usual. That was where she lived. He murdered her in her own home. In her bedroom, actually. I imagine it was a way to show her once and for all that he owned her."

"But to take her across the Gulf, and then drive to Miami, it's what? Two hours away?" Reese presses. "It makes no sense. At least not if he didn't want to get caught. It's so risky."

"It's almost three hours away," Leslie corrects.

"You're no better than he was," Paige says quietly, her voice shaking with anger.

"Don't say that to me." Leslie's teeth are clenched. Her face is stone, her eyes vacant.

"I didn't kill your sister, that man did. You've tormented innocent people for your misplaced revenge fantasy. Including a woman whose husband just died!" Paige shouts, pointing at Courtney, who is out of it on the couch.

"Nobody was supposed to get hurt. If everything had gone

according to plan, you would have been fine if you were smart and confessed."

"But we did get hurt." I'm yelling now, too. I want to strangle her. "Paige is right. You're a psychopath, just like the man who killed Janie. And nothing you've done or ever could do will bring your sister back. She's gone."

Before Leslie can respond, an explosion shatters the front window and she slumps over.

58

REESE

"Everyone down! Shut off the phone light!" I shout, pulling Courtney to the floor. She whimpers but doesn't resist.

There's a huge bullet hole in the window. From the bullet that hit Leslie in the temple, killing her instantly. I don't have to check for a pulse to know.

"Fuck," I whisper.

"Cut me loose!" Rawson yells.

"Shut up," I say. "You want him to know your exact location?"

I can't believe I left the curtains open. And I allowed light in here—that was stupid. My headlamp and Paige's phone were shining on opposite sides of the room. It wasn't a whole lot to see by, but someone who knows what they're doing could work with it. Especially with good positioning outside.

Keith must be a sniper. Or one of the men is. My hands tremble as I crouch on the floor, covering Courtney. We're on the other side of the window, by the couch, and out of sight. I look around. Rawson is hidden from view too, to the right of the window. Tori and Paige are huddled on the floor by the kitchen entrance, totally out of sight. Leslie was a direct shot.

"Everyone stay perfectly still," I say. Then I army-crawl to the window and pull the floor-length curtains closed. There are two other windows. One next to this one, and one on the other side of the door. I get the second window nearby, but we can't chance trying to close the one by the door. There's floor-to-ceiling privacy glass that would be impossible to pass by without exposing ourselves.

My mind races while I crawl toward the door. I sit, pressing my back against the wall, and feel upward for the light switch. My hand hits the plastic plate—and I feel two switches. One turns the lights on in here, and the other turns them on out there.

I can't remember which is which.

"Does anyone know which switch turns on the porch lights?"

"The left one," Tori replies immediately.

"Paige and Tori, get all the way into the kitchen."

I flick the switch, and light floods outside, but it also comes in through the uncovered window and privacy glass. Light streams across the floor, hitting Rawson's foot, which he pulls back. He has to contort himself since he's still pinned to the banister.

I do a mental inventory. I have two guns. The bolt-action rifle from Keith's shed and the AR-15 from the man in the boat. The bolt-action has a full five rounds. The AR-15's magazine is about half empty, so I estimate fifteen rounds. We also have the Beretta, which I brought extra ammo for. It should be enough if I'm careful. And if there isn't an army of men out there.

And if there is?

There's nothing I can do about it. Our ammo situation and this unknown turn my stomach sour.

I slither to the couch and sit with my back against it as I trace the light across the floor with my eyes. I might be able to get upstairs, and from there, I'd be in a much better position to fight back.

Another shot barrels through the front door, splintering a hole at eye level. It hits the stairs next to Rawson.

"Cut these ties!" he demands again.

"You guys stay here. Tori, you still have that handgun?" I ask, ignoring him.

She holds it up.

"Good. Hang on to it in case you need it. I'm going upstairs to see if I can pick some of them off."

I move across the tile on my stomach, but when I get to Leslie's body, I realize I'll have to crawl over it to avoid the light. I try not to think about her still-warm body under me and instead focus on what I need to do next: get upstairs. There's no way to be perfectly quiet as I crawl up them, but I manage to reach the second floor without triggering any more gunfire from Keith and whoever else is out there.

The porch light is blaring into the room I need to access— Tori's. These two windows have wide slat blinds, not curtains, thank god. Between that and the men probably not expecting anyone up here, I'm optimistic about my idea. I move to one of the windows and peek out.

The covered porch blocks a huge area from my view below, but it's unlikely anyone is that close to the house anyway.

"Can you see them?"

I jump and turn to press my back against the wall. It's Tori.

"Jesus," I say, trying to catch my breath from the scare.

"Sorry. But I can help." She crawls low across the floor to sit beside me. "I'm a good shot. Pass me one of those."

"How do you know guns?"

"My husband was a U.S. Marshal. We used to go to the range together. You know, date night, but make it Idahoan."

I know. And I know more than she realizes about her husband, Agent Tucker Carrington. I've been fucking praying she'd never find out, but part of me thinks everything has been leading to this moment. It's time to tell her.

59

REESE

I was just a kid.

Max had repeated that to me in the seconds after it happened and before the police made it into the house.

"You're just a kid. You didn't know any better."

He made me call him Max so nobody would find out our connection as father and daughter and use it against us. He had trained me to be a deadly shot. I could consistently hit a deer from three hundred yards and be sure to drop it. But that day, he'd specifically told me to stay down and not pick up a gun. Told me that this was his fight.

The morning had started out normally. Max and I at our property in middle-of-nowhere Idaho. I was nothing like a typical fifteen-year-old because I was so isolated from society. I was homeschooled, and I had no friends. Nobody but Max. Instead of attending slumber parties, I was attending mock bugout simulations with him. He didn't trust a living soul, and after my mom died when I was three, he moved us away from Boise and deep into the Idaho panhandle where I could practically toss a rock into Canada.

He reasoned we would be safe there when shit hit the fan, as he was always sure it would.

I now know Max was mentally unstable. But for the life of me, for so many years, I couldn't see him as anything other than smart, kind, and insanely resilient. Sure, he had weird ideas, and I would have liked to have had a normal childhood. But he taught me so much, and I'd go on to use it to stay safe throughout my life, wherever I was. He was the one who taught me how to listen to my gut. He taught me first aid, which was how I knew I wanted to be a nurse.

Max had started collecting firearms a few years prior to that day. He had so many.

Having a lot of guns meant more ways to defend ourselves. They could also be bartering tools because money would mean nothing when all hell broke loose. It was good enough for me. I didn't know any different.

A few months earlier, some men wearing black vests that said "ATF" had shown up. I had a feeling right away that it wasn't good. It turned out Max hadn't only been collecting the guns, he'd been selling them too—illegally. He'd been charged with a crime but skipped his court date. He didn't recognize the authority of the U.S. Government. In his mind, his court appearance was optional.

So all of this had been brewing for months when the feds showed up. They set up what looked like a camp at the edge of our property. They were hidden in the woods, but we could see the Humvees.

Days had already passed.

Finally, that morning, Max was sick and tired of them being on our property, so he flung the front door wide open, pulled out the Glock he wore at his hip twenty-four seven, and shot it in the air. Then he slipped back inside, slamming the door behind him.

The feds returned fire.

"It's red tag day," Max shouted.

It was one of the phrases he used a lot. There were some that meant we needed to bug out, or that an EMP had taken down the grid. "Red tag day" meant the government was coming for us and we needed to go into lockdown and prepare to fight. In retrospect, I don't know why he fired that warning shot. I think he wanted them to attack us first so he could feel better about returning fire.

Max was crazy, but he had his own moral code.

I ran to get my rifle, but he stopped me.

"No. These aren't deer, and I don't want you to get hurt. Hide."

The confusion inside me mirrored what was going on all around. This was what he'd trained me for. They were shooting at us. Didn't he need my help?

I watched him set up at the window on the right side of the door, lining a few rifles up before he started firing.

I slunk down the wall and covered my ears. It was so much more terrifying than it had been in our many drills. Nobody had ever shot back before. But I wouldn't cry. I refused to. I would be strong and help even though I was scared. We were outnumbered. He *did* need me; I didn't care what he'd said. And I knew that Max was so preoccupied with what he was doing that he wouldn't notice if I reached for my rifle.

So I did.

When I stole a peek out the window on the other side of the door, I saw a man in matte black armor, holding a ballistic shield.

I exhaled all my breath and squeezed the trigger.

The man in black fell to the ground.

Max noticed. He crawled over to me as bullets pinged our cabin, some breaking through.

"What were you thinking?" he shouted, shaking me, tears in his eyes. "I told you not to pick up a gun."

I was paralyzed. I couldn't speak. Couldn't even move.

"Listen, you didn't shoot him. You hear me? You didn't do that. I did. *I* shot that cop."

I nodded.

"You're just a kid."

And that's what I've always told myself, until I grew up and "I was just a kid" felt too thin. Maybe I was just a kid. But I still knew I was shooting at a human being.

60

TORI

As we're setting up at the window, getting ready to fire at these assholes, Reese whispers something to me.

It sounds like "I have to tell you something."

"Okay," I say. Why is she being cryptic? And why is she suddenly the most nervous I've seen her?

"I killed your husband."

"What?"

"I shot him. Tucker."

My world narrows to this moment.

All I can hear is my own pulse.

The freefall of my thoughts as they reach for anything to grab on to.

My body, ice cold, starting to shake.

"No, a man named Max Dorman shot my husband, and went to jail for it. He died there," I say.

"Max was my dad, and he took the blame to protect me."

Her words land fast, deliberate, crushing.

I can't see her face clearly. She's across the window from

me, shrouded by night, but I don't need to see her. I can feel the truth of this, even though it makes no logical sense.

"I'm so sorry," she says, her voice shaking.

An anchor drops in my gut, marking this moment. The before and after of the truth of my husband's death.

The crack of a gunshot outside startles me, but it brings me back to reality, and I turn to point my gun out one of the tilted blinds.

Reese does the same.

Just like she must have done the day she shot Tucker.

Movement in the palm bushes beyond the porch light draws my eye. I take a shot, but I must have missed, because nothing happens.

Reese fires and a dark figure lands, rustling the brush. She hit him.

Glass shatters, and both of us pull back to our sides of the window, holding our guns with barrels pointed at the ceiling. They shot a hole through the window we're using.

"At least they're shooting at us now," Reese says. "Not at Paige and Court."

I still can't find words to speak. The combination of adrenaline from a shoot-out and the revelation that Reese killed Tucker—it's still too much.

Reese turns and squeezes off another shot, dropping a body, but the gunfire doesn't stop. "That's two. Jesus fuck, how many of them are there?"

Again, I don't answer. I can't. I keep picturing her doing this exact thing, but aiming at Tucker. And killing him.

I need to focus but my mind is ablaze, and that's when my fingers and palms start tingling, going numb.

No.

"Aries in the first house of self. Taurus in the second—material possessions," I whisper, getting up to find my pills. I'll just take one and hope that does the trick.

"What are you doing?" Reese asks, but just then, a shot comes through the other window, splintering the blinds. She returns fire.

"My pills—Gemini in the third house of communication. Cancer in the fourth house of family. Leo in the fifth house of creativity," I mutter as I fumble around in my suitcase.

Where did I put the pills? Rawson brought them downstairs before, but I made sure to put them back. I know I did.

"Oh god, you're having a panic attack," Reese says, setting her gun down.

I want to shout at her to leave me alone. To go away. But I need the help, and she's the only reason we aren't all dead right now, so I don't say anything as she feels around on the nightstands.

"Is this it?" she asks, holding up the pill bottle.

"Yeah," I say, and she shakes out two, handing them to me.

I take one.

"Lay down on the floor." Reese tosses a pillow onto the side of the bed away from the window.

I do what she says, while keeping focus on my recitation of the astrological houses. My hands are sweaty, and my vision is bursting with stars. It'd be blurring at the edges if the light was on. Why did she choose right now to tell me she murdered my husband?

From downstairs comes a crash of glass.

Then a gunshot inside the house.

61

PAIGE

WHEN REESE RUNS UPSTAIRS AND THE MEN START SHOOTING AT the second floor window instead of down here, I silently thank her. Now I need to get Courtney into the kitchen, which certainly feels like a safer spot than where she is on the living room floor.

"Get me out of these!" Rawson shouts again.

Rawson is a fucking idiot, and I don't think he's dangerous. But do I want to risk cutting him loose? Nope.

I keep ignoring him.

Tori shoves the gun at me and runs upstairs. I push it into the back of my shorts and snake over to Courtney, staying as close to the ground as possible.

"Let's get you into the kitchen," I say to Courtney, feeling the pinch of tears as I try to get her up. "I'm so glad you're back. I don't know what I would have done if something happened to you."

"Bryce," she whimpers. "This trip … wasn't his idea."

I pull my bottom lip between my teeth. "I guess not. I'm so sorry."

This whole time we thought we were fulfilling Bryce's last request, but it was a lie. A plan concocted by an unstable, grieving woman.

It would only take someone a quick internet search to learn I'm the owner of SoulMatch, and I know I've talked about my brother's illness in interviews. And like Leslie said, social media filled in the rest. It's not a stretch to see how she took advantage of that information to lure us here. Just like any stalker would.

The irony is thick.

But it's also my fault because of my shitty response to her sister's situation. Because I put myself and my company ahead of everything else.

I help Courtney roll onto her back and pull her across the floor by her armpits, trying to crouch low because I still hear gunfire.

"Come on! If they start shooting at us down here again, I'll die," Rawson shouts.

I groan because he's probably right.

"I need to know you're with us. Not him," I say, dragging Court into the kitchen.

"Of course I am! Jesus. My job was to keep you guys in the house. Not hurt you. This is not what I signed up for."

I believe him. He hasn't done anything to actually hurt us, unless you count being an idiot. But there's one other thing I have to be sure about.

"Okay, but when we get off this fucking island, you're going to lose Tori's number and never speak to her again. Even if she hounds you. Got it?"

He scoffs. "She doesn't like you, you know." His eyes are empty and his face pale, likely from blood loss.

Of course I know. But what *he* doesn't know is that Tori and I have been like this for decades. So, she told some new fuckboy she hates me? It means nothing. Tori and I are solid on a level nobody else will ever understand.

"If you contact her, I'll ruin you. You have no idea what I'm capable of," I say.

Rawson groans. "Fine, just cut me loose already."

I cut the fishing line so he can move into the kitchen, but leave his hands and feet bound. He bitches about it, but I just roll my eyes. He can cry me a river.

Just then, a man crashes through one of the living room windows.

It's almost graceful. A planned tuck and roll.

Everything slows down as I watch him.

I stand and tighten my grip on the gun in my hand.

He recovers his balance and starts to find his footing.

I point the gun at him. My knees are rubber; I can't stop shaking. But if I don't shoot him right now, he'll shoot me.

I squeeze the trigger, panic shearing through me, and a blast goes off that makes my ears ring.

I hit him in the chest and he falls to the floor. Doesn't move.

An eerie silence blankets the darkness. I just killed someone. Actually made them die. Not even my husband has ever done that.

I sink to my ass on the kitchen floor, numb and unable to move.

The shooting stops, and Reese and Tori come downstairs.

"How many men does Keith have?" Reese asks Rawson as Tori appears by my side on the floor. Tori sits close, and it feels like she wants to say something, but doesn't.

I look at her face, softly illuminated by the faint light coming through the exposed window. Her eyelids are droopy and her head hangs slightly. She's taken Klonopin. I wrap my arm around her and hold her close.

"It's okay," I whisper. "You're strong. All those placements in independent signs like Leo and Aquarius. All that Sag. You have everything you need inside yourself. And you're not alone."

"You remember my placements?" she turns to face me, but still her eyes are unfocused.

"Of course. I love astrology. It's just that what the sky looks like the moment we're born doesn't speak to our traumas, our experiences, our morals. It's not the full picture."

Tori nods. "I think I agree, actually. I just wanted one thing to be undeniably true in my life. I wanted one thing I could count on."

"I know," I say, laying my head on her shoulder. "But that's not how life works. There are no guarantees."

She nods and looks down.

My own words sink in, and I think of all the times I've tried to control outcomes at SoulMatch. Control Bryce. Control Tori.

"How would I know how many men are out there?" Rawson argues with Reese.

"I'm betting you do." Reese points the rifle at him.

"Fine, I could guess. Three? Four, maybe?"

"Three men showed up here for a drug deal? Why? It doesn't take that many."

"He said they had to neutralize you before the buyer would show up."

"And you didn't consider that maybe *neutralize* us meant kill us?"

"Look, *I* wasn't going to hurt you. But I can't control other people."

I want to walk over there and shoot Rawson in the face. I look at Tori, but she's staring straight ahead, and her mind must be somewhere else.

"Okay, so why didn't Keith just wait until we leave to do the deal? We're gone tomorrow."

"The buyers were probably putting pressure on him to do it sooner."

So he had to get rid of us. Rawson doesn't say it, but that's the fact that looms large in the silence.

Nobody responds. It's as if we're all too wiped out to get emotional.

Finally, Reese says, "Okay, even if there were four, I think we got them all. The one in the boat, who I took out when I got Court, and the three others we shot tonight."

"But we don't know if any of them were Keith," I add quietly. It's a truth I know none of us want to think about.

"If any are left standing, Keith is one of them. That bastard would use a kid as a shield to save his own skin," Rawson says.

"Well, we don't know if we got them all, but the boat is coming in a few hours … " Reese looks at her watch. "It's about four thirty."

Hope bubbles up inside me. The boat is coming at eight a.m. It seemed like such a fucking early check out time when I booked it, but it was all the marina could swing since the trip was planned so last-minute. Now, it feels like a life raft.

"We just have to wait him out. He won't kill the boat captain," Rawson says.

"But he'll use a child as body armor?" Reese asks.

And he'll kill us*?* I want to add. I never liked Rawson, but in this moment, I truly hate him. Again, I look over at Tori, and see nothing but blank resignation.

Rawson doesn't answer Reese's question. He probably realizes how stupid he sounds.

"I'm certain his plan is to kill the boat captain," Reese says. "He has to. It would give him a head start so he could be in the wind by the time someone discovers what happened here."

It's grim and terrifying and I can't help but picture this island left littered with our dead bodies.

"That's not the way this is gonna go, though." Reese checks the ammo in her gun. "We're not sitting here, waiting for a boat to save us. We have to fucking save ourselves."

62

REESE

CLIMBING DOWN FROM THE SECOND-STORY PORCH, MY BODY screams in protest; I can't get my mind in gear. Not even the military compares to this level of physical and mental exhaustion.

Nothing in me wants to go after this motherfucker. I'm cashed out, sore, and ready to be done with this nightmare. But it's becoming clear Keith won't give up.

He wants us dead.

It's still dark out, but daylight will show up around 0600 hours. The last thing Keith will expect is that he'll become the prey. Especially to a woman.

Before tonight, I'd never killed anyone except Tucker, and I've spent my life after that focusing on saving people, even in the military. It's been some attempt to balance the cosmic scales and do penance for taking an innocent life.

Now I've killed four more people. Soon to be five.

I didn't set out to tell Tori about Tucker, it just happened. I've always wondered if confessing would alleviate some of the guilt I've carried. But I don't feel any different. And I've created a burden for her.

I squeeze my eyes shut. They're heavy and stinging from lack of sleep.

I need to focus.

Keith isn't right outside the house, I'm certain of that. If he were, he'd be making a move. But I don't think he's far away, either. I suspect he's rallying for a second wave before the boat arrives.

So, where is he if not at the house? I half wish Leslie were here to direct me. Leslie, who is in a way a victim, but also a perpetrator.

Both things are true. Just like so many situations in life.

Just like how I feel about Max.

After the Boundary County standoff, I went to live with my aunt and uncle. My aunt stayed home with me and my cousins fulltime, and my uncle was a detective. I took their last name, and started calling them Mom and Dad to try and fit in at school. I didn't want people asking why I lived with my aunt and uncle. I wanted as normal a life as I could get. So, Mom and Dad it was, even though I was fifteen and it was beyond weird to call them that.

They refused to let me visit Max. So, the first time I went to the prison was on my eighteenth birthday. It'd been almost three years since I'd seen him. He looked a decade older than I remembered.

I cried and told him I was sorry for what I did, but he wouldn't hear it. He just said again that I was a kid and I didn't know any better. That he'd lived his life, and the government would lock up his little girl over his dead body.

I know Max had issues. I still loved him.

My feet finally drop to the ground, and I slow my breath to

try to silence the thrumming of blood in my ears. I need to hear everything.

Then, what sounds like a metal can falling to the dirt ground in a soft thud comes from the garage.

I pull my little Beretta up and cock it. Keith's armed, so I'll only have this one chance to ambush him.

I tiptoe over and slink alongside the garage, under the cover of darkness. A beam of light swings around, slivering through the tiny slats in the structure.

I place every footstep with soft precision, then, with my back pressed against the outside of the garage, I sneak a quick peek inside.

"Keith! She's coming for you! G.I. Jane!" Rawson's muffled voice yells from inside the house.

I curse myself for leaving the upstairs sliding door wide open.

The light inside the garage clicks off.

63

TORI

Taking only one pill was the right decision. I feel calm but in control.

When Rawson shouts for Keith, giving away Reese's location, I stand up from my spot on the kitchen floor by Paige and Court, and rush him with the rifle. I'm operating one-hundred percent on this rage-fueled instinct. I whack him on the head with the butt of the gun. He goes limp. Not dead, surely. Just out.

I curse myself. I was so goddamn stupid. How many times am I going to trust people, only to be fucked over?

Like Paige. Then again, she's always been there. Always showed up for me. Even when we don't agree. Even when she isn't doing what I want her to do. Even when she's being a selfish bitch, she's there. And maybe that counts for something.

And Reese. It isn't like I've been open enough to truly trust her. I didn't even have the chance to get to know her until this trip. But that secret. The truth that I've lived all these years without knowing who actually pulled the trigger and killed Tucker. Yet, she's out there right now, hunting down the motherfucker who is trying to kill us. I owe her my life based on the past few days alone.

How old would Reese have been when she shot Tucker? I do the math and land on fifteen. A child. She's more than made up for something she did as a minor, brainwashed by a crazy prepper dad.

I'll sort through all of that another time, but right now, I have to get out there and help her. What Rawson did just now will surely fuck her over; I want to make sure it doesn't kill her.

64

REESE

In the moonlight, by the garage, Keith is standing just inside.

Everything happens in a split second. I point my gun at him and squeeze the trigger once.

Two rounds discharge.

Keith flails backward, gripping his shoulder at the same time my leg screams in pain.

I grapple to make sense of the scene.

We're both on the ground now. I shuffle for close cover behind a workbench and the dock box. I can't see him anymore.

I register silence. Did I kill him?

I feel around my leg for the exact point where the hammer-force pain has landed, praying it isn't serious. Praying it isn't my femoral artery. That would only leave me minutes of consciousness.

I find the entry wound on my outer front thigh, and an exit wound in the back, thank god. I peel off my filthy white tank top and tie it tightly around my leg.

Flicking my headlamp on, I lean over and survey the garage.

Keith is gone.

It's totally empty.

"She's coming for you! G.I. Jane!"

Rawson's words ring in my mind. He must have already told Keith about me, and now Keith is moving on the rest of them while he thinks I'm out.

I stumble, trying to get to my feet, and then, dragging my hurt leg behind me, I shamble out of the garage. I have to stop him.

Once again, the sound of gunfire explodes across the night.

65

TORI

Keith lays there before me, completely still, blood expanding across his chest and soaking his faded blue tee shirt.

My hands tremble and I drop the rifle while my body shakes until it starts convulsing and I have to sit in the dirt between the garage and the house.

"Fuck you!" I scream, letting my voice reverberate across the silence. Something releases from deep inside of me. It feels like I've just murdered every foster parent that hurt me. Like I'm giving the finger to Rawson, to my dynamic with Paige, this trip, my entire shitty life. Like I'm embracing my power for the first time ever, using my open palm to wipe the fucking slate clean.

Reese limps over to me and awkwardly sits close. She hesitates, hugging her knees, and I can feel her Cancer sun wanting to wrap her arms around me. Nurture me, somehow.

I let the awkwardness linger, trying to decide if she falls under the "fuck you" category too, but when my belly softens and I can breathe again, I realize that she doesn't, and I lean into her, melting as she wraps her arms around me.

I sob.

"I'm sorry. So, so sorry. I didn't know what I was doing. I thought we were fighting for our lives against the government." She snivels. "And there's more … "

I stiffen at this. I can't handle much more, but I can tell she has to get it out, so I don't stop her.

"Leslie found out about Bryce because of your social media pages, right? Well, I did, too. About two years ago, I was at a particularly low point in my life. The guilt of what I'd done to Tucker weighed on me so heavily that I started digging into his life, something I hadn't let myself do before. That's how I discovered you were his wife. I found your social media, and your profile was public. So, when you posted a year later that your friend Paige was looking for a qualified nurse to take care of her brother, who was also Tucker's best friend, I jumped at the chance to redeem myself. What she needed for Bryce was the very thing I had already been doing, so my credentials were real. I thought if I could bring some light into your lives during his illness, it might begin to make up for what I took. But then Courtney invited me on this trip, and I was so afraid of the truth coming out. Afraid I'd just erupt with it, even though I didn't want to. Then, after spending more time with you, I realized it was exactly what needed to happen. Except I don't think my timing was great."

Reese abruptly stops talking and watches for my reaction. On the surface, what she's telling me is creepy. Stalking at worst, targeting at best. But when I lay that card right next to the one where we wouldn't be alive if she hadn't taken the job and come on this trip, my response is a no-brainer.

"I forgive you. You were a kid. Your dad was right. And Tucker knew the risks of the career he chose. I knew the risks when I married him. If you weren't on this trip, we would all be dead. I'm so glad you're here, and I don't care how you became

Bryce's nurse," I say, and something more releases inside me. Like a dagger being pulled out of my stomach.

"It's over," I shout to Paige and Court.

Paige comes out, propping Courtney up, then helping us to our feet.

"What happened?" she asks.

"Tori blasted him like a fucking badass," Reese says, wiping her nose.

I give a rough laugh.

Paige laughs too, and then smiles at me. Even in the dark, by the faint moonlight, I can see enough of her face to know that we're good. Things will be better from now on. More like how they used to be.

"You guys, I'm so sorry about all of this," Courtney whispers, clearly still very weak. I imagine Paige dragged her out here so she wouldn't be left alone in the house with that unconscious asshole and a dead body.

"Court, this isn't on you," I say. "Time to ditch the people-pleasing and channel some of that justice-oriented nature of Libra. This is on Keith. And Leslie. And Rawson, a little. Not you. Not any of us."

"It's probably on me too, though," Paige says, and I don't argue. She isn't making it about herself. She's owning up.

"But … I did something else. Something horrible," Courtney says.

I fully doubt that, but we all stay quiet.

She takes Paige's hand. "I killed Bryce."

"Court, that's not how it happened," Reese says. She doesn't seem at all surprised, and I find that I'm not, either.

We all watch Paige.

She falls into Courtney. It's gentle, not a full-on trust fall, but she definitely doesn't give Courtney a chance to dodge the hug. "I couldn't do it." Paige cries. "He wanted me to, but I couldn't, and I've felt such shame about that, thinking he died alone and I let him down. Reese is right. You didn't kill him. You made his last wish come true. A lot of why I didn't question him when I thought he asked me to take you on this trip was because I'd refused to help him do it. I owed it to him."

Courtney only cries, and I imagine the release she's feeling, too.

I clear my throat. "So, Reese, I take it the military wasn't where you learned how to make weird chicken alfredo or Gross Gatorade?"

She smiles. "Nope, that was Max Dorman."

Looking around our dirty-faced, sweaty, even a little blood-smeared circle of friendship, I realize that soulmates can come into our lives in a lot of ways. Maybe I've elevated the romantic aspect of a soulmate far above what it should be. Because right here, I have everything I need. Friends who are cheerleaders, but who don't shy away from telling me the hard truths. Women who will literally fight to the death for me. I will do the same for them.

These are my soulmates.

FIVE MONTHS LATER

66

COURTNEY

THIS TIME IT'S MY IDEA.

Paige, Reese, Tori, and I are sprawled across loungers on the beach in Maui. I booked the place—a hotel, not a vacation rental, because fuck those.

It's Christmas Day, and even though at first the others said no, I told them it was what I wanted and I'd done enough caving to all of them over the years, so I was calling in this one favor. I told Reese no guns. Or knives. Or random extra food. But a first aid kit was acceptable. I told Paige no matching outfits. We needed to create some new traditions. And I told Tori absolutely no men on this trip.

Speaking of men, it turns out Rawson had a warrant out for his arrest—one of those DUIs he mentioned happened to be his seventh, and he didn't appear in court. So he went to jail. He won't be there long, but it's a comfort to know that's exactly where he is right now. Keith had a criminal record a mile long, including assault and manslaughter charges. Sure, he's a veteran who saw combat, but so is Reese. PTSD might be an explanation, but it isn't an excuse for what he did.

The police believed what Leslie told us about being kidnapped by Keith. But we're not so sure she intended on playing as nice as she claimed with obtaining Paige's confession. There was no other explanation for the creepy haul Tori found in the garage. Items on a burying-the-body bingo card. Still, it was likely things fell out of her control once they'd found the wash-ups. It made sense that Keith would bail on Leslie's plan as soon as something with a higher payout came into play.

Like twenty-three kilos of cocaine.

The police found it hidden in a third structure on the island. Smaller and more run-down than the one Leslie was kept in. Obviously, that means Reese was right: Keith hadn't done the drug deal yet. The police thought the buyers wouldn't come anywhere near the island while there were guests staying there, and it was too risky for Keith to move the cache.

When we got back to Boise, Paige went to the police about SoulMatch's involvement in Janie's death. They didn't consider anything she did to be criminal, but the press got a hold of it, and that wreaked havoc. SoulMatch was canceled for a few months, but it's already starting to come back around. I reached out to a few press contacts for advice, and one of them put me in touch with someone at *Forbes* who agreed to write a bio on Paige, Tori, and the company. That smoothed out the edges. Really, though, Paige herself is the reason SoulMatch came back from the brink. Something about a CEO who owns up to her mistakes and actively tries to do better resonates with people.

Paige made Tori a co-owner of SoulMatch, and she's currently flying high on Tori's new idea to make it an app that openly favors women. Heterosexual online dating has a power dynamic that's inherently unequal. Men usually don't have to worry about whether they'll be attacked or physically overpowered on a date. Women always have to consider this.

To even the playing field, Paige and Tori hired a language

specialist to set up a screening process for hetero men who want to use SoulMatch. They have to fill out their dating profile and apply to use the app. This specialist uses Critical Discourse Analysis to find toxic language patterns that controlling and manipulative people (men, in this case) use unknowingly. These are not only red flags that women can learn how to spot, but if the SoulMatch algorithm recognizes any of the toxic key phrases in a man's bio, he will be rejected from using the app. They expect it will cut back on the amount of users, but Paige has decided she doesn't care about that. She wants to keep women safe.

Paige has changed a lot in a very short time, but I think it's Tori who has changed the most. In the days following the Florida trip, she apologized for taking me for granted. I wouldn't have put it that way, but since then, I can see how she's made good on that promise. She's proven to have more depth of character than I'd seen in her yet. That restlessness that'd marked her for as long as I've known her is gone, and she even says she's not sure she wants a partner. At least, not right now. Instead, she's focusing on her friendships, traveling, and helping Paige at SoulMatch.

I think something about Reese's confession allowed her to make peace with losing Tucker. It settled something inside of her.

When Reese connected the dots for me that the person she killed, the one she alluded to on the beach that last night, was Tucker, it blew my mind. I was overwhelmed—she was the child inside the house that day I went to report on the standoff. Since she'd changed her last name, I didn't put it together. All I'd ever heard relating to the standoff was about Max Dorman. She'd effectively hidden herself while finding us.

I roll over onto my back and prop my lounge chair higher so I can look out at the sea, and it acts as a silent reminder for everyone else to shift positions too. We've shared a quiet afternoon together in the warm Maui sun. Tori and Reese are reading, and Paige has her eyes closed with earbuds in, probably listening to a podcast.

Staring at endless azure water, I smile to myself. I'm so grateful to be here with them, but I'd be content to be here by myself, too. I'm working on tapping into that spark inside of me. Learning how to experience my own energy and be my own best friend and partner.

It's tempting to categorize things into neat columns in life: this or that. Happy or sad. Partnered or alone. But since Bryce's death, I've learned the hard way that life is lived more in shades of gray than in black and white.

I can assist my husband with the death he wants without being responsible for it.

I can cry oceans of tears at the tiniest memory of the man I thought I'd grow old with, and anything can trigger it. A song played in a grocery store, an inside joke remembered, or those precious seconds after waking up from a beautiful dream before you grasp that it wasn't real.

I can do all of that, *and* I can smile. I can laugh so hard my stomach hurts.

One doesn't diminish the other. In fact, it's more true that one illuminates the other.

Now, I look forward to my future, eagerly anticipating whatever is ahead because I know who will be there for me every step of the way. I have my friends, yes, but more importantly, I have myself.

And nothing on this side of death will change that.

ACKNOWLEDGMENTS

This book was so much fun to write—it felt like play time. I'm so grateful to the people who supported and assisted me in bringing it to publication.

Thank you first to the cult: Noelle Ihli, Faith Gardner, and Caleb Stephens, for reading, giving feedback, and providing endless encouragement throughout the process of my time drafting this book. I say it a lot but it's never enough—I'm intensely grateful for all three of you and excited to be on this journey together.

For everyone who beta read this book, thank you! Your time investment means so much to me and I appreciate your thoughts about the book in the early stages: Kelsey Zedwick, Rebekah Dresback, Kiersten Walmsley, and Marissa Hayes.

Thank you, Audrey J. Cole, for reading and offering a blurb for the book. I'm so happy I met you last year and am looking forward to getting to know you more. (And read more of your books!)

Thanks to my editors who helped calm the chaos of my drafting style: Kristen Tate, Maddy Leary, and Patti Geesey. Especially Maddy who provided some last-minute insights that landed as a breakthrough for me.

Thank you to Ezra and Ethan Ellenberg, for your generous wisdom and advice, and to Jason Pinter at Simon Maverick for bringing the audiobook to life.

I want to give a shout out to Jennie Young of Burned

Haystack Dating Method. She teaches women how to use Critical Discourse Analysis to spot abusive patterns hiding in men's dating profiles, which was the inspiration for the new iteration of SoulMatch.

I appreciate every BookToker and Bookstagrammer who has picked up one of my books and told other people about it. I wish I could pay you back.

And to you, reading this right now. Thanks for giving my story a chance. I have an agent who helps me with foreign translation rights and film/TV deals, but at the core, I'm an indie author and word of mouth is my bread and butter. If you liked it, would you leave a review on Amazon? Reviews help other readers decide if the book is for them (or not).

XO, Steph

ABOUT THE AUTHOR

Steph Nelson is an author living in Boise, Idaho. Her books have been featured in *The New York Times* and *Library Journal*. She started out writing horror, and her first two short stories were published in anthologies that later went on to become finalists for a Bram Stoker Award.

Steph loves to stay active—walking, pickleball, and yoga are her favorites. She also adores traveling and gathering inspiration from anywhere it might appear.

You can find her on Instagram, Facebook, and TikTok.

LAST ONE OUT

A THRILLER

STEPH NELSON

PART I

AUGUST 1999

CHLOE

I hope we don't die tonight—that's what I'm thinking as I crack open the window of Amy's car. I need fresh air, and the wind relieves my nausea, but not my anxiety about what we're doing and how dangerous it is. Only a short guardrail stands between us and a steep drop into fast-rushing whitecaps of the Payette River. The edge is close. Way too close, and the Payette is wild enough to whitewater raft.

Amy, Kristi, and I aren't here to raft, though.

My friends and I drove over an hour from Boise to take a midnight soak at the isolated Skinny Dipper Hot Springs. A last blast before we start our senior year—Amy's idea. None of our parents know. They'd flip their lids because not only is Skinny Dipper far away, but it's tucked into the Boise National Forest, only accessible by a steep half-mile hike.

Nobody tries it in the dark. In fact, people don't even come out here this time of night. It's secluded enough that you don't need the cover of dark.

Amy parks her Corolla and turns to her twin sister, Kristi, in the front seat. "Let's do this!" she says in that chipper tone that's equal parts cute and demanding. It's her don't-argue-with-me voice.

Kristi claps her hands and they both get out.

I watch from the back seat as Kristi busts out this squirmy little happy dance on the empty road, but I don't buy that she's this excited. Like me, she was nervous when Amy first floated the idea. She's either changed her mind or is pretending. Either way, I'm sure the goal is to avoid upsetting Amy.

Amy and Kristi may be fraternal twins, but they're inseparable and it's like they made some agreement in the womb where Kristi obeys without question, and in return, Amy makes sure Kristi, who is painfully shy, has friends.

As I slide out of the car to join them, the white noise of the plunging river below is deafening, and the way it sits against a backdrop of night makes my stomach turn again.

Being up here feels worlds away from the safety of snuggling on the couch and talking about it.

The girls move to the other side of the deserted two-lane highway, using a flashlight to search for the trail up to Skinny Dipper. My eyes track up the steep mountainside and I let out a little gasp.

I expected a hike and a late-night soak in the woods, but I didn't sign up for this.

This is isolation and wilderness and everything bad that could happen. I'm grateful for the full moon, so at least we can see a little, but that doesn't remove the fact that we're choosing danger. And while the risk is kind of the point, I'm having second thoughts. Where are the hot springs, even?

"I found the trail!" Amy shouts and plants a Nike runner on a patch of dirt while shining the light in my face.

"Hey, stop that." I shield my eyes.

"Well, hurry up," Amy groans.

It's not like I'm lagging. I'm just a few steps behind them, but Amy gets annoyed with everything I do lately. Even when I'm following her ideas and trying hard to be what she wants, she complains. Her voice has a manic edge right now, like she's afraid I'll pull the cord on this whole idea.

I want to, but I also don't want to piss her off, so I tread carefully.

"That hike looks super hard. Worse than I pictured," I say. "Plus, it's creepy enough right here that we can just say we did it. We don't have to go all the way up."

"No," Amy says. "You're not weaseling out of this. We're here, so we're gonna do the whole thing. This little walk isn't going to kill us."

It might though, I'm afraid. It may very well kill us.

After all, it's so … vertical. Switchbacks are supposed to make an uphill hike easier, but they don't do much for this trail. I alternate my gaze between the dirt ribbon leading up and the twins, who are both in one-piece swimsuits covered by jean shorts. Amy's brown hair is in a sloppy bun, and Kristi's is in a French braid. They're a whole head taller than me and I find myself once again envying their long legs. I hate being so short.

I follow as the girls start up the trail, because what else am I going to do? Stand out here alone in the dark, next to the road? That's just as scary.

The wind is cooler than I expected for summer, which makes me wonder why I didn't wear a tee shirt over my bikini top. These Umbro shorts aren't cutting it, either; the fabric is so thin. I drape my beach towel over my shoulders so my hands are free in case I need to catch myself, but it adds a little warmth, too.

We go single file, and I stay behind Kristi, trying to watch where she steps to avoid slipping on the dirt and scree, but she's moving so fast it's nearly impossible to keep up. I have to leech off her flashlight or I'll fall off the trail, so staying close isn't optional. I should have brought my own flashlight.

After a while, even Amy in the lead has to stop to catch her breath.

Thank god.

"This is so much harder than you said it would be," I mutter.

"Well maybe you should have come to the soccer workouts this summer."

I don't reply because whatever comes out won't be nice. I couldn't go because my mom is single and works all day. Unlike Amy, I don't have my driver's license, and even if I did, Mom can't afford to buy me a car. Plus, Amy and Kristi live too far away to pick me up. Not like I'd ask them for a ride anyway because it'd be one more thing they'd hold over me. So, yeah, no soccer workouts. Instead, I spent the summer with my cousin, Frankie. Which was fine by me. Sure, she's two years younger, but she's my best friend in the whole world, even though the twins never want her around. I'm pretty sure they're jealous of how close we are, but the official reason is Frankie's too young to hang out with us. So dumb since she's going to be joining us in high school this year.

Amy and Kristi are hiking again, and Amy acts as if she didn't just say something super rude to me. I follow along in silence, willing this spark of irritation to ease up.

Soon, we're far enough up the mountain that the trees muffle the sound of the river, and the telltale sulfur scent of natural hot springs hits my nose.

My stomach jolts and I pause on the trail for a moment, feeling sick.

"You okay?" Kristi calls from a few feet ahead, shining her light back on the trail so I can see where to step. "We're almost there. Looks like this path dips down to a tiny pool. It's not big enough for all of us, but Amy thinks there's another one above it."

Awesome. More climbing.

"Yeah, I'm fine," I say.

Fine.

I sigh at my word choice because, yeah, I'm fine as in *not ill*. But that doesn't mean I won't throw up.

I've been throwing up for weeks because I'm pregnant.

CHLOE

I don't know how far along I am. I've been tired for what feels like forever, but I'm still not showing. Mostly I try not to think about it because I don't know what to do.

The baby is *his*.

I refuse to even think his name in my mind because I hate him so much for doing this to me. I have to figure it out, but I keep putting it off because it's so overwhelming.

If I have the baby, my life will be over. I can't even think about his response to it because a deep hole digs into my gut when I do. He can't find out. But if I don't have the baby … no way to think about that either because while I'm not ready to be a mom, I also don't want to end the baby's life.

Every option feels bad, and so these thoughts keep dancing circles in my mind, all the while the baby grows, which only stresses me out more. I feel paralyzed, which is why I haven't told anyone I'm pregnant. Not even my mom. Definitely not Frankie. She would be so disappointed in me, and I can't handle that because I'm already so disappointed in myself.

Steam threads up toward the starlit sky and the pools come into view.

I take in the entire scene as best as I can in the dark. It looks like a trickling waterfall landing in shelves, or pools, in the crevice of a mountain. It reminds me of an oversized backyard water feature, but much less perfect. My stomach flips when I see that the pool we're aiming for has an edge that ends in a cliff. You could be in the pool and overlook everything below, which would be an incredible view if it were daylight. There's the mountain we hiked—you can even see the tiny highway below. If it weren't so dark, I bet I could find Amy's car.

Except to get there, we'd have to lily-pad-hop across a few big rocks.

Kristi shines her flashlight on a makeshift carved wooden sign that says "Skinny Dipper Hot Springs," and this weird summer-camp feeling crawls over me. It's not the s'mores and day-hikes kind. More like the horror-movie kind.

A whisper of fear skims against my neck, and I shiver. "We shouldn't be here," I say quietly.

Amy groans and moves the light along the rocks and brush to highlight the empty liquor bottles and beer cans littering the area. I even see a used condom, and that makes me wince thinking about what people do up here. Then she trips while rock-hopping across to the larger pool and teeters over the cliff for a beat, but catches herself and lands on her ass.

I gasp—that was such a close call.

Kristi yells her sister's name, and then she goes across, being more careful than Amy was and hunches over, shining the light on Amy's knee. There's a smear of dirt and red liquid beads pushing through a small cut.

"You okay?" I call out.

"Yeah, it's only a scrape."

"You could have fallen over that cliff and died. Maybe we should go back," I say.

"No, I'm fine," Amy says, pushing Kristi's helping hands away.

"Truth?" Kristi puts her hands on her hips.

"Jesus. Yes, Truth. It's a baby scrape. And I *didn't* fall over the cliff." Amy stands and brushes away dirt and blood.

Truth with a capital "T" is how we operate. High school is full of so much bullshit, so much preening and pretending, that the three of us made a pact last year, swearing that we would always be honest with each other.

Even if it hurts.

Even if it causes a fight.

Because lying would cause fights too—probably more. We pricked our fingertips with a safety pin and solemnly swore.

So, my friends and I don't lie to each other.

Mostly.

I think of my pregnancy, but immediately dismiss it because that's different. It feels much bigger than lies about who we have a crush on or who we're mad at. My lie is necessary. And anyway, is it even lying? It's more like not confessing.

"Come on, Chloe!" Amy calls out, shutting off her flashlight and dropping it on the ground. She removes her shorts.

Kristi points her flashlight on the rocks I need to move across, and I go slowly, even more carefully than she did, until I'm standing next to the pool.

Amy steps into the water and Kristi shucks down to her swimsuit, entering the water without hesitation. "God, it feels so good!" she says with a sigh.

The sulfur scent triggers my nausea a bit, but I have to get in or the girls will wonder why. It does sound nice to soak, and I should enjoy this moment. Let my worries fizzle away for now.

When I finally do slip in, my body practically sighs with relief after that intense hike, and I can feel tight muscles relaxing.

Nobody speaks, and I look at the twins, both of them with eyes closed, like they're in heaven. I take a deep breath and, for the first time tonight, stare at the sky and enjoy the quiet.

After a few minutes, something rustles above us on the mountain. I catch it in my peripheral vision and startle.

"Did you see that?" I whisper, pointing to a small locust tree bursting through two boulders. A few of its branches are still moving against the moonlight. The girls strain to see what I'm talking about, but it doesn't happen again.

"It's just the wind. You need to chill out, Chloe. Jesus," Amy groans.

There's no wind up here. We're sheltered in this crevice.

Minutes pass in silence where nothing happens, and I guess I should take Amy's advice and calm down. The air feels even colder now thanks to my wet skin, so I crouch lower into the water and sit still until my face throbs. It's actually really hot in here.

The baby.

What if this high temperature is harmful to it? I pull myself out and sit on a rock's edge, dangling my feet in. I reach to the side for my towel and nearly knock my shoes into the water.

"Why did you get out?" Amy asks. "What are you doing?"

I sense a challenge in her tone, so I remind myself again to be careful with my reply.

"Oh, I'm good. Just got a little too hot. And I don't feel great."

Amy looks at Kristi, and I swear a little smirk passes between them. Right in front of my face.

"Why are you always sick, Chloe?" Kristi asks in a voice that sounds more like Amy. It catches me off guard. This isn't her. She's usually more non-confrontational.

"Yeah. It's not normal to get the flu for weeks and weeks on end," Amy adds.

What the hell?

Before I can come up with something to say, Amy speaks again, moving closer to me in the pool. "Are you pregnant or something?" But her tone—there's a certainty that makes my gut flop. It feels like she already knows the answer.

"Chloe had sex," Kristi adds.

"Are you having *sex*, Chloe?" Amy whispers in a mocking voice.

"What? No."

"Whatever, *mama*. So much for Truth. We found the used pregnancy test in our bathroom trash can. You didn't even try to be discreet. But don't worry, we haven't told—"

A small avalanche of rocks falls behind us, coming from the spot I saw movement before.

I slip back into the water and duck down as if to hide.

We all stare at each other in silence, and I swear I can feel their panic rise to the same level as mine.

The twins know about my pregnancy and that's a huge, scary deal, but it's overshadowed by this fear thrumming below my skin. Who or what made that noise?

"Guys," I whisper. "That is *something*!"

The air grows charged while we sit as still as possible, trying to make ourselves invisible. I'm fighting the urge to go inspect, if anything, to discover that I'm wrong and it's nothing.

"Get the flashlight," I whisper to Kristi, pointing at it.

"You get it! You're closer," she protests quietly.

"Jesus Christ, you two, it's nothing. I'll show you," Amy says, moving through the water toward the light.

She pulls herself up onto the large rocks that form the rim of the pool, when there's a whirring noise—something flying through the air. It hits her in the back.

An arrow. I can see it sticking out.

Everything slows down and Amy turns as if she's simply changed her mind about the flashlight and now she's getting back into the pool. But her movements are stilted, her face contorts in fear, and then she lets out a shriek of terror that makes it feel like the blood stops pumping in my veins.

I should go over there and help her, but I'm stuck in place. My body won't move.

Amy falters, flailing her arms as if to grab hold of something, but there's nothing. Just the edge of the pool before the massive drop to the bottom. She loses balance and disappears over the cliff.

CHLOE

All noise dampens, funneling into a quiet hum that zings in my ears. Kristi's mouth is open as if she's screaming, but I don't hear anything.

I reach for her hand and grab her by the wrist instead. I want to tell her to stay here. Stay at the back of the pool where we're hidden from above, where the arrow came from. But I can't get anything out.

She shakes off my grip, and I watch her lips form her sister's name, but it's muffled. She repeats it over and over while sloshing across to the place where Amy fell.

No. Stay down. Don't go over there.

The warning is there, but the words stay stuck in my throat.

We need to run. Get out of here. But still, I'm locked in place.

Another arrow flies through the air and lodges into Kristi's chest. She stumbles, crying out as her body goes limp and slides back into the pool.

Everything spins, dreamlike, as if I'm outside of myself watching this happen. As if there are two Chloes, and the first

Chloe moves through the water, ducking low to both hide from whoever is hunting us and to grab Kristi to turn her face up so she doesn't drown. The other Chloe sits, unmoving and observing like an idiot. Someone sobs.

But I'm the only Chloe. I'm the one pulling at Kristi, turning her over, and I'm the one crying. A dark blotch of blood where the arrow sticks out soaks Kristi's pink swimsuit and seeps into the water. Her eyes are open, blinking, and blood trails from the corner of her mouth down her cheek. I wash it off gently, as if that's important. Her mouth gapes open. Is she dead? No—can't be. She's blinking.

Then she's not.

I whimper, looking around and trying to figure out what to do.

Kristi is dead.

What about Amy?

What about me?

If I stay put, *I'm* dead. But if I get out, he may shoot me like the others. Plus, the steep trail back down the mountain would be impossible to run in the dark. How would I do it without falling? Either way, I die.

These thoughts ping in my mind rapid-fire. I have to do something. I can't stay here.

Branches snap from above in the same place the arrows came from. Then I hear nothing. He knows I'm here and he's waiting me out.

Something about that terrifies me even more. I gasp and cover my mouth.

Think.

An idea sprouts and I remove my locket from my neck. I throw it to the other side of the pool, opposite of the trail and into the bushes. If he thinks the movement is me, he'll shoot off another arrow and I may have a split second while he reloads. That's when I'll run.

But nothing happens. The locket is too small to make any noise when it lands.

I pick up a rock and throw it in the same direction, and it crashes against a pine tree.

He doesn't stir. Doesn't take the bait at all.

He can see us.

Whoever this is, he's not going by sound, he's going by sight. And I have to take my chances and run down the hill or he could close in on me. Possibly cut off my access to the trail if I don't move now.

I take a deep breath and rocket out of the pool. The cold air is an instant assault, but I ignore it, crouching to make myself smaller. It's a short incline up and then all downhill switchbacks to the car. If I could get over the hump, the mountainside would shield me. Unless he follows.

I make it past the short incline, and on the way down the trail, I slip on hardpack dirt over and over. Every time, I get a new scrape or open cut on my legs, feet, hands. I move down the mountain, barefoot, drenched with sweat and blood, the whole time trying to focus on what to do next. Need to keep my mind from squirreling off to thoughts about my friends. I lose my balance and skid, but stick my legs out to gain footing again. My whole body throbs with pain.

He's not shooting at me. Why?

Almost to the car. But—shit! The keys are in Amy's pocket!

Can't think about that. I have to keep going, avoid tumbling to my death, figure out what to do next, and also somehow stay out of firing range.

Where is he?

Don't look back.

It'll slow me down, but I want to figure out why this person isn't trying to shoot me. In fact, I can't tell that anyone is chasing behind, and that's way too good to be true.

The road below comes into close view. There's Amy's car, and behind it, a truck with its headlights on, purring while it idles.

No. I stop dead in my tracks. Is that the shooter's truck?

Doesn't matter because I have no choice. I have to go that way, and so I push harder down the last leg of loose scree until I trip and fall, torquing my ankle so hard I can't help but scream out in pain.

Instinctively, I touch the injury, but even that hurts. Standing up is impossible because I can't put any weight on the leg.

But I'm almost there; Amy's car is just ahead, dark and quiet. I know I left my door unlocked. If anything, I can get into the car.

That's not a plan! My instincts scream, but I crawl toward it, dragging my wounded leg. My vision is blurry, blinking in and out, as if I might faint.

Focus. Get to the car. Push a little more.

Then someone is behind me, panting, and there's a slight growl on the exhale. It's deep, like a man's voice even though he doesn't speak. A rag comes over my face and I try not to breathe the sickly sweet smell, but his arms are a vice grip, and eventually I have to.

Everything goes black.